SPLIT

by

Mel Bossa

A Division of Bold Strokes Books

2011

SPLIT
© 2011 BY MEL BOSSA. ALL RIGHTS RESERVED.

ISBN 13: 978-1-60282-220-7

THIS TRADE PAPERBACK ORIGINAL IS PUBLISHED BY
BOLD STROKES BOOKS, INC.
P.O. BOX 249
VALLEY FALLS, NY 12185

FIRST EDITION: APRIL 2011

CREDITS
EDITORS: GREG HERREN AND STACIA SEAMAN
PRODUCTION DESIGN: STACIA SEAMAN
COVER DESIGN BY SHERI (GRAPHICARTIST2020@HOTMAIL.COM)

Acknowledgments

Thank you to Radclyffe for her guidance in the early stages of the manuscript. Special thanks to my editor Greg Herren for his keen eye and spot-on advice. And a very resounding thank you to the Bookish Butch for being such a great critique partner…and friend.

Dedication

For Dan

CHAPTER ONE

A unt Fran dropped by today.

She wanted to see the new condo. Her face had some color to it this afternoon.

She set her thin fingers on my cheeks and kissed my mouth. She still smokes those rotten cigarettes, even with this terrible prognosis hanging over her head. She thinks I don't smell it on her breath, but mint or not, I do.

"Very neutral, Derek." There was a hint of dissatisfaction in her raspy voice. "*Modern,* I suppose."

I helped her slip her coat off.

"A little bland to my taste." She ran her finger along the mantel and cocked her head, scanning the premises with her sharp, keen eyes. Though the cancer has eaten half her weight away, she still carries the same energy, and because of her frail build, that energy seems to have expanded. "This is new."

Of course it is. Everything in the condo is brand-new.

From the rugs to the blinds.

"Looks expensive too." Her eyes shrank a little.

Yes, expensive too. Very. She has no idea.

And as a matter of fact, neither do I.

"The lighting is nice. Very crisp. Soothing."

I suppose. I haven't really had time to pay attention to the lighting. I do work eighty hours a week.

"Can I see the bedroom?"

I bowed, pointing to the far end of the three-bedroom condo.

She walked slowly, as one walks through a museum, stopping often to observe and comment.

I followed.

"This it?"

It was.

White blinds. White oak bedroom set consisting of two nightstands, a six-drawer dresser, a commode, and a corner desk. The white room is punctuated with black and red accessories. A large painting of oriental birds hangs over the four-post bed.

They may be oriental, I'm not sure.

"And you and Nathan have sex in here?"

I flicked the light off. "Aunt Fran, you promised."

She gave a quick nod and turned on her heels.

She went straight to the kitchen.

Stainless steel appliances. Marble counters. Bay window overlooking a third-floor terrace.

Aunt Fran plucked the cupboards open, and pulled a bag of dried Porcini mushrooms off the shelf. "Thought you hated mushrooms."

I held her ardent green gaze. "It's an acquired taste."

Her eyes were two slits of suspicion. "I see." She set the bag down. "Let's have a glass of rouge."

She isn't supposed to drink, but what's chemotherapy to Aunt Fran?

I uncorked a bottle of Jacob's Creek. "How's Dimitri?"

She ran her painted fingernail along the rim of the glass and sighed. Very theatrical of her. "Still trying to find himself. I've cut him loose."

A soft chuckle escaped my lips.

Dimitri is Aunt Fran's new boy toy.

Was, I guess.

"I thought Nathan would be here." She had already finished her glass and was pouring herself another. "Or maybe I misunderstood. Those filthy drugs they've been pumping me with have me just about as clear-headed as Keith Richards."

"Aunt Fran—"

"Oh please, don't get all mushy on me." She slapped my hand. "Why is it that every time I see you, you look more beautiful? Look at you. You're candy for your old auntie's eyes."

Aunt Fran always managed to fluster me. I think she enjoys it. She winked. "So where is Mr. Alpha anyways?"

"Why do you insist on calling him that?"

"Let's see. Because Nathan is domineering, arrogant, completely self-absorbed—"

"He's also consistently charming, immensely driven, quick-witted, and passionate."

"And what about his—" She cleared her throat and leaned in. "Performance in the sack?"

"Aren't you dying to know?"

She exploded into a fit of laughter, but soon, the laughter turned into a coughing spree that had her wheezing and struggling for the next breath.

I clutched the counter and watched helplessly, waiting for it to subside.

Her eyes filled. Her fingers turned white from the effort. Slowly, the air settled into her dying lungs and she cracked a sardonic smile. "That one wasn't too bad, now was it?" She left her stool and went to fetch her bag. "I've got something for you, hon."

As she pulled a black binder out of her large printed purse, my cell phone buzzed on the counter.

On the other end of the line, Nathan's voice was full of sleep. "Hey, babe."

I glanced down at my watch. Montreal. Eight p.m.

One a.m. London time.

"Hello, stranger," I said discreetly. "Can't sleep?"

Aunt Fran refilled her glass before stepping out on the terrace. She huddled in the far corner, hunched over like a thief. Obviously smoking.

"How was your day off?" There was tension in Nathan's voice.

He'd been pushing it lately, but there's no sense in trying to slow him down. The man is a machine.

"Nice. I got ahead on a few things."

"Derek O'Reilly. Tell me you haven't been working on your only—"

"Nathan Ross, if you intend on lecturing me about over-achievement, I suggest you rethink your—"

"All right." A smile seeped into his smooth voice. "But promise me you're going to take it easy tonight. Get yourself a movie, or read one of your dreadful books."

"I will promise no such thing. Now go to sleep."

"Not until you tell me you love me and miss me."

Aunt Fran gently inched the patio door open, as if a smooth entrance would absolve her of all guilt.

"Der? You there?" asked Nathan.

"Yes, Nate. Consider yourself loved and missed. Good night."

An uneasy silence filled the line.

"Derek, why don't you ever say it?"

Aunt Fran's eyes roamed over me as if she had heard Nathan's question.

I pressed the phone closer to my ear. "My auntie is here—"

"That old bat? She better not be smoking in our—"

"Nate. I have to go, call me in the morning, okay? Good night, sleep tight."

I flipped the phone shut.

Aunt Fran pushed the black binder my way. "Found this in the old Verdun apartment. I was there today, cleaning it up a little. New tenants are moving in in three weeks."

I glanced down at the binder. "What is it?"

Her eyes danced on my face. "Open it."

I stared at her a little and flipped the cover back.

My heart leaped.

Memories rushed through me in one big jolt of past tense.

My dearest Bump.

I had forgotten about you.

Seventeen years have passed since I last wrote to you.

"I have to tell you, Derek, I was dying of curiosity, and I did read a few pages. Hope you don't hold it against me?"

My eyes were still glued to the page.

"You have a gift for storytelling." Aunt Fran's voice grew stronger. "Hon? You listening? I think you should pick that habit up again. Would do you some good."

That long winter of 1987.

Seems like a million years ago.

I set my fingers on the pages written by a skinny redheaded boy who had struggled to make sense of the world around him.

And that beautiful name, the one I had managed to push into the deepest corners of my soul, now, like a forgotten prayer, an ancient chant, echoed through my mind.

Nicolai Lund.

"Wonder what happened to them all," Aunt Fran murmured, her gaze searching the horizon.

I tore my eyes away from the meticulous handwriting of a boy I don't know anymore.

❖

July 1987
Dear Bump,

I didn't know it was possible to be brand-new, then dead on the same day.

You know, I waited a long time for you. I had marked August second with a red X. Instead, you came the day before yesterday. You came, but never home. I'm not really supposed to talk about it though.

Dad said, "Derek. You better be quiet when Mom gets home, and you don't say his name. Not one time."

I don't think I'm supposed to write about you either, so I'll just call you "Bump." That's what Mom used to call you when she found out you were coming. I had an asthma attack that morning. I sucked on my medicine and let her comb my hair. "Don't get so tight, Red," she said. "Your little brother's gonna like soccer. Your dad won't mind so much about all your reading anymore."

I was looking forward to that.

Now, not only are you not going to play soccer with Dad, you're not even going to be alive.

Since she came home, Mom's eyes are like Grandma's dish soap and our apartment is like an empty coconut. Dad is the only one allowed in the bedroom.

I'm not allowed past the bathroom.

That's the second to last door before hers.

❖

Dear Bump,

After dinner, I have to yank some weeds, but when I'm done, Boone says he has a surprise for me.

Boone is my best friend. He's a Lund kid. The Lunds are our neighbors. We share the same yard. Their parents are from Norway, but the kids are from here. Born in Verdun, same as me. All three of them. Boone is the middle one. He's been in my class since kindergarten.

Their father is a locksmith, that means he opens doors when you need a door opened.

Dad is, *was* an electrician for a company called mothahumpinasslicor, but he was laid off last fall. That's probably why he was upset when Mom said you were coming.

They fought about you until June.

You were supposed to come in August, but you came in July. Like me.

July is a good month to have your birthday. You can have a pool party. If you have a pool. We don't have a pool, but we have a sprinkler. It belongs to the Lunds, and they let us use it sometimes.

It rained on my birthday, so we didn't get to use it.

❖

Dear Bump,

Mom cut all her hair off yesterday.

She left some on top, but not much in the back. I noticed how small her face is. Or maybe her eyes are bigger than I thought. Dad doesn't like it. I can tell because he keeps staring at her ears. They stick out a little.

Like an elf I guess.

I didn't tell you about Boone's surprise.

It wasn't much. Just a dirty magazine he stole from his cousin. He made such a fuss over it. I thought he was going to reveal something important to me. Thought maybe he'd found a treasure map, but it was only a bunch of jiggly boobies.

He asked me to meet him by the river, behind the auditorium.

"O'Reilly, you're not gonna believe this."

I waited for him for ten whole minutes.

Boone shot out of nowhere, riding his BMX down the steep hill like he was made out of rubber. He almost rammed into me.

"Check this out," he whispered, pulling a sticker album out of his backpack. "But you can't have it. Not even for a day. I gotta bring it back before my cousin finds out it's missing."

"What is it?" My heart thundered with sweet anticipation.

His blue gaze scoured the bank. "It's naked girls. All kinds."

Boone is obsessed with girls. In kindergarten, he'd have pockets full of bubble gum and coax the girls into showing him their privates. He thinks I don't know that, but I used to watch him do it. It's funny, none of the girls ever asked for the gum afterward.

I ended up chewing a lot of gum that year.

"Lene wants to kiss you on the mouth on Tuesday."

We were trekking back home.

"No, Boone. Don't want to-to."

Lene is Boone's sister. She's nine. She has a crush on me. She always sticks love notes in my running shoes. I'm probably going to marry her, but first I need to travel to Asia. All the grown men I know have two things in common: they drink too much brown liquor, and have never gone to Asia. I think there's something there. If I want to be successful, I need to visit Peking.

Mrs. Lund asked me to stay for supper. She was making something colorful. It wasn't meat, and it smelled nice. I wanted to stay, but the last time I stayed for supper, I puked. On account of my nerves, you know. My throat closes up like Dad's fingers around his beer mug. I can't blink.

I forget how to breathe.

My face burns.

My brain hums.

And sometimes, I get this funny feeling deep inside my stomach, like a hot liquid pouring into my shorts.

It only happens when Boone's older brother sits at the table. He mostly doesn't because he's fifteen.

But I can't take that chance. Sometimes, Boone's brother doesn't come until dessert is served, and that's the worst because I love Mrs. Lund's tapioca pudding, but I just can't seem to swallow it when Nicolai Lund is around.

❖

Dear Bump,

I plan on winning the chess tournament this year.

I'm tired of getting the second place. Jesse Chao has won first place since the first grade. His smile looks like a string of gray pebbles. Everyone in the math club knows I can beat him. I need to practice some more, that's all. I've been asking Mom, but she says she can't remember how anymore. I don't understand, she remembered fine last month.

I don't know who I'm supposed to play with now.

When I asked Boone if he could help me hone my skills, he laughed. "No way, Red. Gonna be way too busy. JF told me Julie wears a bra now."

Boone said I should ask his father because Johan and Nick used to play when Nick was little.

It's hard to imagine Nick Lund as a little kid. I try picturing his eyes on a smaller face, but can't do it. His eyes are so different from little kids' eyes. Little kids' eyes look like cough medicine bottles.

Nick's eyes look like a picture I saw of a coral reef.

Except the coral reef wasn't as beautiful.

Boone has blue eyes too, but when he looks at me, it doesn't feel like I've been punched in the stomach.

I'm shy about asking Mr. Lund. He's always so busy. I think that's why Dad doesn't like him. "That man came to our country, hardly speaks any French or English, and he's going around stealing people's jobs." I asked Dad if he wants to be a locksmith, and he just glared at me.

Dad likes Mrs. Lund, though. He's always so nice to her. She used to be in magazines in Norway. Her hair is the color of my beige dresser and her eyes are almost bigger than her ears. They're blue. She wears lipstick and smells like Grandma's rose potpourri. She never wears

pants, just half-skirts. She doesn't take off her shoes in the apartment, and when she walks down the hall, they make a clacking sound I like.
She came by yesterday. She brought some cold fish, and she also had brought some kind of red soup. Her and Mom sat at the kitchen table, and Mrs. Lund made Mom eat like a baby.
Mom cried the whole time.
Some girl with a belly bigger than a pumpkin came by with some boys this morning. Dad helped them load your crib and dresser in the back of their truck. He lit a cigarette and watched them drive away. I was standing next to him, but he never said anything.
Tomorrow's Sunday, and we're going to church. Father Neil is going to say something about you. Everyone is coming.
Even the Lunds, and they never go to church.
I don't really like church, except for the communion.
I like the way Jesus tastes.

I've been debating about writing again.
Really, how healthy would it be to hash up the past, or dwell on the daily shortcomings of my life? What twenty-eight-year-old man keeps a diary? Seems like an odd and self-indulging thing to do. Yet I can't help wondering if Aunt Fran is right. Perhaps writing is something therapeutic to me, and could only provide me with some healthy introspection. Alas, only time will tell.
Let's see. How does one sum up seventeen years?
I suppose one does not.
The Lunds moved away that same year. Johan bought a house on the south shore. Boone promised we would keep in touch, but we never did. Aside from a love note I received from Lene that Christmas, I remained without news of them all these years.
Mom never truly recovered from your death. I used to tiptoe around the apartment, even when she was awake. In 1994, she bought a piano at a garage sale. From that day on, she spent countless hours teaching herself to play. When I left for university, she could play fairly well. That piano was her lifeline. Still is today. I enjoy watching her thin fingers dance on the keys.

Only then can we really connect.
Only then does she ask about me.

❖

Dear Bump,

I saw Jesse Chao in church yesterday. He said he's been practicing every day for the last month. I haven't played chess since June. Dad said, "you gonna let some little chink boy take first place again?"

Jesse isn't Chinese. He's from Australia. His mom sang opera in Sydney, and his father is a cowboy, but he used to be an astronaut until the war broke out in the west and he and Jesse's mom had to go undercover to fight against the rebel snakes that had taken over a place called Pennsylvania.

Dad says, "That's a bunch of bullshit, son. You just got the kind of face people enjoy lying to, Derek."

After the service, all of us were invited to the Lunds' for lunch. I tried to fake an asthma attack, but Mom got too upset, so I had to stop. There was no use.

I was going to have to eat around Nick Lund.

In the Lunds' apartment, I carefully hugged the hallway wall, tiptoed down the stairs, and slithered into Boone's bedroom.

I found him sitting on his bed. "O'Reilly. Check this out."

Boone's face glowed like a red party lantern.

I walked up to his bed and sat on the edge. "What?"

"Smell this." He held something white and crumpled like an old Kleenex.

"Are you-ou cra-azy? I'm not gonna smell some old used up-up tissue."

My stuttering has become a problem in the last year, but Boone doesn't seem to notice.

His eyes darted up. The sun poked yellow into them. "Red, trust me. You need to smell this. Remember the fancy Italian chocolates Mrs. Bastone used to give us on Easter, the ones with the plastic cup at the bottom?"

I remember those. They were sweet and tangy all at once.

"This is how these panties smell."

At the sound of that word, my nose met my mouth, like my face had folded over itself. "Ew! Boone, whose panties are—"

His bedroom door flew open.

And my eyes popped out of my head.

It was Nick.

Boone and I jumped to our feet.

Boone is quicker than I thought, because he had managed to stick the underwear in his back pocket before Nick had passed the threshold, but from where I was standing, I could see it plainly sticking out.

Nick cocked his head a little. "What you got there, Bunny boy?"

My heart beat hard against my ribs. Could Nick hear it?

Nick took a step toward Boone, and Boone stiffened at my side. "We were talking about Hulk Hogan," he said in a small voice.

Nick shrugged. "Hogan's a fake." He looked Boone up and down, and turned around.

I tried to swallow all the spit that had gathered inside my mouth.

Thankfully, we were going to live until lunch.

But just when Boone's shoulders dropped an inch from relief, Nick lunged at him. We both shrank back in shock.

Nick yanked the evidence out of Boone's pocket. "What the fuck is this, you little cumstain!" When Nick unfolded the underwear, his eyes widened. "Oh man," he said, grinning from ear to ear, "you're so fucked. Mom's gonna flip."

Everyone knows about Mrs. Lund's temper. Especially her youngest son.

"Nick, please don't tell her."

Nick's eyes seem to sharpen, and he gave a little snort.

Boone pleaded harder. "I'm already in trouble for the *Playboy*, and—"

"Don't whine. Only losers whine. Where d'you get these anyway?"

Boone seemed surprised. He squinted, and mumbled, "In your bedroom, Nico. Under your bed."

Nick's pale eyebrows curled. He stared at the panties for a few seconds, twisting them between his long fingers, and scoffed. "Huh. Well, shit. Guess she was right." The hardness settled back into his face. "Bunny boy, I catch you taking stuff from my room again, I'll make you wear these, and nothing but these. Then we'll take a nice little stroll around the block, got it?"

Boone nodded. "Got it."

"And one more thing, you should never touch a girl's panties, even if she ain't wearing 'em. Unless she lets you. Don't be a jerk, Boone. Lunds aren't jerks."

From the moment Nick had stormed in, my knees had been locked. I don't think I took a whole new breath, either, but he hadn't even looked at me once.

Like I wasn't there in the room with them.

Like I was watching TV.

"O'Reilly." Nick didn't make eye contact. "Sorry 'bout your brother."

A river rushed through my ears.

Was someone blow-drying my face?

I opened my mouth but couldn't move my lips, so I moved my head up and down instead, letting a sound stream out of my mouth, something half between a grunt and a moan.

Nick left the room.

My knees were roasted marshmallows. The skin around them couldn't hold the middle. I plopped down on the bed, staring at the empty doorway.

Boone sighed, then bounced up. "Hey, my dad taped last week's wrestling match. You wanna go watch it?"

❖

Bump,

Me and Mr. Lund are going to play chess together every Saturday morning.

He has a beautiful board, and all the pieces are handcrafted, made out of pink and black marble. They're heavy too. I think he's happy about it. He says he hasn't played in a long time.

I went to the dentist this morning. I was supposed to go with Mom, but she wasn't dressed. Aunt Frannie came instead. We rode the bus together and she let me use her Walkman. Aunt Frannie works for a lawyer, and her office is on the twenty-first floor of a building I can see from my window. I don't remember the name of it, though. Something Marie.

On the way back, we shared a peanut butter cup.

"Your mom's gonna feel better soon. She's got the blues, that's all."

The blues.

I'm not sure what that is. It probably has something to do with blood. I read that blood is actually blue. It only becomes red when it's out in the open. That's my nickname. Red. A lot of people call me that. Because of my hair.

A lot of people call Nick blue. I don't know why, though. Maybe it's because of his eyes.

They're so blue, they make the sky look green.

Aunt Frannie says she might move in with us. Just for a while.

When I came home, I took my finger paint out of my closet. It was still pretty good, so I mixed the red and blue together.

They turned into purple. I made a purple heart and wrote Nick's name inside.

Then I gagged.

I cut it all up with the kitchen scissors and flushed the pieces down the toilet.

Bump,

School starts in two weeks. I already packed my school bag.

This summer is really long. All the days seem to be wearing the same clothes; it's hard to tell them apart. Aunt Frannie says grown-ups feel like that all the time. "Sometimes I have to check the calendar to remember what year it is."

I think grown-ups don't know what year it is because they don't celebrate their birthdays.

Mom's blues haven't healed yet.

Aunt Frannie says, "It's like when you empty the tub, Red. It takes a while to fill it back up."

I wish I could fill Mom up.

The only days I enjoy are Saturdays. That's when I get to play chess with Mr. Lund. *Johan.* He asked me to call him Johan. It's pronounced *Yo Ann.* We play on the back porch. Mrs. Lund, Helga, makes iced tea and ham sandwiches. The ham isn't the kind Mom buys. It doesn't have any purple spots on it, and doesn't sweat. The bread is almost black, but I like it. Sometimes Helga makes a fruit salad and tops it with whipped cream.

Dad doesn't like me eating their food. "We got plenty of food in the fridge. It ain't good enough for you now?"

It isn't true. We don't have plenty of food in the fridge. Since the day you didn't come home, all we eat is Spam and tuna. Sometimes Dad buys bananas. I had cheddar popcorn for supper last night.

Aunt Frannie lived with us for three days, but she left. She called me later that week. "Have you read *Treasure Island?*"

I haven't.

She seemed to hold her breath, and then whispered, "Red, I'll bring it over next time I come. Be a good boy."

She hasn't come yet.

❖

Dear Bump,

I dreamed about you last night, but I don't remember what we were doing, only that you were in your crib, the one the pumpkin girl took, and there was a snow storm outside.

I was in the hospital yesterday. On account of Boone, you know.

None of it is my fault. It was all his idea. I just did what he asked.

I was in my bedroom playing my records (most of them are scratched, but the Michael Jackson one Aunt Frannie got me last year is still good). I like his music, but can't play it too loud because Dad says, "Only sissies listen to that junk."

I was practicing my moonwalk dance, going from my dresser all the way to the mirror, when Boone knocked on my window.

I climbed on my bed and slid the window open. "Aren't you grounded?"

He frowned. "Dunno."

Lene told me Boone gets in so much trouble that Mrs. Lund has a special calendar to keep track of his different punishments so she doesn't forget any.

Boone took out a little notepad out of his pocket. "I need a plastic bag and some cotton balls, okay?"

I didn't like the sound of that.

"What fuh-fuh-for?"

"And make sure it doesn't have any holes in it. Meet me in the school yard, behind the green Dumpster. In five minutes."

I shouldn't have gone, but you don't know Boone, and you haven't seen him smile. Boone is the only happy person I know. If it weren't for him, I would have never made it to the fifth grade. At recess, the boys don't mess with me anymore because they're scared of Boone, and the ones that aren't, well, they're terrified of Nick. Everyone knows about what happened to the boy who tripped Boone last year.

He walked funny for three weeks.

I got a bag out from under the sink, those tiny white ones we use for the kitchen garbage, and some cotton balls from the medicine cabinet. I didn't know how many he wanted, so I grabbed two handfuls and put those in the bag.

I snuck out from the back door and walked to school. The fence was locked, so I climbed over, being careful not to rip my shorts.

I found Boone and JF crouching behind the Dumpster. "Finally." said Boone.

"What took you so long, carrothead?" JF added with a smirk.

I hate JF. He hates me too, but he can't do anything about it. Boone doesn't let him be mean to me. "Shut up, JF. Besides, O'Reilly's hair isn't even orange, you dimwit, it's red."

I smiled victoriously and handed Boone the bag full of cotton balls. "What do-do you plan doing with this stu-uff anyway?"

JF giggled.

Boone shoved him in the ribs. "You'll see." He had brought his WWF backpack, and when he opened it, I think me and JF held our breaths. Who knew what he would pull out of that bag? There is no limit to what Boone can do. So when he pulled out a small flask with what looked like water in it, our mouths sagged with disappointment.

JF scoffed. "Wow. *Water.* How exciting."

"It isn't water, you idiot. Here, Red, smell it and tell this retard it isn't water."

Boone handed me the bottle. It looked like a maple syrup bottle, only smaller. On the label, there was a drawing of a woman's hand. I didn't really want to smell it, but they were both staring at me with wide, eager eyes. I twisted the cap, and right away, got a good whiff of it. Made me gag. "What is this-this stuff, it smells like your dad's gaara-a-age."

Boone grinned. "It's nail polish remover," he whispered. "Remember that cop that came to school last year?"

I remembered him. Officer Di Paglio. He had brought his German shepherd dog and a whole bunch of other things. He'd stretched a black cloth over a desk in the gym and laid out all of these things. We weren't allowed to touch them, but we could all go up and look at them. He had made a sign that read *Drug Paraphernalia.* I didn't really understand all of it, but I remember Boone's face that morning.

I had never seen him so focused and attentive.

JF still wasn't impressed. "So we're gonna do our nails like a bunch of girlies?"

Boone shot him a mean look. "Weren't you two paying attention that day? We're not gonna use it. We're gonna *sniff* it."

I should have said something, but I was way over my head already.

JF was quiet all of a sudden. "All right," he finally said. "What's the big deal? I mean, what's gonna happen if we do?"

Boone shrugged. "Dunno. Get high, I guess."

My hands were beginning to sweat.

"Okay," said Boone, "this is what's gonna happen. I'm gonna pour a few drops into the cotton balls and then I'm gonna sniff 'em. Then I'm gonna write down everything I see or hear."

He was making it sound like a lab experiment. "Why do-do you need to write everything duh-duh-down?"

He looked at me like I was stupid. "So I can compare."

"With what?"

He winked. "With the other drugs I'm gonna try."

I knew Boone wasn't gonna make me sniff anything if I didn't want to, but JF wasn't going be so lucky. "After I do it, you do it," Boone told him.

JF only nodded. He was paler than a pair of my oldest socks.

We watched Boone pour the nail polish remover into the bag. He poured a lot more than I thought he would. Almost half the bottle. I wanted to say something, but I didn't. I should have said something. I really should have.

When he wrapped the opening of the bag around his mouth and nose, my heart jumped. Boone's clean blue eyes stared at me from over the bag, and I heard him mumble, "Here goes nothing." Then he took a deep, long breath through the nose. I watched the bag shrink around his face.

I couldn't stop staring into his eyes.

They didn't look normal.

He twitched, and his eyeballs rolled back into his head. He fell back like a rag doll—like he had no bones.

My mouth was open, and my arms were outstretched, but I couldn't move for a second. I couldn't even work my legs. They were like two spaghetti noodles.

JF flipped. He screamed and started crying. "Go get Nick! Hurry! Go get Nick!"

And I just ran.

I'm not a fast runner, on account of my asthma you know, but yesterday, I ran so fast, my feet barely touched the ground. I kept thinking of Boone's blue eyes rolling back into his head, and I wondered if I had just seen my best friend die. What would I do without Boone? What would his parents say? They would hate me. Mrs. Lund would never fix me a ham sandwich again, and Johan would point his finger at me. "You killed my best son."

When I got to the Lunds' apartment, my knees were shaking.

Their front door was opened.

I thought I was going to have an asthma attack, and prayed I wouldn't. I climbed the front steps up to the balcony. "Mrs. Lund?" My voice was shaky. I took a few shy steps into the house. I could see the kitchen. It was empty. I walked in farther. "Mrs. Lund!" This time I yelled.

"She isn't home."

I recognized Nick's voice. He was lying on the couch, but I couldn't see him, just his huge feet sticking out. My heart raced. There wasn't any time to lose. If he was going to kill me, then so be it.

Boone needed help.

I took another step inside and tried to make my voice sound lower. "Your brother had an accident."

"What?" Nick jumped to his feet and into his big black boots "What happened?" He frowned and hissed something under his breath, but I didn't catch it.

I started running back to the school yard, with Nick hot on my heels.

The whole way there, all I could think was, "I'm alone with Nick Lund and I'm not puking."

When we got to the school yard, Boone had come around. He was lying on his side, moaning like a kitten. Nick crouched down beside him. "Hey, Bunny boy, what's going on? Talk to me." Nick's voice was soft. I had never heard him speak so quietly. "What happened to your head? Can you sit up?"

Then Nick's cold blue gaze fell on the plastic bag, and I almost ran off, but I knew he would catch up to me and kill me anyway. Nick picked the bag up, looked inside, and brought it up to his nose. "What the fuck are you guys doing with this shit? Huh? What the fuck is going on here? Tell me you haven't been sniffing this shit." Nick's voice quivered with anger, and his eyes were like blades on our faces. "What's wrong with you? This is nasty shit. This is dangerous stuff. You guys are stupider than I thought."

Boone moaned louder. "Nico. It's not their fault—"

"You shut up. You hear me? You fucking shut your piehole. What am I suppose to do with you now, huh?" Nick slowly shook his head. "You need a doctor, and I can't drive you the hospital because Dad's home. We have no choice, I gotta tell him. I gotta tell all your folks—"

"Oh no! Please Nick, please don't tell my parents," whined JF with crocodile tears in his eyes. "You don't know my dad, you don't know how crazy he can get—"

"Okay. Okay. Stop your bitchin' and lemme think here, okay? Shut up and lemme think."

Nick closed his eyes for minute and rubbed his face.

I stood like a glass-eyed doll, watching him. None of us moved until he opened his eyes. Finally, Nick exhaled a hard breath through the nose and glanced up at JF. "Go home. Get outta here."

JF gunned down the street as if his undies were on fire.

"All right. I'm gonna send O'Reilly to get Dad. We stay here and wait."

When Nick looked up at me, my lips pulsed from wanting to say things I'm not even allowed to think.

Nick drew in another deep breath and pointed home. "Go," he whispered, "but tell 'em you guys were wrestling and Bunny bumped his head against the wall. I'll take care of the evidence."

My eyes filled up, and I knew if I blinked, or talked, I would start bawling like a big sissy boy.

"Come on, go," he said more urgently. "Before I change my mind. But if you two ever pull a stunt like this again, I'll whup both of your asses, got it?"

I got it all right. I ran back, but this time my feet had trouble carrying me. When I got there, I was really out of breath, and could hardy get a word out without wheezing.

I supposed it made it even more convincing.

You know, that none of it was my fault.

Johan sprang out the door, and I watched him climb into their van and tear down the street. I wanted to go with him but knew Mom wouldn't let me. So I sat on the porch and stared at the sidewalk for a long time. I sucked on my medicine, that helped a little, and petted the neighbor's cat. After an hour of that, I couldn't wait anymore.

I had to know if Boone was all right.

Mom was taking a nap and Dad was watching TV.

I cleared my throat. "Going for-for a bi——"

"Don't go too far," Dad grumbled without turning away from the TV screen. He never has the patience to let me finish any of my sentences. "It's suppertime soon and I'm making your favorite. We're having sloppy joes."

I gagged.

I rode my bike to the Verdun hospital. It isn't very far. Just down the street, then four or five blocks going east. That's the opposite of where the sun sets.

I left my bike in the parking lot and walked into the emergency room. There were a lot of people in there. Mostly old people. Some kids too. None of them looked like they were dying. I had never been to the hospital. Except once, but that doesn't really count. I was very small, and I don't remember why I was there, except that they made me eat a lot of Jello.

I looked around for the Lunds, but didn't see them anywhere.

I sat down next to an old man who smelled like mothballs and steamed broccoli.

I watched the nurses and doctors. The doctors were all men and carried clipboards. The nurses were girls and frowned a lot. One of them looked at me from across the room and squinted. She whispered something to another nurse, and then walked right up to me.

"Are you alone here?" Her eyebrows met in the middle and her lips looked like they were on a diet.

I thought I was in trouble. "No ma'am. I ca-came here with Da-Da-Dad."

People never believe a word I say, on account of my stuttering.

She looked over at the old man snoring in the chair next to me. "Come with me. Come on. Let's go."

What now? Why couldn't she ask the girl chewing on her piggy tails to come with her?

The nurse took me to a smaller room. There was a sign on the door: *Triage.* "Sit down. What's your name?"

"Derek O'Reilly."

She squinted again. "How old are you, Derek O'Reilly?"

"Eleven."

"Why are you here?"

"I'm waiting fuh-for my friend."

"Who's your friend?"

"Boone. Boone Lund."

She tilted her head, and frowned. "You shouldn't be here alone. The emergency room is a dangerous place." She picked up the phone. "Lydia, can you tell me what room the Lund boy is in, please?"

I stared at my toes. My shoes are torn at the edges and I need new laces.

"Okay," she said after she hung up, "I'll take you to his room. He's upstairs. Next time, you ask your mom or dad to come with you."

"Yes ma'am, tha-thank you."

In the elevator, there was hardly any room to stand. There was a man on a stretcher, and his face was all gray and yellow. There were tubes coming out of his neck and arms. He kept farting out of his mouth.

The nurse pulled me close to her. "Stay close."

When the doors opened, I hurried out. I was glad to be free of that awful man. The nurse tugged on my T-shirt and pointed ahead. "You go straight. It's a few doors down. Room two thirty-four."

When I got to 234, I stopped short.

The door was ajar.

I hugged the wall, listening.

Mrs. Lund was crying.

Had I made a mistake by coming?

Then I heard Johan. He didn't sound too angry. His voice was more like warm maple spread, and before too long, Mrs. Lund had stopped her whimpering.

I knocked on the door, and pushed on it a little, poking my face in the wedge, but I didn't say anything.

Boone lay in a big white bed. His face was the same color as the walls. He had a plastic thing stuck up his nose and a tube coming out his arm. The tube was attached to a bag with some kind of liquid that looked like pee. Johan sat next to him, directly on the bed, and Mrs. Lund sat in the armchair with Lene on her lap. She kept blotting her eyes with a tissue. Her cheeks were smeared with black makeup.

Nick stood in the far right corner of the room. His hands were buried deep inside his pockets. His eyes were like that thunderstorm we had last year. The one that tore the roof off the shed.

Johan was the first to see me. "Derek. What are you doing here? Do your parents know you're here?"

At that moment, I remembered Boone's blue eyes rolling back into his head and my throat tightened. Tears stung my eyes. I couldn't speak. I just shook my head, pushing the bad thoughts out of my mind.

"Well, I'm not sure what to make of all this, Derek." Johan's eyes shone too. "I don't understand. I would think that you'd know better. I'm real disappointed with you boys."

It was the way he said those words. He wasn't yelling, but I think I would have preferred if he had. He simply shook his head and sighed.

"You know, Boone needs some test done now. Doc says he might have some brain damage. Brain damage, Derek, do you understand what that means?"

I understood.

From the bed, Boone whined, "Dad, Red didn't know what—"

"Not a word from you. Understood? I don't wanna hear it, Boone. You put your mother through hell this afternoon. You lay down like the doctor said, and you be quiet now."

Boone glanced over at me, and my eyes quickly darted down to the dirty floor. I couldn't look into his eyes. I don't think I can ever look into his eyes ever again.

At least, not until next week.

I didn't know what to do with my arm and legs, so I held my breath and stayed close to the door. They're all so nice to me, and I've disappointed them. I don't mind disappointing Dad so much, matter of fact, I think I do so all the time, but Johan, that's different.

Finally, Mrs. Lund spoke to me. "Go home, Derek. I don't blame you for what happened. I know my sons. When they get an idea in their thick skulls, no one can change their minds." She stared Boone right in the face. "One of them is crazy," she said, and then her eyes went, like a poisonous dart, from Boone's face to Nick's. "And this one over here is a beautiful liar."

My heart exploded inside my chest.

No. Nick isn't a liar. He was just trying to protect Boone, that's all. My cheeks burned up, but all I could do was bite down on my lower lip.

Nick's nostrils flared. He looked like a bull trying not to lunge at the red flag. His cheeks had darkened, and for a second, I thought he was going to throw something at his mom, but instead, he threw his hands up and bolted out of the room.

"Nicolai!" Johan yelled. "Come back here!"

Nick didn't slow down. And for some reason, I couldn't stop myself from chasing him.

I caught the back of his head as he shoved open the door to the staircase, and I followed. I heard him running down the stairs. His steps were heavy and quick.

I skidded down those stairs, nearly breaking my neck at every landing, and caught up to him on the first floor.

I flinched, drawing back a little.

Nick was throwing punches in the air, cursing in Norwegian. His hair had come undone, and with every hook he swung, it whipped his face. He was breaking a sweat, fighting this invisible person.

Who could it be?

Then his long arms dropped at his side, and he stopped.

I opened my mouth, but nothing but a small breath crawled out.

Nick leaned back on the wall, breathing hard and fast through the nose, staring straight ahead. Straight through me. "I fucking hate her." I think he meant his mother, but I didn't dare ask.

He ran his fingers through his blond hair and tied it back again. "Well shit." The light flicked on inside his eyes. "Better go back up there 'fore my dad comes down here looking for me."

I nodded, chewing on my lip.

For some odd reason, Nick laughed. Not a big laugh, just a small chuckle.

His eyes moved over my lips like they were tasting a candy cane. "Man," he whispered. "You sure don't say much, O'Reilly."

I shook my head.

My penis jumped.

Nick squinted and ran up the stairs, leaving me to stare at the blank wall.

CHAPTER TWO

Dear Bump,

It was nine in the morning when I heard some voices in the Lunds' yard.

My heart skipped three beats and I almost ran to the patio door. It was Saturday, and I wasn't sure if Johan would let me play chess with him on account of me helping Boone break his brain.

Lene pushed her Cabbage Patch Kid on the tire swing.

Looked like she was giving it a good sermon.

My eyes jumped from one corner of the yard to the next, but I didn't see Boone.

I slid the door open. "Hey, Le-Lene."

"Hello, Derek." She turned around. She had Nutella on her chin. "You be the daddy, I'll be the mommy."

"No."

"Do you wanna see my special place?"

"No."

"Can I see your special place?"

"No."

She shrugged and went back to pushing the fat-headed baby. I sat on the steps and watched some ants carry a dead ladybug across the tiles. "Is your bro-brother okay?"

"Which one?"

"What do-do you mean which one? The one-one that was in the-the hospital yesterday."

"They were both in the hospital yesterday."

I sighed. "Lene, I'm talking about-bout Boone."

She plucked her doll out of the tire and inched up her shirt. She tucked the doll inside it. "Oh, he's fine. He's sleeping. Do you wanna help me give birth?"

"No."

"I plan on having a c-section."

Lene reads a lot of magazines. I got to my feet. I didn't plan on spending my day with her. She scares me. "Well, tell him-him I went fuh-fuh-for a bike ride."

"Aren't you gonna play checkers with my dad?"

I stopped. "You mean chess, and yes, if he still wa-wa-wants to."

"Why wouldn't he?" She squatted down and started moaning.

"Is he in-inside?" I tried not to pay any attention to her shallow panting.

She fell back and started twitching on the grass. "Come cut my stomach before the baby dies!"

I shrunk back. "No-no way."

She kept rolling her head from side to side, moaning louder and louder, getting dirt in her hair. "Hurry, Derek, save me! Save our baby!"

I looked around. There was nobody listening to her lunatic ravings. I found a twig and dragged my feet up to her. In one quick motion, I pretended to slash her belly open. "The-there."

She screamed, then made like she had passed out.

I watched her for a minute, shrugged, and went inside to find Johan.

He was in the living room.

And Nick was there too, asleep on the couch. He was on his side, with his knees curled under his belly and his rosy cheek resting against his palm. The sunlight filtered through his yellow eyelashes.

My belly burned.

I paused by the oak chest and cleared my throat. "Hello."

Johan looked up from his book. "Shh." He tossed his head to where Nick rested peacefully. "Nicolai didn't get much sleep last night." Johan then eased himself out of his armchair and went to the kitchen.

I followed.

He smiled as he pulled a chair out for me. "Glad you came. Have you had breakfast?"

"Yes. I di-did. Thank you."

"Okay then. I'll get the board."

❖

I haven't played chess in over fifteen years.

I never could find another opponent who could teach me about life as we moved marble across a board.

I am thinking of Johan Lund tonight.

Him and his beautiful sons.

What happened to me?

I grew up, and then caught a deadly virus called adulthood.

After three years at Dawson College, I was accepted at Concordia University, where I earned a bachelor's in commerce.

Following graduation, I began my apprenticeship in the glorious world of finance. I maxed out my credit card on tailored suits and trendy ties, and got myself dolled up every day only to sit at my computer, under blinking neon lights, sealed into a cubicle the size of my toilet. For six months, I crunched numbers through Excel pads, plugging data day in day out, drinking bad coffee, and sucking every possible ass I thought could get me ahead. Every time I moved an inch closer to a position worthy of eight years of studying, the ass I had been kissing was either fired or quit. The economy was beginning to plummet, and the first reaction from the major corporations was to panic and scrape off a whole layer of executives, leaving us poor middle men and women, picking up the slack with no financial rewards and little recognition.

After nearly a year of this, this idealistic Irish boy was about ready to quit the game.

Then I met Nathan.

We met at a sales conference, in the Charlevoix area. Though I was merely a staff accountant, I had been ordered to attend.

Nathan was one of the guest speakers.

As Nathan approached the podium, the audience, which had been quite distracted, and at times, just plain rude, quieted down. He plucked the microphone out of its stand and tapped it. His voice rose and fell perfectly. His tone was determined, yet nuanced with sympathy for the "hardworking men and women who strive to provide the customer with the best experience possible." Within moments, the tough crowd of salesmen and jaded administrative assistants had fallen into a mild stupor. Everyone seemed completely smitten with him. His hand swooped the air as he spoke of "cutting the expenses out and raising the bar." His dark eyes glimmered with ambition and straightforwardness. People around me, the very same people who had been doodling and yawning minutes ago, were now hunched over the tables, hanging on his every word.

Of course it helped that Nathan is drop-dead gorgeous.

The essence of him resembles a landslide.

And me? What did I think of him?

I hadn't slept a wink the night before, on account of the party the sales team were having in the next room. Nathan's speech, though compelling and perfectly delivered, was no match for my drooping eyelids. As he spoke of "going back to the basics, the core of customer service," I struggled to keep my eyes open. I tried widening them every other minute, blinking and grimacing.

People must have wondered if I suffered from Tourette's.

"You're drooling on my presentation," was the first thing Nathan ever said to me.

I had dozed off.

At the sight of this arrogant salesman towering over me, grinning devilishly, I popped up on my chair and wiped my damp cheek with the back of my hand.

"Hey, easy now. You'll give yourself a head rush." Nathan seemed perfectly amused.

I shot him a puzzled glance, and adjusted my jacket.

His dark eyes quickly moved over me, and I flinched, as if he had seen me in my boxer shorts. "Lunch is up in the next room," he said. "They have liters of coffee. Not very good, but by the looks of you, I don't think you'll mind." He extended his hand. I stared at it for a moment, and then reached out. "I'm Nate." He pumped my hand as if we were sealing an important transaction. "Nice to meet you, Derek."

I frowned. How could this jerk know my name?

He laughed, then flicked the plastic badge I had clipped on my jacket. "Your name tag."

I glanced down.

Right.

"So," he asked, pulling me out of my chair as if it was the most natural thing to do, "accounting or marketing?"

That afternoon, we were tormented with more presentations, but though I had rarely witnessed such blatant disregard for engaging talk, I was excessively alert. Every time I turned my head, I would catch Nathan's gaze devouring my face. By the last interminable presentation, Nathan's persistent stare had worked itself under my skin, and I began holding it.

Soon, the chemistry between us had reached levels fit to dizzy any inhibited, guilt-tripping Irish Catholic boy.

I could barely swallow.

When the VP of communications broke out the projector, my will left me. I dared a glance Nathan's way. His eyes gleamed with desire. I lowered my gaze to his full lips and caught them mouthing the words, "I want you."

That was it.

Nathan's room was on the second floor. We shot up the steps, ripping at each other's clothes.

We nearly did it in the staircase, but managed to make it to his room. He dropped his key card twice before he could open the door, and I huddled against him, whispering, "Hurry. Oh God, hurry."

That was two years ago.

Since I've met Nathan, my life has changed. Through his mind-boggling social network, Nathan has helped me secure a job as a financial analyst with the Bank of Canada. He's paid my school loans, put me in touch with a wonderful speech therapist who, through grueling exercises and persistent coaching, has completely rid me of my stuttering problem (though, at times, when cornered or nervous, I do have some small setbacks).

Nathan has made my dreams come true. I owe him much. I'm very grateful to him.

What does it matter if I don't particularly like modern art or sushi?

What does it matter that I prefer a Guinness to sake? Or popcorn to soy nuts? None of these things matter. What is important is our commitment to one another.

Yes, he works a lot. Travels a lot too. But that's normal. That's to be expected. Patience is a virtue I intend on cultivating. No sense in placing blame. I knew what the score was when we agreed to take this dive. This lifestyle doesn't come cheap, and with my less than impressive salary, my contribution is mainly domestic.

Aunt Fran can squint at me all she wants.

I'm perfectly happy with my life.

❖

Dear Bump,

Dad is leaving for two months.

On account of a job in the Hudson Bay. I'm going to be responsible for the garbage and snow shoveling. Some of the cleaning too, but mostly the scrubbing of the toilet bowl. Aunt Frannie is coming to stay with us until Christmas. Dad is leaving on a train, and he's leaving on Tuesday. He said, "Take care of your ma and don't let Aunt Frannie drink too much."

I've never been on a train, but I've been on the subway a lot, so that counts for something.

Next week is Halloween. I'm going as a pirate. Boone is going as a mass murderer. Him and Nick have been working on some sort of graveyard set. They plan on "having little kids shit their *E.T.* costumes." When I was there yesterday, they were trying out a home recipe for fake blood and human tissue. Mrs. Lund warned, "If one of you ends up blind because of this revolting mixture, don't expect me to drive you around for the rest of your life." But she stuck around the kitchen anyway. I think she was fascinated by the result.

I didn't know this, but Nick is really good at arts and crafts.

I tried not to watch him, but that's like trying to keep my eyes on a book when the TV is on.

I noticed everything Nick picks up always looks so much more interesting in his fingers. He made a mask out of papier-mâché. It's in the shape of a human face, except it has no mouth, just two slits for the eyes, and a pair of small holes for the nose. When Nick slipped it on, he looked terrifying. Then he tried on Johan's old work clothes and walked around the house for an hour. I played my worst game of chess ever. Every time I caught a glimpse of him out of the corner of my eye, I squirmed in my seat. I think he grew two inches since August. Nick must be close to six feet tall now. His voice is just as deep as Johan's. His shoulders are wider than the fridge.

It was his sixteenth birthday on August eighth. Johan gave him a car. It doesn't work, but they're going to fix it up together. Nick knows a lot about cars and mechanics. It's a Chevy Nova.

I hope we don't encounter problems, you know, on account of us living without Dad. I don't know if Mom knows how to change a fuse. Dad showed me where he keeps his shotgun. It isn't loaded, so it doesn't matter much that I don't know how to use it. "Just to scare 'em," he said.

Mom's hair is growing back, but she's skinny. I don't like it when she hugs me because I can feel her bones on my stomach.

Aunt Frannie said, "I'm going to show you how to cook. If your mom knows you made it, she'll have to eat it."

I don't mind learning how to cook. I just don't want anyone knowing about it. If JF or his friends find out that I'm spending Sunday morning baking cookies, even Boone won't be able to stop them from torturing me.

They've started calling me a homo, and yes, Bump, I know what a homo is.

Well, I'm pretty sure I know.

Jesse Chao quit the math club. Can you believe him? "I kissed a girl on her privates," he said.

But it's a lie, of course. Boone and JF cornered him during recess and demanded to know what it looked like. Jesse said it had a pair of lips and five small holes. Boone gave Jesse a wedgie while JF slapped his ears pink.

Boone got detention again, but JF got off with a warning.

❖

Dear Bump,

I really need to start using my head if I'm going to become an accountant.

I'm grounded until next Saturday. I've never been grounded before.

It all started with an argument during gym. We were playing volleyball. I don't mind playing volleyball, but I don't like to serve. My wrist ends up looking like a lobster tail, and I hardly ever get the ball over the net. I was lucky yesterday, because of Boone and Sebastian's fight, I didn't get to serve.

Boone and Sebastian have been sworn enemies since the first grade. Sebastian lives on Gordon Street, where the "decent people live," and he constantly brags because his father owns the building. Also, on top of that, when Sebastian's white Adidas get too dirty, his mom buys him a new pair.

Everybody hates him, but no one ever says it to his face.

Except for Boone.

Sebastian has an older brother. *David.* David is the same age as Nick. David and Nick are also sworn enemies, but the two of them were once best friends. They used to share a paper run and build the best snow forts in the neighborhood.

Until Miguel Santos moved to Verdun.

Miguel was only here for a year, but he left a disaster area behind him. After Miguel moved back to Toronto, Nick and David never spoke to each other again. Now David goes to Loyola. It's an all-boys Catholic school. Nick goes to Monseigneur Richard. It's a French public school. It's brown and looks like a jail. Yesterday was the first time Nick and David spoke in two years. I think they might be friends again. Even though Nick had to give back the Chevy Nova on account of what he did to David's house.

What happened was this.

Yesterday morning, in gym class, we had been playing for ten minutes when Boone's turn to serve came up. He and Sebastian had both been named captain of their teams. Sebastian's team was winning, on account of them cheating twice. Coach Angelos hadn't caught Sebastian's double hits (he never does for some reason), so we hadn't gotten the points for them.

Boone's eyes had shrunk a size and his mouth was a straight line on his face.

He was going to pop his lid.

"Watch this." Boone grabbed the ball and made his way to the back of the court. "I'll show 'em."

I took my position and held my breath. I know how hard Boone can hit that ball, and somehow, I had a feeling he wasn't going to be aiming it at the ground.

I was right.

Boone looked straight at me, bounced his eyebrows like Groucho Marx, and before I could try to reason with him, he had tossed the ball up, slamming it over the net in a powerful jump serve. We all heard the ball as it bounced off his skin and flew across the court like a stray bullet. Boone's aim is near perfect. It's hardly ever off. When it landed on Sebastian's cheek, I cringed.

Then someone whispered, "Ooh...that must have hurt."

Of course, Sebastian had to play it up. He fell to his knees and started screaming. "My face! My face!" Coach Angelos blew his whistle and ordered Catherine to get the nurse. Sebastian only yelped louder, moaning that he couldn't feel his face anymore.

Boone sneered. "How come it hurts, then? Huh? Liar."

I tried to keep Boone quiet. I knew Coach Angelos was going to get on his case as soon as he was done tending to Sebastian's swollen, reddish cheek.

"Don't say-say anything el-else," I pleaded softly. "Tonight's Hal-Halloween, remember-ber?" I didn't want Boone to get detention. We had plans to go trick or treating. This was going to be our last year. "Go ask if he's okay-kay." I suggested in a whisper.

Boone only scoffed. "Are you crazy? No way. He had it coming for him." Then he raised his voice. His words thundered through the gym. "Bastian, you cheater! I hope your face stays like that! You should thank me, now you don't even need a mask for—"

"Mr. Lund." Coach Angelos was getting to his feet. His usually warm brown eyes were sharp on Boone's pink face. "Out you go. Change your shorts and go to Principle Strozuk's office."

"But—"

"Now."

Boone threw his hands up and kicked the ball across the gym. "No fair."

As Boone passed out the gym doors, Sebastian cried out, "I'll get you back for this, Boone! You and your retarded brother!"

Boone spun around. "What did you say?" His face was white with anger.

Coach Angelos set his humongous hand on Boone's chest. "Easy, Lund."

But Boone's eyes were on Sebastian, who was still on his knees, glaring up at him. "You heard me," said Sebastian. "Your brother's so fucking dumb, he can't even read a license plate."

I don't know how Boone got past Coach Angelos, but somehow, he did. He lunged at Sebastian and fell on top of him. All I could see were Boone's arms going up and down, and Coach trying to pull him off. "Stop it!" he kept saying to Boone, but Boone wouldn't stop. "Don't ever call my brother a retard! My brother's dyslexic! You and your faggot brother don't even know how to spell that word."

Later that night, after we were all safe in our beds, I looked the word up in the dictionary. *Dyslexia: any of various reading disorders associated with impairment of the ability to interpret spatial relationships or to integrate auditory and visual information.*

I guess it means Nick can't read or write without thinking about it for a long time. That's probably why he always looks so serious.

Boone is suspended from school until Friday.

He's not allowed to leave his apartment until Christmas.

That's two months. I think he got lucky.

Here I was, all dressed up in my pirate costume, but no one to go trick or treating with.

I could have gone with JF, but I didn't feel like taking his abuse all night. Lately, JF has been getting meaner and meaner with me. I don't know why he hates me so much. He keeps staring at me all the time. His eyes move over me the way Aunt Frannie's eyes move over the deli counter.

Aunt Frannie helped me with my makeup and lent me her red scarf to tie around my head. I had an eye patch, and she even made a hook out of tin foil to stick inside my sleeve. I wore my black shorts and my dad's white shirt. I was aiming to look like Long John Silver (I read *Treasure Island* four times since Aunt Frannie gave it to me), but when I stood in front of the mirror, all I saw was a skinny boy dressed up like a gypsy. I decided I was too old for Halloween anyway. I would stay home and help Aunt Frannie give out the candy.

Our part of the building wasn't decorated, but the Lunds' front yard looked like something out of the "Thriller" video. They even had creepy music and everything.

I sat on the balcony steps and watched the street.

"Why don't you go out there with your friends?" Aunt Frannie asked.

"I have a sto-stomach ache."

"Red, honey, you're missing out on all the fun." She spoke through her fake teeth. She was dressed up as a woman vampire. Her long red dress hung all the way down to the floor, and her wig was black and shiny. "Are you sad about Boone?"

I shrugged.

"Suit yourself, but I still think you look too darn cute to be sitting here moping around."

Cute? I'm eleven.

"I wanna."

Besides, I wanted to watch Nick and his friends.

Josh D'Amico, who's the only boy I know who had a beard in grade seven, wore a hockey mask and a plaid shirt. He stood quietly at the far corner of the front yard, stiff as a statue, and every time kids came up the steps, he would lunge at them, screaming like a crazy man. Terry, who was dressed up as a headless nun, would then grab the kids by their sleeves, and yell, "Trick or treat? Come on, what'll it be, you little bugger!"

The kids who made it to the front door were finally greeted by Nick.

I liked his persona best.

Nick wore the mask he had made, and a black jumpsuit that made his shoulders seem wider than usual. The suit had a shiny zipper all along the front. His hair was tucked under a black cowboy hat. Nick didn't say one word. Never made a single sound. He would only drop a few candies into the courageous kid's treat bag and nod slowly.

It was beyond creepy.

It was *great*.

Until Mrs. Lund came back with Lene. She had passed a few of our neighbors on her way. Some of their little kids were in tears. "Nicolai!" she yelled from the sidewalk. "You stop frightening the children! Let your dad give out the candy."

Nick nodded slowly. His silence was even creepier than when he had done it for the kids. Josh and Terry, who are terrified of Mrs. Lund, ran off with the Sanchez girls. Nick stayed behind.

Lene was dressed up as Marie Curie. I know because she showed me a picture of the scientist in the Lunds' encyclopedia. She cut loose of Mrs. Lund's firm grip and skipped up our front steps.

She sat by me. "Hello, Derek."

"Hi, Lene."

"Are you the Count of Monte Cristo?"

"No."

"Don Juan?"

"No."

"Our baby is sleeping. The cat ate one of her eyes out, but the doctor said she would be fine without it."

"Lene? Why is your to-ton-tongue bl-u-ue?"

She plucked a lollipop out of her apron. "I was sucking on this. You wanna taste it?"

"No."

"How come you aren't trick or treating?"

"Don't wa-wa-want to."

Then, like some kind of slow, deep dream, Nick's voice dripped down to me. "Come on, Lene." He leaned over the railing. "Mom wants you to take your bath." He wasn't wearing his mask or hat anymore.

Lene pouted. "You know, Nico, baths weren't common practice in the early 1900s, and I—"

"Inside, Lene. *Now.*"

Even Lene knew not to protest. She got to her feet, and Nick picked her up, carrying her as if she were a doll, right over the railing. "Come on, bright eyes, and wash your mouth. It looks like a Smurf had an accident on your tongue."

I got nervous.

There weren't that many kids anymore. Nick and I were basically alone. I wanted to go back inside, but that meant having to say good night at least, and I didn't know if I could manage to do that. My mouth was too dry. My tongue, too heavy. I sat on the first step, trying to keep my breathing in check, with my hands on my lap, staring at the empty sidewalk.

I could see Nick out of the corner of my eye.

He leaned over the front railing, watching the street. "You want some of this leftover candy?" he finally said. "Nothing but toffee and raisins, but I think I saw a few gum sticks in there."

I dared to look over my shoulder. "No-no thank you-ou."

"No? Sure?" He was handing me the plastic pumpkin over the railing. He looked nine feet tall. The street lamp shimmered inside his eyes. "Come on, O'Reilly." His mouth glistened like water under the moon. "Have a box of dried raisins, at least."

I wanted to, but that meant having to reach out and take the pumpkin out of his hand. I wasn't sure if I could do it, but he still stood there, with his arm stretched over the railing, and I had to get myself together. "All right," I said, standing up. "Than-thanks."

I took whatever my fingers landed on, and stuffed that in my pocket without even looking at it. Nick set the pumpkin down, shut the front door, and then stood against the wall with his hands in his pockets. I wanted to sit down again, but instead, I stayed by the railing, staring at the ground.

Nick glanced around. He then took a quick peek into the front window of their apartment and pulled out a pack of cigarettes. He lit one. I watched the orange fire on the tip of the cigarette widen every time he sucked on it. He inhaled deeply, and exhaled through the nose. He didn't cough once.

He didn't say anything else. Just smoked.

Then of course, stupid JF had to show up. "Hey Nico," he shot from the sidewalk. Nick hates it when people call him that. Only his family can. But JF is clueless. He's always trying to impress Nick, on account of JF being a schmuck and all. "Hangin' out, huh, Nico."

Nick tossed his chin up. "Nice costume."

JF was dressed up as a Macho Man, but his wig looked like something Madonna would wear. I caught the sarcasm in Nick's voice, but JF obviously didn't. "Thanks, man. Your brother's still punished huh?"

Nick squashed the end of the cigarette on his heel, then walked over to the street drain and dropped it in there. "That's right."

"Too bad, though," JF said, sniffling nervously. "He was only trying to defend you. I mean, Sebastian was just looking for a—"

"What's that?"

I tensed up.

"Well, I mean—" JF's voice was smaller now. "Sebastian was sort of putting you down and Boone didn't like that one bit, so—"

"Putting me down?' Nick's eyebrows met over his nose. "What do you mean exactly? What did he say? Word for word."

JF was going to have to repeat those words.

He was going to have to call Nick Lund a retard to his face.

I couldn't help smiling.

JF looked up to me with panic in his eyes. "Well, I don't remember everything he said, just that you had some problems or something. Anyways, Boone sure gave him a lesson, huh?"

Nick wasn't buying it. "Problems? What kind of problems?" He took a step toward JF and folded his arms over his broad chest. "What the fuck did he say, exactly? Come on, spit it out, you little pussy."

JF swallowed hard. "He called you a retard." We could barely hear him.

"A what now?" Nick's voice was like an ice storm.

"A retard. He said you couldn't even read a license plate."

"Oh yeah?"

My heart had begun racing. I didn't know if it was from dread, or satisfaction.

"A retard, huh?" Nick repeated, his eyes blazing. "He said that? That little shit? He said I was a retard. Huh. Okay. All right. Okay."

JF had managed to slip past Nick and come up the stairs to our balcony. "Derek, he's flippin' out." he whispered.

Oh yeah, Nick was flipping out.

"A retard huh? I'm gonna fucking break him in half and have him eating out of his asshole for the rest of his life."

I could kind of picture what that might look like, and it wasn't pretty.

"I'm gonna go pay that little pimple squirt a visit. No fair Boone had to take the rap." Nick looked up to JF. "You go get Josh and Terry. Tell 'em I'll be at Dunkin' Donuts." He climbed up the stairs, and then looked over at me. "O'Reilly, if you have some extra toilet paper you wouldn't mind parting with, I'd like it, please."

I nodded. "Yes."

Nick went into the house.

JF made a strange sound, sort of like a snort, and stuck his hands into his pockets. His wig was crooked and his face looked like curd cheese. "You could have said something. You were there too."

I sighed and pointed to the street. "Better do-do what he said before-fuh-fore he comes back out."

"What do you think he's gonna do? I mean, he won't really break him in half—"

"I don't know, but I'm getting him some toilet pa-pa-per."

Inside, Aunt Frannie was on the phone. "Honey—" She folded her hand over the speaker. "Be quiet, your mom's sleeping, but don't worry, she had an egg sandwich before she went to bed. See? It's not so bad."

Aunt Frannie thinks Mom's blues are hungry all the time.

I slipped the silk scarf off my head and washed my face in the bathroom sink. I put Dad's shirt in the hamper and pulled my thick black sweater over my head. It hasn't snowed yet, but it's still cold out there.

I tiptoed to the hallway closet and gently opened it.

"What are you looking for, Red?" Aunt Frannie stood behind me.

The answer jumped out of my mouth before I could even think it. "A flashlight."

"What for? There's plenty of light. Are they calling for a thunderstorm?"

Aunt Frannie could wrestle a grizzly bear, but she doesn't like thunderstorms.

"May-maybe." I said, avoiding her wide green eyes.

"Oh, well in that case, I'm going to get the candles ready. Where does your mom keep 'em, hon?"

We have two white candles in the kitchen. Both melted down to the middle. They're in the second drawer, under the washcloths.

"In the ba-ba-basement, in Dad's corner." I lied.

I thought I could slip the toilet paper out to Nick while she went looking for them.

She threw her white robe on and took the flashlight out of my hand. "Just in case." She headed down the narrow stairs to the cement basement.

She's lucky. I have to sleep down there.

As soon as she was out of sight, I yanked the bulging bag of toilet paper rolls out of the closet and sprang for the front door.

Nick was on the sidewalk. He carried a baseball bat and a bag full of what looked like groceries. I handed him the rolls.

He slid the bag under his arm. "Thanks, O'Reilly."

Before I could say anything, he had taken off on his skateboard. Nick rides that board like he's standing on a magic carpet. Even when he's carrying two grocery bags and a baseball bat.

I went to the corner of Wellington. I watched Nick pop his board into his empty hand, then walk into the Dunkin' Donuts with his ammo. The other guys were already there.

I dragged my feet back to our apartment because I didn't have the courage to follow them.

I sat on the balcony again.

My chest tightened.

I jumped up and went back inside.

It was a school night and I suspected Aunt Frannie wouldn't let me leave now that it was dark. I decided I would tell her I was going to bed and then try to sneak out through the back door. It would be tricky, but if she was watching TV in the living room, I could probably manage to escape for half an hour before she came down to check on me. I had a plan. It felt really good to have a plan.

I never have a plan.

"Aunt Frannie?"

She was still on the phone. "What is it, hon? You know you should be in bed, it's almost nine."

"Did you find the ca-ca-candles?"

"No, Derek. I found two cans of pork beans, though. Good night, hon."

"Good night."

On my way down to the basement, I made sure to land loudly on every step, then I crept back up and tiptoed to the kitchen. I passed Mom's bedroom, but the door was shut.

It's always shut.

I pulled on the back door, making sure not to make a sound, and snuck out.

The yard seemed bigger. The sky, darker. I was the only one awake in the whole universe, and all I had in my pockets were two quarters and some of Nick's raisins.

I pulled the sleeves of the sweater over my hands and headed for Wellington Street.

The guys had already left the restaurant, but I knew where they were. I decided to take the alleys to Gordon Street; that way, no one would spot me and report my whereabouts to Aunt Frannie in the morning. There was a thin coat of frost on the ground and my breath streamed in and out of my lips like I was boiling pasta in my mouth.

I walked fast, with my head down, trying to ignore the barking dogs as I passed. I hadn't brought my medicine and I was beginning to feel a little short of breath, so I slowed down.

Then I heard some voices.

They were coming from the street. Gordon Street. The voices were uneven, some yelling angrily, some hissing low, some pitched high and threatening. All of them were coming from Sebastian's front yard.

I stopped.

Nick's voice was the deepest of them all. I could single it out easily. "Get your hands off me," I heard him snarl. "Or cleaning up your face's gonna take longer than your house."

That's when I decided to step out of the alley and see what was happening.

The first thing I saw was Sebastian's maple tree. It looked like the dress Lene wore when she was a flower girl last year. I guess Nick had gotten toilet paper from everyone who would give it to him, because *my* rolls couldn't have done that. The second thing I saw was the front door. It reminded me of Slimer from the *Ghostbusters* movie. Except thinner.

Then I saw Sebastian rolling on the ground with JF, the two of them punching each other's shoulders and growling like mad dogs.

Then I saw Terry trying to hold Nick back from destroying David.

David kept yelling, "Come on, Nick! Come on, hit me! I know you want to. You've been wanting to hit me since Miguel—"

The last thing I saw before being struck down by David's elbow was Nick punching David.

Something exploded inside my head and everything went black. When I opened my eyes, I was lying on my back on Sebastian's lawn.

"Oh fuck me."

I recognized Nick's voice.

He was pacing around me. "This is your fault, Dave. I swear to God, if that kid has anything broken..."

There was a pounding in my head, but when I wiped my nose, I didn't find any blood. David's elbow must have hit me in the forehead, because I have a small bluish bump there today. Everyone says I was only out for less than a second.

I can't believe I fainted in front of Nick and his friends.

I tried to sit up, but Terry held me back. "No, Derek, stay down. Sebastian's getting some ice."

I heard a woman's voice in the background. It was Mrs. Pinet, Sebastian and David's mom. "What in heaven's name is going on here!"

David looked down at me and winked. His lip was fat. "Mom, it's okay. We were just having a little fun and it got out of hand—"

"A little fun? David, look at my tree! And the door! What happened to my door?"

"I'll clean it, Mom. Bas and me, we'll take care of it. Right, Bas?"

Sebastian had reappeared. He managed to slither past his mom in the doorway and was bringing me a pack of frozen peas. "Right."

"Who's that for? What happened to that boy?" Mrs. Pinet sounded like a baby bird. "Oh my, is that the O'Reilly boy? Derek, is that you?"

I sat up and my eyes moved around the front lawn. JF had bailed. *Predictable.* Sebastian sat on the curb with his head between his knees. Josh and Terry stood a safe measure away from Mrs. Pinet's slimy front door. Both their T-shirts were ripped, and their hair looked like shrubs in the fall. They were almost as out of breath as I get when I'm having an episode.

Nick was pulling the toilet paper out of the tree.

"Nicolas, you leave that alone. Don't touch anything on my

property. I'm calling your father. You stay put. You and your no-good friends." Mrs. Pinet was on her way to me. "Oh dear, look at you. What are you doing with these, these…these criminals?"

I got to my feet and dusted myself off. I felt like I was going to be sick, but I clenched my jaw and held it down.

Mrs. Pinet lifted my face to the street lamp and frowned. "Well, you aren't bleeding. You look all right. Sit down. I'm going back inside to call Mr. Lund." She walked away, and then said, "You know, Derek, your mom's been through a lot. She doesn't need all this extra worrying."

What was Mom going to say? Would she punish me? Would she call Dad? Would she cry and scream?

I was hoping she would.

At least that way, she wouldn't be sleeping.

Mrs. Pinet went back into the house and I sat down like she asked me.

"That bitch is gonna call your dad, man." Josh had taken a few steps in Nick's direction and was trying to make eye contact with Nick. But Nick kept staring at the ground. His long hair hung down into his eyes. I couldn't make out his expression, but I knew it probably looked a lot like the mask he had made. "So fucking what," he whispered. *"C'est la vie."*

C'est la vie. That means "that's life." I don't know why Nick said that. Life isn't that.

It just isn't.

"Oh, Nick man, I can't get in trouble again, you know my dad… Come on, Nico boy, don't lemme stand here with my dick in the wind."

Josh's father is in the army. Josh can do a hundred pushups without breaking a sweat. His stomach is harder than a concrete block, on account of his dad's strict regimen. "Come on, Blue. Fuck, come on! I'm fucking bailing, okay? And you shake my hand on it, man, you promise not to come after me tomorrow."

Nick threw a finger up in Josh's panicked face. "Okay, fuck off," he said quietly. "Get the fuck outta here."

Josh bolted out of the street faster than Carl Lewis. "I owe you one, Lund," he shouted over his shoulder.

David sighed. "Nick, why'd you let him leave?"

David's dark eyes shine every time he speaks to Nick. Like he has fever.

Before Nick could answer him, Mrs. Pinet had come back out. We all stiffened at the sight of her smile. "Okay, boys. Mr. Lund is on his way." She folded her arms around herself. "And you, Nicolas, well, you're just lucky my husband isn't home." She turned to David. "Get all this cleaned up and go to bed. Your father will deal with you when he comes back from his business trip."

Sebastian whined, "But, Mom, I didn't do anything—"

"Shut up, you little shit." David yanked Sebastian off the curb. "You heard Mom, get some trash bags from the shed."

Sebastian kicked a rock into the street and looked over at Nick. "This all Boone's fault, you know. He started all of this."

David slapped his brother's shoulder. "Shut up! You don't know when to shut up, do you? It's over." Then David stared into Nick's face. "Right, Nicolai?"

Nick held David's hot stare. "Right," he said quietly. "We're even."

I never noticed, but David is almost as tall as Nick, and he's got the same kind of eyes, except his are almost black and his hair is dark and curly.

"I'm sorry about what my brother said about you." David's voice is different when he speaks to Nick. It sounds like he's in a lot of pain. "You're not...*you know.*"

"Retarded?" Nick whispered with a half smile.

David's breath seemed to get caught in his throat. "That's right you big retard."

When Nick laughed, it resonated through the street. He laughs like the Green Giant. At the sound of it, everyone seemed to let out some of the extra air in their lungs.

I kind of felt like one of them for a minute.

Nick looked over at me, like he had forgotten I was even there, and frowned. "You all right? How's your face?"

I nodded.

"You shouldn't have come. I'm gonna be in deep shit 'cause of it."

I had never thought of that. Of how bad it would look to Johan. I hadn't planned on getting Nick in trouble, I just wanted to see what he was going to do with the toilet paper. "I ca-ca-came by myself. You-you didn't ask me to—"

"Yeah, well, you try tellin' my dad that."

I bit down on my lip. That nice feeling was gone. I only felt like crying.

"Okay." Nick stretched his arms out and took a deep breath. "I hear the van. You guys don't say a thing. Not a fucking thing. Got it, Terry? You lemme do all the talking."

When Johan pulled up, all my courage leaked out of me. I had never seen his face like that. It hung down and all his features seem to meet in the middle. Johan climbed out. He didn't even look at any of us. He walked slowly to the front door and knocked.

Mrs. Pinet's face appeared in the wedge. "John," she called him.

Johan means John. I didn't know that. That's Dad's name.

"I want you to know that I don't plan on reporting this to the police." she said. "I know you and Helga are good folk and you can handle this matter privately." She lowered her voice, but we could still hear her. "I know he's been givin' you some problems. I heard about what they found in his locker."

What was she talking about?

Johan said something, but we couldn't make out his words. Mrs. Pinet nodded and then called to her sons, "Come on, boys, you'll finish this in the morning. It's late, there's school tomorrow. Get inside."

Sebastian immediately dropped the bag and skipped up the stairs into the house.

David hesitated, but Nick tossed his chin up and whispered, "Better do what she says."

David's body seemed to harden, and his mouth looked hungry for something. "Nick, oh Nick."

Nick tensed. "Go."

David's lips formed a strange smile, and he disappeared into the house.

The front porch light went off.

"Get in the truck." Johan had opened the passenger door for Nick. "Derek, Terry, get in the back."

We all obeyed.

Johan drove Terry home. On the way there, none of us said a word.

I could hear Terry swallowing beside me, that's how quiet it was. When we got to his apartment building, Terry leaned between the front seats. "Thank you, sir. Have a good night, sir."

Johan didn't say anything. He waited until Terry was safely inside his apartment, and drove away slowly.

That's when I noticed I wasn't breathing much. As a matter of fact, none of my breaths made it past my throat. I pushed my shoulders down and forced them there, like Mom had showed me, then I widened my nostrils to try and get some more air inside them. I leaned back into the seat and closed my eyes. Sometimes, if I concentrate and picture the sponges inside my chest opening up like flowers after the rain, I can get my lungs to work without my medicine.

Johan had started talking. He wasn't yelling, just talking real slow, but it couldn't be good because he was grumbling in Norwegian.

Nick didn't say much, aside from a grunt here or there. Once in a while, when Johan raised his voice a bit, Nick would sigh heavily or chew on his thumbnail.

Trying to understand what they were saying helped me keep my mind off my episode and slowly, my breaths became deeper.

Then Johan looked up to the rearview mirror. "Nicolai says we shouldn't tell your aunt you were out with them tonight. What do you think, Derek? Do you think I should lie to your auntie? Do you think a young man should avoid responsibility or consequences for his actions? Do you think it's how good men behave? Should we all connive and deceive the women who care about us?"

I had the feeling he wasn't really talking to me.

"Should we? What do you think? What is the proper and honorable way to deal with this mess? You tell me."

Nick sank back into his seat. "Dad, why don't you leave the poor kid alone?"

The poor kid. Is that what I am to Nick?

"I think we-we shuh-shu-should tell my-my aunt." I said, trying to sound brave. "I want to."

Johan pulled up in their driveway. He sighed. "I think so too." He turned to Nick. "See, the boy's eleven years old and he has more guts than you do. Go inside. Mom wants to talk to you, and I suggest you don't argue with her."

There was nothing I could do for him.

I watched Nick climb out of the van and walk up the stairs. He pushed the front door open and then crept inside. Johan rubbed his face. "What am I going to do with that boy?" He came around and opened the door for me. "You want me to come with you, or can you handle this on your own?"

"I'll be okay by-by myself."

"All right. Listen to me. You're a good boy, Derek. I know you don't have it easy. I know you miss your dad."

I don't miss Dad at all, but I let him say it anyway.

"Derek, I'm counting on you to try and keep Boone straight. His mom and I feel like he's trying to follow down his brother's path, and that's not a good thing. There's not much we can do for Nicolai, he's too headstrong, too angry, but Boone, Boone we can still work on. I want you to be the voice of reason. Okay? You understand?"

The thought of trying to keep Boone from doing anything is kind of funny. But I nodded. "But Mr. Lund, *Johan*...Nick isn't that-that bad, he was on-on-only—"

"There are things you don't know about my son. He's trouble. It's best if you stay away from him." Johan pointed to my front door. "Now go inside, before you freeze to death."

Trouble. What kind of trouble is Nick?

Inside, Aunt Frannie was still on the phone. When she saw me, she hung up without saying good-bye. "Honey? What are doing? Were you outside?" She came to me and put her hands on my face. They were very warm. "Baby, you're frozen. Where were you? I thought you were in bed. Where did you go, Derek?"

I opened my mouth to explain, but a big fat sob came out instead of words. I couldn't control it. Snot and tears shot out of me and my shoulders heaved up and down. "He-he was trying to de-defend himself," I stammered between sobs. "He was only trying to ma-make them take it buh-back. He isn't dumb."

Aunt Frannie smelled like Chantilly, baby powder, and cigarettes. "There, there. Did you get in some sort of fight, is that what happened?"

I pulled away a little, and wiped my nose with the back of my sleeve. "Uh-huh."

"And don't tell me. Boone was with ya."

I shook my head. "No, he's grounded. It was Nick. But-but he didn't ask me to co-co-come. Just wanted toilet pa-paper."

Aunt Frannie chewed on her bottom lip for a second, and then she threw her head back and sighed. "Nicolai Lund. That boy is so dangerous. His looks alone could kill you."

I wasn't sure what she meant, but she had this dreamy look in her eyes. Then they cleared up and she got serious again. "I'm gonna run you a hot bath. Throw your clothes in the hamper and wrap yourself in your dad's flannel robe." She went to the hall closet to fetch a towel. "Now, how should I punish you? What would your mom do?"

I thought about it for a while.

Mom wouldn't do anything.

Then I thought of Nick and Boone. "I should be grounded until-til Saturday. And no-no TV."

Aunt Frannie popped her head out of the bathroom. "Sounds fair to me."

❖

I am dazed, for lack of a better word.

Last night, over dinner (the first Nathan and I have had together since he came back from England, and that was eight days ago), Nathan raised his glass, proposing a toast. "To the man who brings color to my life."

That was sweet.

Of course, I instantly became suspicious.

He set his glass down, peering into my eyes. "Do you like the wine?"

It was spectacular. As always.

He drew in a long breath. "So," he said, staring down at his hands. "I've been thinking."

My neck tensed up. Nathan is at his best when he is doing, not *thinking*. Every time he thinks too much, we end up doing something drastic.

Like moving into a place we couldn't afford if he ever lost his job.

"Listen, Der. You know I'm not a sentimentalist."

Well. That's an understatement.

"But I think me and you, we have something solid."

I poked at my shrimp, feeling my heartbeat pick up the pace.

"Hey, look at me," he insisted softly. "No?"

I nodded.

Yes. Solid. Absolutely.

Like cement.

I chewed on my lip.

I decided to try a bite and see if I could swallow it.

"Derek. After two years, you're still an enigma to me." He sighed. "You know, I used to think that would bother me one day, but I realize, it only makes me crazier about you. Makes me want you even more."

The shrimp was definitely too spicy for my taste. Nathan swears by this fresh pepper puree. He dumps it into everything.

"Der? Hello? You listening to any of this?"

I glanced up. His ebony eyes flickered with a deadly anger for a moment. At least, I think they did.

Maybe it was the candlelight.

"Yes," I promptly returned. "Go on."

"What are you thinking about right now?"

Whenever people ask me that question, my mind goes blank. Imagine a vacant parking lot. Like that. Lots of expensive spaces filled with nothing.

"Der?"

I stuffed some rice into mouth, hoping to buy some time.

"Derek O'Reilly. This is Nathan Ross putting in a request for a full sentence, please. I want nouns, verbs, and if you can manage an adjective or two, I'd be eternally grateful."

I smiled.

He poured himself another glass. "Do you know what that smile does to me?" He took a sip, and I waited, watching the wax drip along the candle. "It kindles me," he said. "Ignites my very soul."

Nathan is a closer.

Life is a good deal to him.

"These last two years have been the best years of my life. I can't imagine a future without you."

The wax had clumped; it was going to tip the stick.

"I know you need your space. I respect that. I can appreciate it. And that's why I think we're perfect for each other. Der—" He paused, then rose. "I guess what I'm trying to say is—" He pulled a box out of his pocket. "Derek, baby."

Please.

A heart attack.

An aneurysm.

A flash of lightning through the bay window.

My heart had begun pounding, and its demented rhythm only reminded me that I was alive. That meant having to hear and answer the coming question.

"Let's do it, Der. Let's take this up a notch. You and me. What do you say? Will you marry me?"

I've long ago come to terms with my homosexuality. I live it in a fairly healthy way. I've worked through many issues through the years, and I pride myself on the progress I have made.

I am not a fag. I'm gay.

But marrying another man? *Marrying.* As in "husband and husband."

A nervous chuckle unfortunately escaped my treacherous lips.

Nathan's handsome features sagged. "Did you just laugh?" He shrank back.

I sprung out of my chair. "No, Na-Nate, I-I just—"

"You're stuttering."

I raised a brow, trying to paint on the cutest possible expression on my face. "No, I didn't."

"Yeah. You did. Just now."

"Okay, so?"

"You only do it when you're trying to hold something back." He sucked in a short but determined breath, then swiftly rubbed his angular chin. "All right. Let's try this again, okay?"

Twice? I mean, *twice*?

"Derek. Marry me."

My knees locked.

He popped that box open and there it was. A silver band. Nice too.

"We're ready for this, Der. I know it. I feel it."

Forever. Monogamy. Forever.

"Look into my eyes." His eyes were like two puddles of shiny petroleum. "Marry me, Derek. We'll have the biggest, most lavish wedding you could ever dream of. The whole deal, Der. Think Hotel Saint James. Think top hats and champagne fountain. Think fois gras and jazz."

My heart fluttered a little. Who can resist fois gras? Except me, of course, as I'm a vegetarian, but what's that to Nathan?

He pulled me close, binding me to his chest. "So?"

The last two years have been the most symmetrical years of my life. Dark and light, bad and good have shared an equal part of my existence.

That's something, isn't it?

I lifted my eyes to his and smiled. "All right."

He spun me around, dipped me, and then kissed my mouth with a ferocious passion I haven't gotten from him in too long. "Oh baby, we have got so much planning to do. We're going to have an engagement party, of course—"

"Of course."

His gaze wandered, as if he was imagining a ballroom filled with power and crystal. "We'll make it chic, but intimate. Only our closest friends and family."

He means, his closest friends, as I have none.

"We could do a Bal Masqué."

Now, how gay is that?

Suddenly, he turned to me and frowned. "What do you think your parents will say?"

I thought about it for a moment.

Visualized myself sitting in their kitchen.

Nathan brought my fingers to his lips. "Whatever they say, you know you have my support and understanding."

How is it possible for a man to constantly say the right things? Isn't that God's job?

"Derek. I want you to be happy. I want the best for you. And I know I'm the man who can make that happen for you."

A closer should know when the deal has been sealed.

No sense in overselling.

He slid back into his seat and picked up his fork. "Okay, babe. Let's finish dinner and go for a walk on the mountain, yes?"

❖

We had a meeting this afternoon. A surprise meeting.
The kind that comes with a tap on the shoulder and a somber face.
We were told there's going to be a merger. One branch will be dissolved. Another will merge with ours.
"This is going to be transitional phase for us," said Goldman (that's my director). "I'm going to need your patience and cooperation. As we go along, you will be informed of the changes and your input will be considered. However—" His voice thickened with impending doom. "Some positions may be jeopardized."
"What the fuck does that mean?" asked Jake, livening up in his chair. Jake is the Q.A.S.T. (Quality Assurance System Testing) analyst. Big title, bigger ego. "You saying my job is on the line?"
His job. Everything is me me me with this guy.
"Jake." Goldman rose and poured himself another cup of coffee from the portable machine.
Why does it always look like he's been sleeping in his Moores suit?
"I don't have any more information, I wish I could ease your mind, but right now, things are being looked into and we still haven't figured out—"
"Well. That's just great. That's fucking great."
Isabelle, our new translator, let out an explosive sigh. "Can we hear what the man has to say, please?"
Jake shot her a mean look, then folded his arms over himself.
Goldman shuffled some papers. "Okay, listen, guys. I know I have the best team here. I'm gonna do everything I can. But I'm gonna need your help. For the next few weeks, I need everybody here to be on their toes. This is crucial, you understand?"
I glanced around.
Everyone's eyes were glued to the table. I could almost hear them subtracting their monthly expenses out of their unemployment check.
I wasn't feeling those fears. Why would I? I've got a boyfriend, *fiancé*, who makes enough money to support a small school. I'm taken care of. No worries.
"I'm gonna turn you loose, I know you all have a full schedule today." Goldman plucked the conference door opened. "But if there is anything you need to discuss with me, you're all welcome to."

I picked up my empty paper cup.

"Derek," said Goldman, patting shoulders and shaking hands, "I'd like to talk you."

My breath burned my chest. Goldman has never even looked my way.

He shut the door. "Sit down, please." His smile was genuine enough.

Okay. He wasn't going to fire me.

"More coffee?"

I shook my head. "Thank you."

"All right." He gave my face a quick sweep of the eye and leaned in. His face is lined with orange wrinkles. One of his hobbies is falling asleep in a tanning booth on Friday afternoons. "I want you to know that your job is safe. I've made sure of it."

I bit down on my lip, but then, made myself stop. I have to try to be more assertive in my body language. Or so Nathan says.

"I know we haven't had a chance to talk one-on-one, you and I, but I've been following your progress, and I have to say, I'm very pleased with your performance." He took a noisy sip of his coffee. "I'd like to ask a favor of you."

The image of him whipping out his Viagra-friendly cock caused my anus to constrict.

"I'd like you to keep things under control, you know, make sure everyone stays calm, make sure no one starts feeding the rumor mill. You know how these things get blown out of proportion. You seem like a levelheaded guy. Think you can do that?"

On a average day, my spoken word count is between four and six. Aside from a nod and smile, my colleagues seldom even acknowledge my existence.

Unless the paper tray is empty.

"I think you're a leader, the quiet type, but nonetheless a leader."

The only thing I lead is a boring life.

"Well." Goldman got to his feet. "I'm glad we talked."

I nodded. "Yes sir."

CHAPTER THREE

Dear Bump,

Dad sent us a check.

It must have been a lot of money because Aunt Frannie tucked it away in her shirt and had a big glass of Dad's whiskey. "Oh boy," she gasped, "we're gonna be having a nice Christmas."

She promised we'd get a VCR and a new snow suit for me.

Also, I think I'm turning into a pervert.

My penis hurts.

I've been rubbing it after lunch, and at night before I go to bed. And I've ruined it because it keeps leaking. Except, when it squirts, it feels so good that I can't stop doing it some more. I can't sleep if I don't make it squirt.

It all started when I slept over at Boone's. That was two days ago. After we got our first snow. It was the day after his birthday. November thirteenth.

He turned twelve, so it's his lucky year.

"If you sleep over there," warned Aunt Frannie, "you better be a good boy."

Of course I was gonna be a good boy.

Why wouldn't I be a good boy?

When I rang the Lunds' doorbell, my stomach twisted all up. My mouth tasted like metal. I clutched my bag and waited for someone to let me in. They hardly ever hear their doorbell, on account of all the noise the Lunds make.

Eventually, Lene stuck her face in the window and came to the door. "Hello, Derek."

"Hello, Le-Lene."

"Boone says you're sleeping over." She looked me over. Her eyes are like a bedtime sky. She wore a yellow sweater and Sylvester the cat slippers. "What you got in the bag?"

"My stuff."

"My bedroom is next to the living room. But I never sleep. You can come up and visit our baby later."

She turned on her heels and I let myself in.

Inside, it smelled like lemon and beets.

I set my bag down by the couch and walked to the kitchen. I stepped over the threshold. Mrs. Lund had her back to me, stirring something in a big ceramic pot. "Hi, Derek," she greeted me without turning around, "Boone is downstairs. You know he's still punished, but I expect you guys will be quiet, right?"

"Yes-yes ma'am."

She spun around and wiped her hands on her pale blue apron. She had lipstick on her shiny mouth and her hair was tied back in a long blond ponytail. "Okay then, off you go." She licked the spoon and smiled. "Supper is in ten minutes."

Supper? I had already eaten. I hadn't planned on eating with the Lunds, on account of me wanting to vomit whenever I do. "Um, Mrs. Lund, I already had a sa-sa-sandwich with my-my aunt—"

"A sandwich? Please, that's not supper. You'll eat with us. You'll like it. It's my specialty."

Mrs. Lund has the same exact eyes as Nick. They find a spot inside yours and make a nest. I couldn't argue with her, so I nodded and left her smiling.

I went downstairs to find Boone.

He was in the playroom, watching *Top Gun*.

Again.

He's been watching it every day ever since he was grounded.

"Hey, Boone—"

"Shh," he hissed, "they're kissing."

I watched the screen. I've seen that scene before. It's gross. Their tongues keep slipping in and out of their mouths like slimy snakes.

It makes me cringe. "I'm go-gonna go read a co-comic in your bedroom."

Boone only nodded. His eyes didn't leave that TV.

When I passed Nick's room, my heart jumped up inside my throat.

The door was ajar.

He wasn't home.

I had to see his things.

I pushed on the door.

My eyes swarmed around like bees over a strawberry patch.

I was terrified Nick would show up and tap me on the shoulder. "Hey pervert," he would say, "what you doing?"

I took a shy step inside.

I could smell him. I could smell his clothes and sheets.

Nick smells like suntan lotion and Ivory soap.

I looked at the walls first. They were plastered with posters. One got my attention. It was the picture of some guy with hair like a spider and white makeup on. His name is Robert Smith. Beside it was a picture of a skeleton face, and the caption read: "Didn't hurt that much." In the corner, there was a brown guitar. It leaned on a dresser whose drawers overflowed with clothes. Nick's blue sweater hung over the edge of the second one. On top of the dresser were a whole bunch of things. Some papers with music on them, some drawings he made, rubber bands, a statue of Rocky, some magazines, and some used Kleenex. On the floor, there was even more stuff. Clothes, socks, more magazines, empty containers of yogurt and Jello, some cracker crumbs and a pair of black boxers.

I never knew Nick was so messy. Even his bed was undone. There was a bag of chips on his pillow.

He's going to need a maid when he's older.

For sure.

Of all the things I saw in his bedroom, one thing stuck out the most: on his bed stand, right beside his Halloween mask, there was a large, hardcover book. I walked over to take a closer look at it. It was least six hundred pages.

If Nick is dyslexic, then I wonder how long it took him to read it.

What kind of book would be worth all that time and energy?

I picked it up and read the title. *Professional Cooking: Learn the tricks of the trade, from classical French cuisine to the newest trends.*

A recipe book? Why is Nick reading this? It can't be for school.

Just as I was passing out of his room, Mrs. Lund called out. *"A table! Et on se grouille!"*

Mrs. Lund insists on speaking French to the kids. I understand most of it, but can't put two words together without sounding mentally challenged. Nick speaks French fluently, as does Lene.

Boone, not so much. "I don't plan on dating no French girls anyway."

Upstairs, Johan set the table while Mrs. Lund poured the soup into the bowls. They were square bowls. I had never seen bowls like that. "Hands cleaned?" she asked.

They weren't.

Boone and I went to the bathroom, followed by Lene and her doll. She made us wait while she meticulously scrubbed the doll's fingers. "Our baby has to be squeaky clean, don't you think?"

Boone barked a laugh. "You're so nuts, squirrels wanna crawl up your ear."

The smell of Mrs. Lund's cooking had begun to make me hungry, and since I hadn't seen Nick around, I figured I would be okay. I felt my muscles relax and I pulled out my designated chair, and then sat down. "It smells nuh-nice, Mrs. Lund."

"Why, thank you, Derek." She turned to Boone and slapped his shoulder. "See? See how polite he is? He has manners."

Boone shot me a murderous stare and picked up his spoon. "That's 'cause he's a suckup," he said with a grin.

Johan chuckled a little, and we all dove right in. The soup tasted like fall, but without the cold. It was purple and really thin, but filling. I was enjoying it.

Then, just like that, Nick walked into the kitchen.

Like magic.

I hadn't even heard the front door. He appeared right out of nowhere. And at the wrong time too. I had just put a piece of bread in my mouth. Now it was stuck there, because I couldn't swallow it. I knew I would choke to death if I tried.

"Where have you been?" Mrs. Lund asked.

Nick tucked a loose strand of his ash blond hair behind his ear and shrugged. "Dave's."

Since that fight, David and Nick have been hanging out again. Boone says they see each other all the time.

"We've already started supper, and you know the rule."

The rule is, if someone shows up after the first bite has been eaten, that person has to wait until the meal is done, and then have whatever is left over when the table has been cleared.

"Helga, let him eat. We have a guest." Johan gestured for Nick to sit down.

Mrs. Lund didn't seem pleased at all, but she didn't say anything.

Nick went to the sink to rinse his hands, and pulled out the only available chair at the table.

The one directly facing me.

My chest tightened as that piece of bread began to slowly disintegrate inside my mouth.

I finally swallowed it.

Nick poured himself two ladles of the soup and then started eating as if he hadn't eaten since last Christmas.

No one was talking anymore. If it weren't for the radio, we could have heard each other breathing.

Lene, who was sitting to Nick's left, tugged on his shirt. "Will you help me braid Cassandra's hair after supper?"

Nick glanced over and winked at her. "Sure thing."

"She has to look pretty for her baptism."

"Honey," snapped Mrs. Lund, "I told you, we're not having a doll baptized."

Lene pouted. Her lips are like an upside-down apricot slice. "But, Mom, she's going to go to hell if we don't. And her father is Irish, we can't expect him to accept that."

Boone snorted a laugh and soup came flying out of his nose.

Nick cocked his head, then looked up at me and grinned. "Irish, huh?"

My cheeks combusted." I'm not-not that doll's fa-father."

"So you're denying your paternity?" Nick seemed very amused. "I think we should have a blood test done."

Boone twitched and yelped next to me.

Mrs. Lund fought back a smile. "Enough, Nicolai. Leave him alone." She stared down Lene. "And you, young lady, you are not to read another one of my lady magazines, understood?"

Of course, I didn't have another bite after that.

After dinner, Boone and I decided to go downstairs to play a game of Monopoly. We weren't allowed to go outside, on account of him still being grounded and all.

Nick had disappeared again.

Boone and I were alone in the basement, playing and eating leftover Halloween candy.

"So when's your dad coming back?" Boone was chewing on some Tire Sainte-Catherine.

"Dunno. Aunt Frannie says after Christmas-as maybe."

"What you gettin'?"

"A VCR."

Boone's eyes widened. "Really. Wow."

He landed on the "go to jail" square.

Again.

"So, your brother had to take the ca-ca-car back, huh?"

"Yeah. But he said he didn't care. He doesn't need a car. Dave's got a car."

David has everything. He doesn't even have to ask. But it's funny, because he looks empty all the time.

"So, are you gonna go to the stupid Valentine's Day dance?" Boone tried to sound like he didn't want to go to the school dance, but I know he's been planning for it ever since Mrs. Saint-Amour announced they were going to have one this year.

And it's only for the fifth and sixth graders.

"Dunno."

"O'Reilly, you have to come. I mean, you have to."

"Why?"

"Because. You just have to."

I frowned, and then shrugged. "Who-who you going with?"

This dance is a couples only dance. Every boy has been encouraged to ask a girl of his choice to escort him.

"Kenya."

Kenya is a black girl. She's from Africa. Her skin is almost blue. She wears flowered dresses and yellow ribbons in her hair.

"Did she say-ay yes?"

Of course I know she said yes. I heard Susan and Marylou whimpering about how Boone was going to take a "nigger" to the dance. Every time I hear the N-word, my fists close up. I want to scream, but I never do. I never say anything.

Just like when JF and his friends call me a faggot.

Boone raised a brow and smiled. "She's the one who asked me. Did you see her eyes? I've never seen eyes like that. I'm gonna try to kiss her. If she lets me. I really hope she lets me. Do you think she'll let me?"

I can't see why on earth she wouldn't. Boone has nice lips. They never have leftover sleep on them, and his teeth are straight and white because he brushes them a lot. He never has bad breath, well, only on Saturday morning after he's had Johan's onion omelet.

Not that I would kiss him. I wouldn't kiss Boone. No way.

"Dunno." I said. "De-depends, I guess."

"On what?"

"On if she-she wants to."

He sighed. "Gee thanks, Red. That really helps a lot." He rolled the dice. "Well, anyway, it's worth a shot, right?"

"I guess."

"What do you mean, I guess? Don't you wanna kiss a girl on the mouth? Besides, it's necessary."

"How so?" I couldn't find the necessity he was talking about.

"To get hair down there. To have your thing grow. For your voice to change. You know. Things like that. That's how Nick got so tall. He kissed a lot of girls. He started way before me. Says he was kissing girls back when he was in diapers."

For some reason, I can believe that. "Well, okay, but-but what if girls don't wa-wanna kiss me, huh?"

"Plenty of girls wanna kiss you."

"Right. Na-na-name one. And Lene doesn't count."

Boone rubbed his chin and looked up to the ceiling. He didn't say anything for at least five minutes.

"Well?" I insisted. "Na-name one."

Boone slapped his thigh and then smiled like he had won an Olympic gold medal. "Sue Ellen."

I wrinkled my nose. "Your cousin-in from Oslo?"

"That's right. Remember, she kept trying to get you to go in the shed with her?"

I remember. She didn't have a neck or knees, and her face looked like yellow Play-Doh. "That doesn't co-co-count either."

"Why not?"

"Just doesn't."

Boone folded his arms around his chest. "You wanna watch *Top Gun*?"

"You're kidding, right? Boone, no-no."

"So what then?"

"Dunno."

Boone's face lit up. "You wanna make prank phone calls? We could do the one where I pretend I'm being murdered."

Boone is the best at prank calls. One time, he actually had a woman in tears.

"You don't think we'll ge-get in trouble?" I asked, remembering my pledge to Aunt Frannie.

"We'll get the phone from the kitchen and plug it in down here. Mom's doing the neighbor's nails tonight and Dad's watching TV, so…"

"What about-bout Nick?"

"Nico? He's with Dave. He won't come home until we're sleeping."

Disappointment and relief were rolling around inside my gut. "Oh. What are they do-doing?"

"Dunno. They go by the river a lot. So, anyways, why do you keep asking me about my brother all the time?"

My eyes darted up. Saliva got caught in my throat. "I don't. I wa-was just making conversa-sation. I don't care what your brother do-does. I mean, what's it to me—"

"Yeah, you do. Don't lie. You're always looking at him."

My heart beat in all different directions. "I never loo-look at him."

"Yeah, you do." Boone casually got to his feet, then turned the TV on. "It doesn't matter if you do, I don't care." He popped the *Top Gun* cassette into the machine. "You can play with my GI Joes if you like. I'm gonna watch this."

GI Joes?

I haven't played GI Joes since last year. And I wasn't even playing really, I was just lining them up and shooting them down with a rubber band. "Fine," I said, "I'll be-be in your room, *not playing*."

I went to his room and plopped down on the bed.

I stared at the ceiling for a long time. Finally, I got Boone's GI Joes out of the shoe box and lined them up. Then I heard some noise. Voices.

I tensed my neck. It was Nick, and David was with him. I shot my last soldier down and went to the door. I heard Nick's bedroom door shut and the voices became muffled, but I could still hear them talking through the wall that separates the boys' rooms. I couldn't make out all the words, on account of Johan doing an excellent job on the isolation in the basement.

I tried going back to preparing the second battalion for combat, but couldn't concentrate. I kept trying to hear what they were saying. Once in a while, I would hear Nick or David laugh, then it would get quiet again.

Before too long, my curiosity got the best of me.

I rose and crept out of Boone's room. Boone was in the playroom. He couldn't see me standing in the small hallway that connects the two bedrooms and the bathroom.

I stood between Boone's door and Nick's.

Now that I was closer, I could hear a little better.

I heard David's voice first. "Why not?"

They were playing some music.

"Stop," whispered Nick. I could barely hear him.

I stood stiff with my back against the wall, listening to them whisper to each other.

"You keep saying you wanna get out of here, Nick, this is your chance. If you come with me, we could—"

"I told you already. No, Dave." Nick's voice had risen over the music. He sounded tense.

"Why? I've got a job lined up and my friend says—"

"A job? You don't even know what kind of place that club is." Nick had lowered his voice again. "And you're gonna dance there?" I heard a thump, and then Nick said, "You're so fucking naïve, Davie. One day you're gonna get yourself into something you won't be able to get out of."

There was a long silence, and I almost changed my mind.

Then I heard David again. "That's why you should come out there with me."

The music had stopped, and I held my breath, pressing my back to the wall, with my ear tuned to their private conversation.

"Nick." David's voice had a strange sound to it. Like he was hurting. "I need you."

My heart skipped a beat.

Had he really said that?

David was getting upset. "I can't do this alone, but Nick, I can't stay here one more minute, I can't stand my life here. You don't know how bad it gets sometimes. You don't have to go to Loyola, you don't have to put up with that shit, I swear, Nick, I'll fucking kill myself if—"

"You shut the fuck up." Nick whispered, but his voice was hard. "Don't say shit like that. You're too good for that. You got talent, Dave, you got something at least, something to shoot for." He paused, and then spoke again. Softer. "What the fuck do I have, huh? I can't even read this piece-of-shit book—"

"Nick, no, that's not true and you know it. You have everything going for you. I think you're the most beautiful—" But David stopped.

I hadn't taken one single breath.

I opened my mouth to let some air in and closed my eyes. I don't know why I felt so weak. There was something in David's voice that made my belly feel tight and warm.

I kept hearing those three words in my head.

I need you. I need you. I need you.

My cheeks were hot.

Then I heard Nick whisper again. "They're gonna kick me out. Cause of the knife. She's gonna flip when I tell her. My dad...Oh fuck, Davie, what's he gonna think of me, you know?" Nick's voice dropped to a whisper again. "I don't know what to do...I just don't know anymore—"

"Nick. Oh Nick. Come here."

I couldn't even swallow anymore. They were barely whispering now. I took a step closer to Nick's door.

"Don't, Dave." I heard Nick say.

"Why? Why can't I just put my mouth —"

"No." Nick's voice was sharp and brutal. "Enough."

"Why? Damn it, Nick. One day it's yes, the next is no." David's tone had changed. He was whining. "You can't keep doing this to me. You're killing me. Look at me. Look how—"

"Get out."

Though it wasn't meant for me, I jumped at the sound of that order and leaped back to Boone's room with my heart in my throat. I shut the door behind me and leaned up against it. My breaths were uneven, and I couldn't seem to get the rhythm right. My eyes pulsed inside my head.

I slid down the door and sat with my head resting between my knees.

I listened.

Had David left?

No. He was still in Nick's bedroom. They weren't talking, though. I couldn't hear a thing. Except for the music. They had turned it back on.

I couldn't get that tightness in my belly to go away.

And it wasn't just my belly anymore.

That warm feeling had moved down into my privates.

I decided to go to the bathroom.

I hurried down the hall, and on the way, I listened for any voices, but heard none. Just music.

I locked myself up in the bathroom and sat on the counter with my back to the mirror.

That's when it happened.

My penis was swollen, like in the morning, but even if I wore my loose pajama bottoms, they still felt too tight. I didn't really wanna touch it, because I know it's a dirty thing to do. Mom says you only touch it when you wash, but I couldn't just leave it inside my pants, it was starting to throb.

What could I do?

The door was locked.

I checked it twice.

I only touched it a little. Just the tip because it was wet.

I need you.

My penis twitched inside my fingers and I shivered.

My knees bent.

I cleaned myself up with toilet paper and flushed three times, but even after I had washed my hands, I could still smell that hot stuff on my fingers. I went back to Boone's bedroom and lay down.

I felt very tired all of a sudden.

Boone came in later and climbed on top.

He has a bunk bed and it squeaks a lot.

"Are you asleep?" he asked.

"I wa-was a little, but not really."

"Sorry 'bout what I said."

"It's okay."

"Do you wanna go for a bike ride down by the river tomorrow morning? We could try to find a turtle."

"Yes."

"Derek?"

"Yes?"

"I think my brother's gonna run away soon." Boone's voice was full of doom. "I know it. He's gonna leave, and he won't say good-bye."

I tensed up. "He wouldn't."

"Yes, he would. You don't know Nick."

"I hope he-he stays," I whispered, half for myself.

Nathan is in Toronto this weekend.

Some sales conference. I swear, if it weren't for salespeople, the hotel and food industry would go bankrupt.

"Be good," he said as he walked out the front door. "I'll call you tonight. Have a good time with your folks."

A good time with my folks.

That's like asking me to enjoy guilt-free anal sex.

I was there tonight, at my parents'. Mom looked well. Dad, not so much, but he always looks like he's been sleeping under a train on Sunday evenings.

"Aunt Fran passed by this afternoon." Mom scooped some instant mashed potatoes on my plate. "Poor thing."

There's nothing poor about Aunt Fran.

"Says she's been thinking about reuniting with God."

I smashed some fried onions into my potatoes.

When Aunt Fran reaches the Pearly Gates, I have a feeling God's going to ask her to hurry up before he changes his mind.

"Have you been to church lately?"

I glanced up.

Me?

"Father Neil was asking about you this morning."

Well. I'm sure he would love to bless Nathan's and my homosexual marriage.

"Maybe you should pass by the presbytery, you know, say hello. He'd like that."

Yes. And we can discuss Sodom and Gomorrah.

"Dolores," snapped Dad, causing the mush to stick in my throat, "why don't you leave the boy alone."

Mom's eyes hardened. "Just trying to get our boy to enter the Kingdom of Heaven, that's all."

Holy shit.

I giggled.

"Derek! I worry about your soul!"

Yes yes, I know. So do I.

I'd like to know where it went.

"I want you to go to Father Neil and repent. Confess your sins."

"Dolores. Enough!" Some potatoes flew out of Dad's mouth.

"But, John, don't you want —"

"Enough, woman. Let us eat in peace."

Whenever Dad calls Mom "woman," I'm always inclined to look under the table to check for shackles on her ankles.

"Well," said Mom, gathering our full plates. "At least I've made my peace with Our Heavenly Father." She set them in the sink. "You two are on your own."

Dad shot an uneasy glance my way, then shrugged.

I leaned back into my chair.

Why not throw a little liquid nitrogen on these open wounds. "Mom, Dad—"

Needless to say, the announcement of Nathan's and my engagement didn't go very well. Mom went through two boxes of Kleenex and Dad emptied the bar. I helped him a little. But it's done. Out of the way. I think they may even come.

By the door, Mom traced her finger along my chin. "Baby, I don't know why you're the way you are. Don't know if it's a malformation or some kind of mental disease, but I love you, regardless of it."

Malformation.

"I don't understand you, Derek. You're so handsome. Smart too. You could have any woman you want. You could give us grandchildren."

Oh no, mother, this disastrous gene pool stops here.

"I love you, honey."

"I love you too, Mom."

"Yes?"

I nodded. "Yes."

Nathan has hired a wedding planner.

The boy is gayer than a bag of Skittles.

He doesn't breathe, he hyperventilates. I can't stand being in the same room with him for more than three minutes.

"Tu vas voir mon petit roux, ton marriage va faire revirer Cléopatre dans son tombeau."

He's French too.

That means expensive.

"Are you sure we can afford all of—"

"Don't talk about money," Nathan says. "It doesn't sound good."

I manage financial portfolios for a living. Money is the only thing I'm comfortable talking about.

"Besides, baby, I got it covered. You don't have to worry about that."

Sometimes I feel like I'm the hired help.

"Gimme a kiss."

Okay, the hired help plus bonus.

Dear Bump,

Dad isn't coming home until March.

You know how long that is? That's a whole lot more than he had promised. But I don't care. If he wants to stay up there until summer, that's fine with me. I can take care of Aunt Frannie and Mom all by myself. I don't need Dad to help me with anything. I already know how to change a fuse. I already know how to unclog the toilet. I already know how to shovel the snow, and I don't even get any piled up on the sidewalk. I can do everything he does. I can make better sloppy joes, I bet.

Except I won't.

I already told Aunt Frannie about my plans to be a vegetarian.

"It's very fashionable," she said while she painted her toenails red. "Lots of sophisticated people are these days."

Oh, and Mom doesn't need Dad either. She only needs you, but you're in heaven. So. Too bad for her, I guess.

C'est la vie.

It's snowing again.

From my bed, I can see the snowflakes float past my window. They're pretty. I wish I could go play outside, but there's no one to play with. I've been all by myself since school let out for the holidays. The Lunds are in Florida. They always go to Florida for Christmas. They drive there. It takes so long that when they get there, it isn't even the same season. It's summer over there, I think. They swim in an ocean. Boone showed me pictures. The water is so big—it takes up the whole frame—and the sand isn't like the one we have in the sandbox, no sir, the sand over there is almost white. Like Mom's wedding band. Also, did you know that there's crabs on the beach? Boone and Lene hunt for them. They have contests, but I bet I could find the biggest one, on account of how patient I am.

The Lunds live in a hotel for two weeks. Boone says you don't have to make your bed. They have people who come in when you're out and make your bed for you, but of course, he's never actually seen them.

Once, I swam in a lake. It was pretty big too. I guess that counts for something.

Nick almost didn't go with them. He wanted to stay here, but Mrs. Lund made him. She threw his bag in the trunk and slapped the back of his head. I watched the whole thing from the living room window.

When their van rolled away, I saw David turn the street corner.

He was running, sprinting really, and he wasn't even wearing his coat. Just a T-shirt.

He yelled out Nick's name, then kicked the snowbank and walked away.

❖

Dear Bump,

I found the Hudson Bay on the map in my dictionary.

You go straight, then left, then straight all the way to the water. It's very far, but I don't plan on walking. I'll take the train, same as Dad. I have three hundred dollars and forty-five cents in my school account. Mom needs to sign a paper, but that's all right because I can almost copy her signature. Just need a little more practice, that's all. I'll go to the bank on Tuesday morning. That's when Aunt Frannie is going to take Mom to fix her hair. Then I'll buy a ticket. It's easy, there's a train station in the city. I know where the city is. I rode my bike there this summer.

I'll find Dad.

When Dad sees how far I've gone all by myself, he'll be surprised silly. He'll forget about the old me. He'll only see the new me, and I can help him with his work at the plant. This way, he'll get double the work done. He'll be the fastest up there, and no one will ever say Irishmen are just good for drinking and sleeping. We'll come back to Verdun and everyone will congratulate us. We'll be heroes.

Can you imagine what Boone would say if he knew what my plans are? His chin would drop to the floor, but I won't get to see his face when he finds out about it, because I'll be leaving before the Lunds get back.

I'll be gone before Aunt Frannie puts our 1987 calendar in the trash.

❖

Dear Bump,

I couldn't go to the Hudson Bay on account of Mom being so sick from nerves.

It happened the day before yesterday.

I was downstairs, playing with my new Transformers, when I heard Aunt Frannie screaming. I widened my eyes and held my breath.

"When are you gonna snap out of it, Dolores! That baby is gone! GONE!"

Then I heard Mom. She was screaming too, but her words were like Dad's sloppy joes. They didn't have any order. It didn't matter what place they took in a sentence.

Aunt Frannie cried louder. "What is that boy gonna do without his mama huh? You're breaking Red's spirit, Dolores, and I won't let you! He's a sensitive boy!"

Then there were some thumps.

Right above my head. Some clanking too. It was raining furniture on top of me. My mouth was still open, but my eyes were closed.

Shut tight.

The fighting and screaming went on for a while.

I kept looking out my window.

Kept hoping to see Boone's face in it. But he's still in Florida.

Building sand castles in the sun.

Finally, just when I thought I was gonna have to go up there and suck on my medicine, it stopped.

I rose.

Put my Transformers away in the red bin.

Sat down and folded my hands.

Aunt Frannie knocked on my door. "Baby?"

"Come in-in please." I sat up straight, holding my chin up.

"I need to talk to you."

Mom is going away for a while. She's going to be staying in a special place where they suck the blues out of you. Aunt Frannie says it's only for a couple of weeks, but Mom packed her big suitcase, the one with the umbrellas on it. Her drawers are empty.

She even took all of her books.

C'est la vie.

By the door, Mom hugged me. For a long time too. Her warm tears streamed down into my shirt. "I love you Red," she whispered, "you're my special boy. Be good to Aunt Frannie. Dad will be home soon."

❖

Could he be?

No. Impossible.

Complete paranoia on my part.

Nathan would never.

No.

But...could he?

Could he be that much of a two-timing snake?

No. I'm being ridiculous. It's self-sabotage, that's all.

I'm compelled to find something negative to dwell on.

It is in my nature to measure loss before it happens.

He would never do such a thing. He has too much respect for me. For our commitment.

Nathan wouldn't play with my life this way. We haven't used condoms in a year. He wouldn't play Russian roulette with my health.

No way.

It was just the bellboy, like he said.

And the laughter?

Nathan made a joke, yes, like he said, and I heard the bellboy laugh.

❖

Dear Bump,

The Lunds are back!

Boone's eyes look like blueberry Popsicles. His teeth probably glow in the dark. I think he grew five inches, but how can that be possible?

Maybe I shrank.

They pulled into their driveway this morning, and I watched them unload their luggage from my living room window. Boone and Lene laughed and tossed snow at each other. Mrs. Lund's lips were the color of raspberry jam and a big smile hung on them. When Johan carried all of their heavy suitcases into the house, his face wasn't twisted, or pulled down with fatigue. No sir. He smiled. A wide smile that stretched far into his scrubby cheeks.

I kept my eyes sharp on his face, and I didn't let them stray. Not one time. Nope.

When Nick stepped out of their truck, I turned my eyes away from his face. I swear. I just caught a blurry image of his hair, but it was hanging down into his eyes, so I didn't even see them. If I don't see his eyes, then it doesn't count. He wasn't wearing a coat. Just a T-shirt.

But I didn't look. I can't even tell you what was written on it.

See? It's over. I'm not going to think about him anymore. I'm not going to let the knot in my belly ruin my promise. I'm not going to touch myself.

I'm going to be so good.

Father Neil says, "Every day we are reborn." I didn't understand what he meant, but Aunt Frannie explained it to me when we were folding the dry clothes.

"He means that every day is a new promise. We get to have a second chance. If you ask for forgiveness, then you start with a clean slate."

Every day is a new promise.

Last night, I asked God to give me a clean slate, and this morning, I checked my eyes in the mirror. They look different. I think God scrubbed my soul clean during the night.

Dad called this evening. He couldn't stay on the phone very long, on account of how much it costs. He mostly spoke to Aunt Frannie. She whispered a lot.

I was watching a movie about this man who experiments with machines and monkeys. This man starts transforming into the most disgusting creature you could ever imagine. I was trying to keep my eyes on my Rubik's cube, but when the man started ripping his nails off, my jelly sandwich crawled up my throat.

My aunt tapped my shoulder. "Baby, you shouldn't be watching this nonsense." She handed me the phone. "Your dad wants to wish you a happy new year."

I took the phone, but my eyes wouldn't leave the TV.

The man's girlfriend was crying now. The man/creature kept asking her to leave because he was going to hurt her.

He was going to hurt her.

He couldn't stop himself.

"Hello, Dad."

No matter how much he loved her, he was going to come apart and hurt her.

"Aunt Frannie says you've been real good. That's good, Red. Real good."

But the woman didn't want to leave him. She didn't care about his nasty face. She didn't care about his sickness. She wanted to stay.

She wanted to help him.

"Dad, when are you-you coming ho-home?"

The nature of the thing inside him was too strong. He wouldn't be able to fight it, the man warned.

"Dunno, Red. Soon. Real soon."

The woman cried, but she ran. Ran all the way to her car.

She left him.

He could only watch her leave.

"Dad. Is it co-cold there?"

"Sure is."

"Dad?"

She should have stayed. No matter how ugly he was. She should have helped him through it.

They should have taken care of each other.

"What is it, Red?"

But sometimes, people get real scared.

"Nothing. Thanks for the mo-money."

"Okay, Derek. I'll see you real soon."

❖

I think I've made a friend.

I was at my desk, working late. I have nothing else to do, as Nathan has been held up for another day of "team building" group activities in downtown Toronto.

I was eating ramen noodles out of a cardboard bowl, scrolling down an impossibly complicated sheet of interest variables.

"You know they don't pay you for the extra hours."

I tore my eyes from the screen.

Jake stood by my desk, smoking a cigarette.

Yes, I know about the nonsmoking law in Québec, but apparently, Jake isn't particularly interested in it.

"What are you listening to?"

I still had my earphones plugged into my ears, though the iPod had long ago run out of power. "Nothing."

Jake scowled, then smiled. "You realize me and you are the only losers still working at this hour?"

I like when people who've never spoken more than two words to me call me a loser.

Reminds me of home.

"Susan says you drive a Ducati. That right?"

A red Monster 1100cc with Desmodromic L-Twin engine.

I nodded.

"Yeah?" Jake looked me up and down. "You must have sold a kidney to pay for the insurance on that little Euro death trap."

I never saw the invoice. Just signed the form.

"O'Reilly, let's go for a drink."

Jake didn't wait for my reply. He simply grabbed his jacket off the rack and punched the code in. "Coming?"

I turned my computer off and tossed the noodles in the bin.

We walked up Crescent Street.

"Ever been here?" Jake asked.

We stood in front of O'Hurley's.

"No."

"And you're Irish?"

I nodded.

Jake opened the door and invited me in. "I thought all Irish boys celebrated their eighteenth birthday here. Thought it was some kind of rite of passage."

I smiled.

Inside, the party was going strong. The place was packed, as if Monday had skipped this place on its way to Friday.

Jake pointed to the bar. "Let's sit down over there," he shouted into my ear, over the thunderous melodies of the Irish folk music blasting through the stereos. "Closer to the action."

I looked over at the bar.

A woman, all curves, sat on the last stool, sipping on a glass of mineral water. The fact that she kept staring at the door, then down to her watch should have clued Jake in. But straight men survive the singles scene on two things: booze and denial.

We slipped into our seats. Jake leaned in and I caught a gust of his cologne. Strong, but not overpowering.

"What's your pleasure?" His almond-shaped eyes were on the impatient brunette at his side.

"Whiskey sour," I returned.

"Good choice. I'll join you." He slapped the bar counter. "Two whiskey sours."

No pretty please or anything. Just a direct order.

I cringed a little. To Jake, manners are for the meek.

The barman raised a brow and tossed his chin up.

Obviously, the man was going to be taking his sweet time with our drinks.

"So," asked Jake, flicking a peanut shell around. "You gay?"

When men ask me that question, I never know if they're offering or judging.

Either way, I end up being screwed.

"Why?" I figured I would play it safe.

Jake laughed. His teeth are pretty. "Just making conversation. Don't get defensive."

"Are you?" I quickly replied.

"Yes, I am."

"You are?"

His face tensed. "Wait. I mean, yes, I'm making conversation." He chuckled. "Oh man, you thought—" He winked. "Yeah, right. You wish."

I smiled. I wish? No way.

Well. Maybe a little.

"I'm straight, but I did let a guy blow me once. At a bachelor party, or maybe it was my birthday—"

"I see."

Jake's smile broadened. "Too much information, huh?"

The barman, who was a cross between James Dean and Colin

Farrell, set our drinks down. He slapped the counter. "That'll be eighteen dollars."

Jake scowled. "For two ounces of cheap whiskey and lemon water? You gotta be kiddin' me." He pulled a twenty out of his wallet. "Here, you bloodsucking vampire. And I want my change back."

The barman's caramel eyes shifted to my poker face. "Your friend here has a major attitude problem."

I've noticed.

Jake scoffed. "Whatever." He took a long swill of his drink. "Let's get loaded."

I came home at two a.m. Drunk out of my mind. I woke up late, with my tie wrapped around my neck and the Sahara Desert sitting on my tongue.

"Who knew?" Jake kept saying last night, his eyes glossy from the whiskey. "Always thought you were an aristocrat."

I've been thinking about that. The expensive shoes Nate insists on buying for me. The suits. The ties. The bike. Everything.

What do people think of me?

What have I become?

But above all, *who* have I become?

CHAPTER FOUR

Dear Bump,

Me and Aunt Frannie visited Mom today. We rode the bus, and then the metro.

We got off somewhere in the middle of the city.

I saw a man sleeping inside a plastic bag. His toenails were so long, they folded over. His hair was like dirty cotton candy. Aunt Frannie kept pointing to things. "See, that's the Mount Royal. We have a mountain in the middle of our island."

Montreal is an island. Same as Hawaii. I don't think I knew that.

"Look, Red, that's the Chinese district."

Everyone there looked just like Jesse Chao, and it smelled like roasted peanuts or something. They have a statue of angry lions guarding the street. They have purple vegetables and big green fruits sitting in cardboard boxes all along the sidewalk. Half of the food, I'd never seen before. They have red restaurants packed with people, and everyone eats their soup with sticks.

"You wanna taste something special, Red?"

Aunt Frannie took me deep into the district. My eyes kept shooting from side to side, and I tripped twice, on account of my curious nature, you know. We walked up to a store that was no bigger than my closet. A man with silky black hair and thin brown eyes stood behind a counter. His face was young, but his hands looked old. He wasn't smiling with his mouth. Just his eyes. He rolled something on a stick. It looked like the stuff that hangs down from the classroom ceiling when a tile is missing. I wasn't sure if I wanted to taste it anymore.

I crinkled my nose.

"Try it, hon," whispered Aunt Frannie through her pressed lips.

I chewed on my lip, avoiding her insistent gaze.

The man behind the counter lifted a finger to my face. "You're a snake."

"Excuse me?" Aunt Frannie's tone had a sharpness to it. "What did you just say?"

"Your son is a snake. 1977, no?"

Aunt Frannie let out a small gasp, and laughed. Her face lit up. "Oh, you mean his Chinese zodiac sign?"

The stuff had made its way to my lips and I was liking it. It kind of tasted like sugar and oil.

"Yes," said the man. "A pure one."

Pure?

I gathered the stuff with my tongue and let it sit in my mouth for a while.

I watched an old woman brush the snow off her doorstep with a broom.

"A wise soul. A seclusive heart. A philosopher."

Aunt Frannie tousled my hair. "Hear that, Red?"

The stuff was melting on my tongue and the more I got of it, the better it tasted.

"What is your day of birth?"

My heart jumped a little. I'm not very good with strangers. Especially if I have to talk to them.

"July seventh, sir."

His black eyes flickered on my face. "The mystic number."

Aunt Frannie squeezed my fingers. "Is that good or bad?"

The stranger lolled his head, and his gaze wandered. He seemed to be watching the end of street.

I took another mouthful of the stuff.

The man then leaned over the counter, and I immediately flinched, but he smiled and handed Aunt Frannie her change. "Yes. Very good." He winked at me. "He is the sorcerer. He is the enchanter."

At the sound of those words, a shiver passed through me.

And before I knew it, a question flew out of my lips.

"What is 1972 plea-please?"

The man squinted, and smiled again. "Ah. The rat."

I grimaced. Nick, a rat?

Don't snakes eat rats?

"Stubborn. Pioneer. Stormy. The endless traveler. Dangerous."

Dangerous.

That word again.

I threw my stick into the bin and followed Aunt Frannie. When we were out of the man's earshot, she tugged on my sleeve. "Who's 1972?"

Her eyes were steady on my face, and a warm liquid seem to fill my cheeks. "No-nobody."

I watched her mumble to herself.

She was counting.

"Nobody," I repeated.

"Sixteen," she whispered. "Who's sixteen? *Ah.* I see."

My cheeks were so hot, they hurt. "It doesn't mat-matter."

She frowned. "What do you mean, it doesn't matter? It matters a whole bunch. It matters more than anything else in the world. Hon, it's who you are that makes it matter."

"It doesn't matter," I said again, louder this time, but my heart shrunk back another inch inside my chest. "And I don't wa-wa-want to-to talk about it."

Mom's room is all yellow.

Everything except the ceiling.

"Yellow is a happy color," Mom said as she busied herself with a box of lemon cookies. "Doctor says it helps."

I looked around. She has a bed, a dresser, a bookshelf, and a TV.

"Come sit with me."

I sat by her on the yellow bed.

I gave her the daisies.

"Tell me about things, Red."

I opened my mouth, but only air came out.

"Are you angry with me?"

Her fingernails are yellow. Her breath smells like yellow.

"Derek, say somethin'."

She doesn't feel the same anymore.

"Just like your dad, Red. Gettin' a word out of you is like pullin' teeth."

Aunt Frannie gave me a quarter and asked me to go get her a coffee in the hallway machine.

I didn't get her one.

I rode the elevator up and down, and then sat in the washroom by Mom's room. Aunt Frannie knocked on the door, but I didn't answer her. I sat on the lid and stared at the wall.

"We're leaving in five minutes. Come say good-bye to her at least."

I shut my eyes.

When it was time to leave, Aunt Frannie knocked on the door again. "Come on, let's go home. She's sleeping. I'll show you how to make pizza dough."

We passed Mom's yellow room.

The door was half-open, but I turned my eyes away.

At home, we made pizza pies for three hours.

Aunt Frannie played her Marvin Gaye records and showed me how to knead the dough. You have to make it smooth like a baby's bottom, and slap it too. My favorite part was making the sauce. She let me season it. It came out real tasty.

"You have a thing for this," she said, smiling real big, swaying her hips to the music. "Maybe you should think about that."

I sprinkled some mozzarella cheese over the pepperoni, thinking of Nick. Thinking of the big book on his nightstand. "I wa-wanna be-be an accountant."

She threw her head back and clapped her hands. "That sounds just about right." Then, she wiped her hands on her white apron and her voice dropped to a whisper. "Look at you." Her smile was gone. Her eyes twinkled. Tears sat on the edges. "I mean, look at you."

I looked down at myself. I had flour on my socks.

She came around to me, and before I knew it, she was pulling me down the hall. She spun me around and made me face the mirror in the entrance. "Look at you." Her fingers dug into my shoulders. Her voice quivered. "Make your eyes look. Make them see."

The whole apartment smelled like yeast. I widened my eyes, staring at my reflection, hoping to calm her down. "I'm loo-looking, Aunt Frannie."

Her grip loosened. "What do you see?"

I saw a boy.

A boy with a crazy woman standing behind him. "Me," I said.

"And who is *me* exactly?"

I watched the boy in the mirror frown.

"Derek, look at your face. Your eyes. Your skin. Your hair. Don't you see? You *are* the sorcerer. When are you gonna start working some of that magic of yours, huh?"

She let go of me and walked back to the kitchen.

My eyes are too pale. Like some kind of washed-out green, and it looks like I don't have any eyelashes, on account of them being so light. My nose looks like a potato. My mouth looks like a girl's mouth.

My hair is the color of coagulated blood. My skin is like skim milk. At least I don't have freckles.

I walked away from the boy in the mirror.

Aunt Frannie can't understand. That boy isn't me.

And I'm not him.

Last night, after I slammed the phone down, ending Nathan's and my one way conversation, I jumped into my jeans and stormed out the door, heading for the basement garage.

When I shot out atop my bike into the quiet street, my mouth was filled with an acidic taste, and my heart thundered with every roar of the motor. I clutched the handles, zooming down Doctor Penfield Boulevard with the wind slapping my jacket and thighs. I reached Rene-Lévesque, checked for incoming traffic, then gunned through the red light.

There was a fire burning deep inside my gut.

I kept hearing that crystalline laughter.

Bellboy, my ass.

Nathan is fucking around on me. Oh yes he is. Hadn't we agreed to honesty? I'm emotionally castrated, butting my head against a barbed-wire fence, and he permits himself to be the stallion galloping the field?

Against the sound of my murderous thoughts, I rolled fast and steady, keeping left, heading East.

My back was stiff with anger as I mentally edited my adieu letter.

Then I heard sirens.

I flicked my gaze to the side mirror, and watched the red and blue flashes spin.

Bloody hell.

I slowly released the gas, trying not to make it too obvious. Of course that would surely fool the cop who was now hot on my heels. I watched the side mirror, and caught him signaling me to pull over. For a reckless second, I had an inclination to accelerate. There was no way his Impala could match my bike.

But I've seen too many *Cops* episodes to try anything like that.

I slowed down, then shot to the right lane to pull over.

I flipped the bike stand and sat back, watching the cop make his way to me.

Tall.

Blond.

Typical prick.

"Helmet." His voice was cool.

Right.

I removed the helmet and set it on my lap.

"License and registration."

Not very talkative.

I pulled the papers out of my wallet and handed them to him. I dared a glance his way. The asshole was still wearing his shades though it was way past sunset.

"You realize you burned a red light."

I had forgotten about that one.

"Ye-yes sir." How could I let myself stutter in a time like this? "I realize."

"Wait right here."

I tapped my fingers on the handle, getting more and more nervous by the minute.

He came back interminable minutes later. "Gonna have to take you in."

"What?"

"You heard me. Don't make me call for backup. Get off the bike. Now."

My heart pumped adrenaline into my bloodstream, filling the

creases of my palms with cold sweat. "Wha-what's going on-on here?"

He slapped my shoulder. "Get off the fucking bike, you little shit!"

Every single nerve in my body flinched. Every muscle contracted. My jaw was so tight, I thought I would break a tooth. I hesitated, but finally climbed off my bike. "Sir? I don't—"

"Shut up." He began scribbling something on a notepad. "Turn around. Put your hands behind your head."

"Wait a minu—"

"Put your hands behind your head. NOW."

By this point, my breath was a little short. I hadn't brought my inhaler, as I haven't had an asthma attack in years.

I obeyed.

"Anything I should know about before I pat you down? Don't wanna be pricking my finger on some fucking—"

"No sir."

Before I turned around, I shot a nervous glance at his wide chest, hoping to catch his name, but there was a piece of paper tucked over his badge.

Like a Post-it of some kind.

Panic rippled through me. "Sir, I have ri—" But I stopped mid sentence.

On account of him groping my ass, getting a generous handful of it.

"Nice. Oh wow. Real nice." His breath steamed my ear.

And there was something like a smile in his smooth voice.

His hand released my butt cheek. "Been working out, I see."

That tone. That bloody tone. I remembered it like one remembers the sounds a lover makes. I slowly lowered my arms but didn't turn around. "Boone? Boone Lund?"

"I told you. It's *Maverick*, you little shit."

I spun around.

Heated blood rushed though my every limb. "You asshole!" I shoved him hard with both hands. "I almost had an-an asthma attack!"

He pulled his shades off and winked. "O'Reilly. Mr. Gullible himself."

Before I could return a clever reply, Boone had wrapped his arms around me and was squeezing me, lifting me an inch off the ground. "How you been? Jesus. How long has it been?" He released his powerful grip on me and cracked a smile.

Same smile. Same eyes. Same demeanor.

I raked an unsteady hand through my hair. "Seventeen years."

His blue eyes clouded over. "Well, shit. That long, huh?" Boone's gaze roamed for a moment, and then he laughed. "I wasn't sure you were the same Derek O'Reilly, but when I saw that head full of red flames, I knew it had to be you. What's up, man? Why you tearing down the street like a bat out of hell? Some girl piss you off?"

I laughed nervously. "Not rea-really," I softly returned, knowing Boone has always had a clear view of the details that make up my composition.

His eyes moved over me. "No." He watched me closely. "Don't think so." He tilted his head, studying my face. "More like *man trouble*, huh?"

Under the brilliant Montreal sky, with the indigo night shrouding us, I held Boone's frank stare. "The second one," I confessed against the urban noise.

Boone squeezed my shoulder and welcomed my simple but liberating statement with a generous smile. "Thought so," he said. "Guess I always knew. Folks know?"

I nodded.

"Yikes. Bet you've been collecting Bibles ever since."

My heart swelled with peace.

Boone. My wonderful Boone.

"I can't believe they let you enter the police force," I teased.

"Hey, watch it, O'Reilly. I'm still debating about the ticket."

Right.

"How long have you been a cop?"

"Four years in November."

"And how did that happen?"

Boone rubbed his brow, then chucked softly. "Blame it on Di Paglio."

Officer Scott Di Paglio. I had forgotten about him.

"After my brother left, Di Paglio sort of lingered around us, you know? Like maybe he felt bad about the things he'd said about my brother back when all that shit went down."

Yes, *that shit.*

I remembered my stay at the hospital, and Di Paglio's warm brown eyes. The way he had courted Aunt Fran in a clumsy but sweet way. He could have been an uncle to me.

"After Nick left, I started acting out. You remember. By the next summer, I was well on my way to Juvy if Di Paglio hadn't stepped in. He got me thinking and moving. He got me interested in the military. In training. Discipline. Those things just felt right to me. I guess they appealed to me. So, I joined up with the cadets and the rest is history."

A question scorched my tongue, but I couldn't even summon the courage to hear myself speak his name.

Nick.

Boone shrugged. "Anyways, what do you do?"

I smiled.

"Lemme guess. Accountant, right?"

I nodded. "Financial analyst," I said with false arrogance.

He whistled, and bowed. "Well done, Red. Well done. I'm impressed."

"Thank you."

"Oh man, I can't wait to tell Lene about this. She's gonna flip. We were just talking about you last week at my parents'. Wondering what you were up to."

Lene. I remembered her toothless mouth. Our baby. The love notes. How old was she now? Twenty-seven years old. A woman.

"How is Lene?"

"She's at Douglas. Since last June."

Douglas. The mental institution. The nut house.

"Oh God, Boone. I'm sorry—"

"It's cool, man, I mean, I wouldn't be able to cope, but she likes it."

"Yeah?"

"Yeah. It's good money too."

"They pay her?"

"Yeah man, expect her to work for free?"

I shook my head, smiling. "She works at Douglas. She isn't a patient."

Boone exploded into laughter. "That's too funny. Oh, she's gonna love that." He caught his breath. "Lene's a shrink. A good one too."

Of course. That makes perfect sense.

"So you got somebody?" Boone asked.

"Yes."

"*Yes*. Okay. Well, what's this guy's name? What's he do? How long have you been together? Is it serious?"

I chuckled, grateful that Boone's curious nature hadn't dwindled with the years. "His name is Nathan. He's in sales. Pharmaceutical industry. It's serious, yes."

Boone whistled. "Pharmaceuticals, huh? So the guy's loaded."

I frowned, then shrugged. "It's a comfortable living, yes."

Boone's eyes flickered for a moment, but he let it go.

We had covered everything important in less than three minutes.

Not *everything*, but I still couldn't bring myself to ask about him.

"Listen," said Boone, "I gotta jet. But hey, what are you and Nathan doing this coming Saturday?"

I thought about it.

Who cares.

"How 'bout you guys come for dinner? I think we should do that. Kenya is gonna fix you the best meal you've ever had, and we can catch—"

"Kenya? You married Kenya?"

Boone's smile nearly knocked the air out of me. "I told you she was my soul mate."

"Kids?"

"No, but we're trying. We got a little house in Crawford Park, you know the neighborhood, right?"

"Of course. We used to ride our bikes up and down the Queen Elizabeth Park."

"So, you wanna?"

"I'd be honored. We'll be there, absolutely."

"Here's my card, and your ticket."

I glanced down.

"Kidding," said Boone. "I'll see you Saturday, then?"

"Yes."

"Derek O'Reilly," he mumbled as he walked away. "I can't believe it."

I stood on the side of the road, inwardly cursing myself for being such a coward.

Seventeen years of wondering and hadn't had the balls to ask.

Boone plucked the car door opened. "By the way," he said, leaning on the door. "In case you're wondering." He winked. "Nico disappeared for more than a decade. The son of a gun traveled the world. Nico worked on cruise ships and beach resorts, bartending and cooking his way to a small fortune. We'd get postcards from every fucking continent. One month he was pushing booze at a Club Med in Saint Lucia, the next he was writing from a boat somewhere off the Alaskan coast." Boone smiled, and then his eyes locked themselves to mine. "We didn't hear from Nico for a whole year, and one morning, just like that, he came back. That was five years ago. He opened a little bistro restaurant in the old port. A place called Split. He's doing well too. Got some fantastic reviews lately. But I don't see much of him. There's still some bad blood between him and my mom. Plus, he's busy. Him being a big-shot chef and all."

A chef.

A jolt of energy shook my insides.

I remembered that thick hardcover book on Nick's nightstand.

Boone laughed. "You should see your face right now. You still have a thing for him, don't you?"

My cheeks filled with heat. "No I do-don't."

"Right. Of course you don't. Then it doesn't matter if I tell you that Nico swings both ways. I mean, I'm just saying."

Swings both ways.

My cock jumped.

I remembered a certain winter night. Private words whispered behind closed doors.

"I'll see you Saturday," Boone shot back before shutting the car door.

I watched him drive away and the silver moonlight engulfed my vibrating soul.

Swings both ways.

A chef.

Oh, God help me.

❖

Dear Bump,

I have an oral presentation due next week.

Do you know what that means? Do you?

It means I'm going to have to stand in front of the whole class and faint.

"I'll do all the talking, you just hold the chart," says Boone. We're allowed to team up, but that doesn't help much. Mrs. Saint-Amour counts the words. Everyone has to speak equally, or she knocks points off.

"You write it and I'll draw the chart," says Boone.

Please. I know. It's the same every year.

"We'll do it on Doc Brown."

"Boone. Doc Brown isn't a real per-person."

"She doesn't know that."

This presentation makes my skin itch. Boone doesn't understand the concept of research. Reality doesn't seem to visit him much.

"We'll say he's from out of town."

We have one week. One week to find someone we admire and interview this person.

I suggested Mrs. Bebelski.

I like Mrs. Bebelski. She lives two doors down from us. She sits on her porch all day and knits. She has a pair of slippers for every day of the week. She has a number tattooed on her arm. On account of her being a survivor of some war called the *hollow cost.*

But Boone grimaced. "Nope. She always makes me eat those dry bananas."

Boone's suggestions don't take us anywhere. Unless we can track down the Terminator and ask him a few personal questions. Oh, and since he got back from Florida, Boone is making everyone call him Maverick. Says he's going to be a pilot when he grows up. Says he's going to fly jets.

I've been thinking about what Mrs. Saint-Amour said.

"Anyone who you feel has done something of significance around you. May it be grandiose, or small. It doesn't matter. This is your chance to sit down and talk with this person. Get to know this person more deeply."

More deeply.

There is only one person like that around me.

But it would be easier to sit down with Indiana Jones.

❖

Dear Bump,

So, we were discussing the presentation over a bowl of tapioca, in Boone's basement.

"We could ask your aunt some questions." Boone flicked a crumb off the coffee table. "Make it look like she's some big shot."

"No."

"Why not?"

"Because I don't wanna ask m-my aunt per-personal questions."

"Why not?"

I puzzled over his question for a moment. "Because, then she'll ask them all right buh-buh-back."

Boone skimmed his tapioca. He always carefully removes the first layer because he doesn't like the cinnamon Mrs. Lund sprinkles on top. "We could ask Coach Angelos. He's in the *Club Optimist*. They do charity work and stuff."

Boring. "No."

Boone sighed impatiently. "You keep saying no to everything. What's wrong with you, anyway? You're acting like a prissy boy."

My eyes darted up.

Boone sank back into the couch and folded his arms over himself. "You haven't said a word to me since I got back."

"What? I'm talking to you-you right now."

"Not really, no." His blue eyes fastened themselves to mine. "You're different. You walk different. And you never smile anymore."

Boone's words poked at something raw inside me. I dug the spoon into the pudding, and then stuffed it in my mouth.

He shook his head. "Fine. Be like that."

I didn't want to be "like that." I wanted to be at the opposite side of "like that." I wanted to tell him about Mom's yellow breath and Dad's empty promises.

And how his brother's smile makes me want to take my pants off.

See if Boone ever heard of something like that.

"We could ask your duh-dad," I finally said.

Boone fiddled with a couch pillow. His eyes kept swooping the room, as if maybe, if he looked hard enough, the person would magically appear before us. "Not my dad. Too busy." He slapped his thigh. "What about Jesse Chao's dad? He writes for a paper. He went to Iraq last year."

"I thought he was a cow-cowboy."

Boone rolled his eyes, and picked up his cup again. "So? Should we call Jesse and ask him if his father would wanna do it?"

The very thought of asking Jesse Chao for anything makes me angry. "No-no way. Nope."

"You're just mad 'cause he's been winning every chess game since we got back from the holidays."

It's true. I don't know why, though. I can't think straight anymore. My head is filled with fog. I keep forgetting Johan's strategies. Like something has sucked the normal thoughts out of my head and replaced them with fragments of someone else's mind.

It's been like that since the Lunds came back from Florida.

Finally, Boone set his empty cup down and threw the pillow on the ground. "Forget it. We don't have anyone. It's a stupid idea anyway. Why couldn't she do like Mrs. Jenkins and ask us to pick our favorite animal?"

I picked up the cups and placed them on the first step, then went back to the couch. "I guess we could do it-it on Doc Brown. We cou-could change his—" But, I couldn't finish my sentence.

Because Nick's feet had appeared on the top step of the staircase.

Then his calves.

His thighs.

And when my eyes reached the bulge in his jeans, I averted them, and glued them solid to the carpeted floor.

"Hey," said Nick as he walked past us, straight to his room.

"Hey," returned Boone.

I could only mouth the word *hello.*

Boone watched me. "What were you saying?" He had a funny look in his eyes.

I tried to compose myself, but that liquid fire was burning through my whole tingling body again. "That maybe-be we could change his na-name. Like, instead of Doc Brown, we could say his name—"

"Wait here."

"What—"

"Gimme a minute." Boone shot up from the couch. He tucked his *Star Wars* T-shirt into his black jeans and walked off to Nick's bedroom.

I sat up.

Waited.

Listened.

I wiped my wet palms down my pants and fixed my socks, then stared at the TV screen. It wasn't on; I could see my reflection in it.

I looked like Mrs. Bebelski's canary after he flew into the window.

Dazed. Confused. Wild-eyed.

Nick's door opened.

I stiffened up and held my breath.

Boone tapped my shoulder. "Hey."

I slowly turned around, and found Boone grinning from ear to ear. That's when terror iced my blood, sealing my lips together in a straight line.

Nick plopped down next to me. "Go"

I caught a gust of his beach scent and my head spun.

Nick spread out his long legs on the coffee table and yawned. "Shoot."

The couch is in an L shape, and I sat in the shorter part, with my legs folded under me. Nick sat in the long part.

No matter where I looked, his face was in every frame shot.

Boone flicked the TV on and sat in the arm chair. "Go ahead, Red," he said without looking at me. "Nico says he'll be our subject. Him being dyslexic and all. As long as we say that he's been prematurely accepted at McGill University. Pre-med, no more, no less."

I glanced over at Nick.

A cocky half smile hung on his lips. "That's right. Saint-Amour flunked me twice. Said I was a lost cause." He leaned forward and then pushed a strand of his ash blond hair out of his eyes. "So, you got your questions ready? I got somewhere to be."

His eyebrows are alive. He has a thousand different smiles. His eyes are like glaciers floating in the deepest, bluest of all seas.

I shot a nervous glance over at Boone, but when I realized that he wouldn't acknowledge my panic, I cleared my throat and took a deep breath. "I-I-I haven't prepa-pared anything really. I mean, I thought that—"

"So," said Nick, lying back into the couch. "Wing it, O'Reilly."

Wing it.

I've never winged anything in my life. I wasn't even sure what that meant.

Nick ran his tongue over his lips and raised a brow. "Jesus. Let's go already."

I pulled some paper out of my school bag. A pen too. "Let's see." I looked over at Boone again. "Aren't you go-go-gonna ask some questions?"

Boone shook his head. "I'm drawing the chart, remember?"

There is no chart for this presentation.

Nick closed his eyes and started to snore loudly.

I got the point.

I took another deep breath. "What made you-you decide to go into me-medicine?" I asked, without looking at him.

"The pay."

"Okay." I scribbled my question and his answer down real quick, but my fingers were sweaty and the pen kept sliding down my thumb. "Where do you plan-an on being a doctor? I mean, what hospital-al do you plan—"

"What's a good one?'"

"Okay." I scribbled down his words, trying not to let the ink get wet.

"O'Reilly, that's not my answer, I'm asking you somethin'."

I looked up.

His skin is immaculate. His Adam's apple moves up and down

when he swallows. His feet are the size of my calves. His hands are broad. His fingers are long and always busy with something.

"What?"

"What's the best hospital on this shithole of an island?"

I thought for a moment. "Dunno."

Nick rubbed his chin, then his eyes. "I plan on working in New York."

I jotted down his answer. "How did you sur-sur-mount the obstacles—"

"Surwhat?"

"I mean, how did you-you overco-come your learning disabilities to achieve this goal?"

I witnessed a shadow move across his crystal blue eyes, and I wanted to reach out and snatch the words that still hung in midair. Wanted to push them back into my big stupid mouth.

"I found a way to make the words make sense," he finally said.

I could barely hold my love inside my chest anymore. It expanded with every breath Nick took, until I could feel it on the very tip of my scalp and toes. There was darkness all around me. The only light I could see was the one in Nick's eyes. "I see," I whispered.

And the light in his eyes swallowed the darkness.

Like a blue vacuum.

His face makes me want to cry.

I blinked. "What words of wisdom could you pa-pass on to-to someone who may be suffering from dyslexia-a?" I asked, trying to keep my voice steady.

Nick shrugged, and smiled. "Don't jerk off so much."

I don't know what the joke was, but still, my penis moved inside my pants.

Nick slapped my knee. "Kiddin', man. I don't know. Guess I'd say…Learn how to use your brain upside down."

I nodded. "Okay."

"Okay," Nick echoed softly.

His eyes were like blue flames warming my mouth.

I didn't know where to go from there, so I stared at the paper.

Nick pulled a thread on his sock, letting out a long breath. "Is that it?"

I glanced up. "You—you said you fo-fo-found out how to make the words make sense. How?"

"I draw things." He yanked the thread out and stuffed it under the couch. "Little words I get wrong. I draw 'em. Make symbols."

I wasn't sure I understood. "You mean, like pictures of the words?"

Nick shook his head, and reached his hand out. My stomach churned. His fingers almost touched my hand.

"I'll show you. Gimme the paper."

I couldn't give it to him, but he slipped it out of my fingers. The pen too. The breaths were coming fast now. Too fast.

He tucked a loose strand of hair behind his ear again, and using his knee as a hard surface, began to scribble something.

Finally, now that his eyes were on something else, I could stare at him undisturbed.

I let my eyes move over him. He wore his old blue jeans. There was a big tear around the left knee, but it was patched up with a red bandanna. He wore a white T-shirt with the sleeves rolled up all the way to his shoulders, and it was skin-tight. I could see his stomach under it.

It's hard. Like a flat rock.

His chest heaved lightly with every deep breath he took. He has a small mark on the bottom of his neck. Looks like a scar. His right ear is pierced, but he doesn't wear an earring. His thighs are bulky. His forearms are covered with blond fuzz.

I almost puked when my eyes got caught on his mouth. I felt sweaty.

Cold.

Hot.

Dizzy.

"Here," he said, handing me the paper. "Like this."

I forced my eyes to look away from his face, down to the paper.

The first word I read was: Taepoons. There was a square. Then, Liert. There was a circle with four lines in the middle. When I read the last word, I caught on. Tablespoons. Three small squares.

These were cooking measures.

Nick was watching me. "That's how I do it, O'Reilly."

I thought about the book on his nightstand. How many hours would it take to map out every single recipe this way?

"It's impressive," I said. "You do-do this a lot? I mean, with every wo-word?"

"The ones I need, yeah."

Every thing Nick says is clear. As if every single word has been assessed for quality. For purpose. There's no gray about him. I never lose track. I always know what page we're on.

Like reading a picture book.

"Gotta go." He was already on his feet. Towering over me. "You got what you need out of me, right?"

I need you. I need you. I need you.

"Yes. I think so-so."

Nick stretched his arms out and then jumped over the couch. "Anyways, the rest, you can always make up."

I stared down at the paper in my hand.

The nerve of him.

I haven't socialized with anyone in years.

The only people I ever see are all in Nathan's circle of power executives, or divorced fag hags. One lousy happy hour, and he flips. Have I ever complained about his overpacked schedule, his weekend getaways, his evening meetings?

The man's life is one big PR event.

I go out for drinks with Jake, and come home to find Ike Turner sitting in our living room.

Nathan hit me. Whacked me right across the mouth. Yes, I hit him right back. How mature is that? The two of us rumbling in our living room like some kind of boxing exhibition.

"You crazy little paddy!"

"You imperialistic bastard!"

The awful thing ended in a very anticlimactic manner. I stepped on the remote and Michael Bolton's voice shot out of the sound system.

Some corny love song Nathan insists is good.

At the sound of it, Nathan's eyes filled up. "Baby." His voice cracked. His lips quivered. I should have been moved, but you haven't seen Nathan when he's crying. Not a pretty picture. Very messy too.

I was still quite wired, but willing to let it go. I tucked my shirt back into my pants and sucked in a long breath.

"Der—" Nathan's nose was running. "How can you accuse me like that? How, baby?" His pitch was high. Dramatic. "You know I would never do you like that. What we have is sacred to me. Der, look at me."

He always makes me look at him. I guess he prefers lying to me straight in the face.

"You know, Derek—" His tone had shifted. "Maybe I should be the suspicious one. I mean, I'm never home. And you have shown absolutely no interest in the wedding planning, nor the engagement." His dark brown eyes sharpened. "Hell, you haven't even told your aunt yet. I'm starting to think you might be having some doubts."

Then came the conveniently-slotted silence.

I picked up the remote to turn the abominable whining down, and sat on the edge of the couch. My mind drifted for a moment, and binding itself to the past, it guided my thoughts through a darkroom where pictures hung here and there. My inner eye roamed over them: Boone shooting down the hill on his bike. Johan pulling a fast checkmate on me. Aunt Frannie licking the back of a spoon full of vanilla frosting. Helga Lund's strawberry jam lips. JF. David. Sebastian. Coach Angelos.

And Nick, my Nordic King, my gypsy warrior, singing "Heartbreak Hotel" into a broomstick.

"Derek? Where are you right now?"

I glanced up. "Huh?"

"What is up with you lately? You keep staring into space like you're watching a fucking movie in your head." Nathan sat by me. "Talk to me. Let me in a little. Is that too much to ask out of you? For your trust, a little faith in my ability to understand you? You think I'm beneath it?"

Finally some authenticity in his voice. I began to warm.

"Shit, Derek." He reached for my fingers, and I let him hold my hand. "You think I don't hear you moaning in your sleep? You think I don't see the circles under your eyes? You're fighting something. Let me fight with you. Der, you can't do everything alone all the time. You don't need to be so strong—"

"Nathan—"

But that's all I had to say.

"Come here." He pulled me close and kissed my head. "I love you. And I'm not messing around on you. I swear, baby. I swear on my father's grave."

"You hate your father."

He laughed and his chest shook against my cheek. "Good point," he said. "Okay then, I swear on our love."

If you swear on the very thing you're destroying, doesn't that cancel everything out?

Chapter Five

Dear Bump,

One morning, just minutes after the red sunlight had flooded my bedroom, I crept out of the room and tiptoed to the washroom.

I closed the door behind me and sat on the cold ceramic floor, with my back against the door.

I couldn't feel my body anymore. Not even my head.

I knew I was alive because my heart was pounding.

Nick.

How can I love someone so much, but be invisible to him?

I closed my eyes and tried to make my heart stop beating. I prayed to God, "Make this heartbeat be the last."

But it never was.

There was always another one, then another, and another, until all I could hear and feel was my stupid heart thundering inside me. I clenched my fists, bit down on my lip, and prayed harder.

It never stopped.

I slapped my chest.

It kept beating.

Boom. Boom. Boom.

I slapped it harder.

Boom.

Harder still.

Boom. Boom.

I hit it again and again, but it kept beating, so I hit it again.

And again.

With my palm, then my closed fist, but it kept going like a ghost drum.

Going without a soul, or an order.

I pounded my chest, pounding now with both fists, hitting until the air was knocked out of me, and with every strike, my head bounced against the door, but I kept hitting and slapping my chest. My neck. My face. My head. Banging myself up. My nose. My mouth.

I need you.

There was blood now. On my hands and fingers. But I couldn't feel anything.

So I kept hitting.

"Open the door! Baby, open the door!"

The last blow brought an explosion of color. Some purple, some white.

Then darkness.

The first thing I saw when I came to was the deep blue Arctic Sea dripping down into my eyes.

"Hey." whispered Nick.

I was floating. Moving along the surface of the world. The sky raced by. Bare trees. Buildings. Flashing above me. Voices hummed near my head.

"Johan. Slow down." I recognized Aunt Frannie's voice.

I moved my tongue inside my mouth, except it wasn't really my mouth, just a bruise stretched over my gums and teeth. I moved my fingers. A sharp pain rippled up my arms, then stabbed me hard in the throat.

I moaned.

"It's okay," whispered Nick. "It's cool."

I closed my eyes.

"Dad, faster. He passed out again."

I moaned. "Mom."

Then something soft moved over my head. A gentle touch full of restraint.

"Mom." I moaned louder.

"It's okay." Nick whispered again. "I got you now."

There were fingers in my hair, brushing my bangs gently out of my face, and every time those fingers grazed my forehead, the pain let up a little. I tried opening my eyes again. I focused my gaze. "Where am I?"

Aunt Frannie's voice streamed to me. "On your way to the hospital. How do you feel, baby? Can you see? Can you feel everything on your body?"

I moved a little. I could feel everything. "It hurts."

Nick chuckled softly, and his stomach shook against my neck.

I was lying on his lap, and those fingers caressing my hair so sweetly were his fingers.

"O'Reilly," he said quietly. "The way that it stands, you're gonna have to start talking a little more."

I looked up to his face. My heart leaped. My lips trembled. "I'm scared, Nick."

"Don't cry, O'Reilly. Everybody's scared. *Everybody.*"

The tears stung my eyes. "But not Boone." I tried not to choke on the sob in my throat.

Nick's blue gaze drifted. He stared out the car window. "No. Not Boone."

I closed my eyes again, listening to the tires rolling on the street— listening to Nick breathe against me. The pain in my face and neck was like a pulse, beating in time with my own heart. I tightened my jaw and fists.

Nick's fingers moved inside my hair, but his touch was different. Distracted.

I opened my eyes to look up at him.

His eyes were fastened to the winter sky.

We stopped.

I was pulled away from his body and lifted into a chair, then rolled down a brightly lit hall.

The doctor asked Aunt Frannie to leave.

She hesitated by the door, then slowly turned around and left. "I'll be right outside the door, hon." Her voice was like a bell in a hurricane.

The doctor shut the door. His colorless eyes looked like dried chickpeas crushed under Coke bottles.

"Remove your gown, please."

I could hardly lift my arms, but I obeyed. I slipped the gown down my shoulders and pulled it off. I wondered if my underwear was clean.

"Lie on your back, please."

The paper sheet rustled under my back. It was cold too.

"Turn your face to the left."

The doctor's hands were warm. His skin was loose, as if he wore a mask of secondhand skin.

"Look into the light, please. Follow it."

I watched the light at the end of the black stick. Left. Right. Left. Up. Down. My teeth clattered. I bit my tongue twice. My back lifted from the table on account of my body shaking like a leaf.

"Sit up."

I tried. I rose halfway, but fell back. My belly was soaked with fire. My hands were sore and bruised.

"Hold my neck." The doctor pulled me up. Gently. "Reach your arms out." He helped me slip the gown back on and left the room.

The shivers running through me had become too powerful for my body. They jerked it wildly, sending waves of hurt all through my arms and neck. I bent my knees, wrapped my arms around my legs, and held on as hard as I could, trying to contain the vibration.

The doctor walked back in. He was carrying a large brown blanket, and when he wrapped it around my shoulders, my body loosened a little.

"I want to talk to you."

My heart jumped.

He dragged the chair closer and sat down. He removed the Coke bottles, and tucked them into his jacket pocket. "Do you play soccer?"

I knew my eyebrows had met in the middle, because my forehead hurt.

He leaned in. "I'm just asking because my grandson plays soccer. Thought maybe you knew him."

I don't know anybody but the people I know.

And I've never played soccer on account of my asthma.

The doctor sighed.

I figured I should ask his grandson's name. That was the polite thing to do. I pulled the blanket closer to my chest. "What's his na-name?"

Something moved inside the doctor's eyes. "Pete."

I don't know anyone named Pete.

The doctor's beige eyes were steady on my face. "He's your age. Eleven, right?"

I nodded.

"His dad is my son."

That makes sense.

"Sometimes they have arguments. Just little things. They fight about Pete's homework, or the mess in his bedroom."

My mouth was dry, but I was too shy to ask for a glass of water. I kept staring at the sink, hoping.

"One time, my son came back from a very bad day at work. Pete had kept his soccer shoes on in the house. There was a trail of mud from the entrance, all the way to the living room."

I looked up.

"My son was very angry. Not so much at Pete. Just angry about everything, but he hit Pete across the shoulder and slapped him in the face."

My lips came apart a bit. I sucked in a short breath.

I felt warmer.

"My son called me that night. He was crying."

Who ever heard of a grown man crying?

"You see, my son felt terrible about what he had done. He thought the worst of himself. He asked me what he should do or say to make things better between him and his son."

There was a knock at the door. I looked over at it.

So did the doctor. He rose. "Excuse me."

In the door frame stood a policeman. He was taller than a tree and his dark eyes found mine in a blink.

The doctor shut the door behind him. I heard them talking outside the room, but couldn't make out the words. I did hear my name *twice*.

I looked down at my feet.

Swung my legs under the table.

The pain wasn't that bad anymore. Maybe it had something to do with the white pills the nurse had asked me to swallow. I was feeling a lot better. I wondered if Nick and Johan were still in the hospital.

I slid off the table and folded the blanket, then set it on the chair.

I looked around for my clothes, but couldn't find them. The gown was silly looking. There was no way I was going to be seen walking around in this dress. I sighed.

What could I do to make this doctor give me back my clothes and send me home?

The door swung open and the policeman walked in. The doctor was two steps behind. There was some color in the doctor's grayish cheeks. "Derek. This man would like to talk to you for a moment. Just a few questions. Is that okay with you? Standard procedure."

Standard procedure. I liked the sound of that.

The giant policeman smiled. He had big white teeth. "Good boy."

The doctor stood nervously by the door. "All right then," he muttered before leaving.

The policeman leaned against the sink. "Sit down son." His voice was like Darth Vader's, but without the noisy breathing. "Says here…" He squinted, staring at the clipboard in his humongous hand. "Says here…Your auntie found you in bad shape. Says you were unconscious and pretty banged up."

I swallowed hard.

"Doc says you don't have anything broken. No signs of concussion. Nothing but some bruises, some marks."

I reached up and folded my fingers over my neck.

The policeman lifted a finger to me. "Like that one there, for instance."

The heat raced from my belly up to my cheeks.

He reached for my fingers and I flinched.

"Easy now. Easy. I'm not gonna hurt you." His milk chocolate eyes moved all along my shoulder and neck, like a flashlight over the shadows. "You wanna know what I think?"

My heart beat inside my ears.

"Your friend. The Lund boy. We know him. He's got a pretty good rap sheet for a kid his age. I'd almost say impressive." He took a step back and leaned on the sink again. He rubbed his chin. "Your auntie says you were in some trouble, some brawl 'round Hallow's eve. That true?"

Why would Aunt Frannie tell on me like that? I felt my eyes harden.

"That Lund boy was with you. Wasn't he?"

Something was crawling up my chest, tightening all the loose ends inside me. My jaw locked.

I jerked my chin up.

The policeman's eyes darted back to my face. His furry eyebrows curled. "Well. Tell you what. I think he has somethin' do to with this. I don't know how, but I'm itchin' to find out—"

"No." That word felt like ice on a fresh burn. I had to say it again and again. "No sir. No."

His gaze deepened. "No?"

"No."

No. No. No. No. And no.

That word felt like the only thing worth saying. I couldn't stop it from shooting out of my mouth. "No."

Couldn't let a yes ever betray me. "No. No. No!"

My hand flew up. "No!" It hit my cheek. "No!"

My hand bounced off my sore skin, coming at it again and again, but some force restrained it.

Something strong enough to snap my wrist like a dry twig.

It was the police officer's fingers. "No more of that," he whispered.

I looked up. My hand had disappeared inside his. His eyes weren't scanning anymore, they were looking. At me. At my face. My trembling lips.

"Enough of that. No more, son."

My hand became putty. I let out some of the air in my lungs. "No," I whispered again. "No."

He released my hand. "Okay. I believe you. Okay. The Lund boy is clean as a whistle in this here story. I got it. Okay? I got it."

"No."

"Kid, contrary to popular belief, you gotta have some kind of brains to be a cop. Okay? So I got the *no* part. I got it."

"My heart kept bea-beating."

He opened his mouth, and formed a word, but it hung on his lips, as if he had changed his mind. He cocked his head and stared into my eyes. "Talk to me," he said quietly. "You can talk to me. That's my job. You understand? I know how to listen. Talk to me."

I looked down at his tag, and my heart skipped a beat.

Di Paglio.

He was the one. The one who had come to school that afternoon. With the dog.

"Bubba," I murmured.

A faint smile turned up his lips. "You know my furry partner."

I nodded.

"You've seen me before. At school maybe."

I nodded and sniffled.

"See. I'm the good guys. I'm on your side. Talk to me."

I sighed heavily and chewed on my lip some more.

Swung my legs.

"Derek. I know your dad had to go up north for a job. I know your mom had to be sent away for a while. That's a rotten deck you're holding right now, but you never know, kid, life might deal you a royal flush someday. Now talk to me 'fore the doctor comes back in here." He smiled. "Hit me with the ugliest thing you got floatin' around in that head of yours."

Ugly.

All right then.

"I beat my-myself up-up."

Nothing moved between us.

Officer Di Paglio's face was like a picture. His arms hung like dead branches. Then his chest moved forward, followed by his head. Like he was stepping out of a cookie mold. He turned around and ran some water. He filled a cup and drank it in one straight gulp.

It looked nice.

"Can—I have so-some please?

His back was to me. "Sure thing." Officer Di Paglio filled another paper cup and slowly turned around. His face was the color of chalk dust. He handed me the cup.

I drank half of it and gave it back to him. I felt better. A whole bunch. "Can I go ho-home now—"

"Why did you do this to yourself?"

His question filled my eyes with tears.

"Derek? What made you lose your head like that?" He knit his thick eyebrows. "Did somebody ask you to? Maybe someone inside your mind, like—"

"I want to-to tuh-tuh-touch him so much."

Officer Di Paglio ran his hand over his face. "Him who?" His voice was flat. Like the sounds our guitars make in music class.

His honest eyes turned my secret thoughts into words.

"I wa-want him to ki-kiss me—"

"Okay. Okay." Officer Di Paglio set his clipboard down on the counter. "Okay."

I nibbled on my thumbnail, watching him pace back and forth.

"Okay," he said again. I don't think he was talking to me. He picked up the clipboard again. "Okay."

I began to worry.

He then took a piece of gum out of his pants. "Okay." he said again. He dropped a piece in my hand. "Want some?"

I nodded.

He frowned. "You're saying you like boys. I mean, in a—" His voiced tired. "In a special way."

I glanced up and thought about it for a moment. "No."

"No?'

I crinkled my nose. "Nah-uh." The gum was spearmint. I don't like that kind, but I like Juicy Fruit. "No. Just hi-him."

"Him who?"

I smiled. "Nick."

Officer Di Paglio didn't smile back. His eyes were dull like butter knives. "Okay," he repeated again.

"Can I throw my-my gum out pl-please?"

The corners of his mouth sagged. "Yeah, sure thing." He handed me the basket. I threw my gum in.

"Nick, you mean that bum sitting in the waiting room?"

My body hardened and I tasted blood on my lip.

He looked up. "Listen, maybe you just admire him. You know? That happens between boys sometimes, when—" He stopped. "Never mind. I'm gonna go get your auntie—"

"No. Please—"

"Derek—"

I shook my head. "No."

"Derek." Officer Di Paglio's voice was quiet, but firm. "Look at me. Okay? I won't tell nobody about the whole wanting to kiss that juvenile delinquent thing. You don't like boys the way you think, or you'd like all the boys." He sighed. "I don't know much about these things, but I know I have to tell your little auntie that you did this to yourself, 'cause right now, she's your legal guardian. She needs to know about these things. It's the law. I have no choice."

The warmth was gone from me. Fear soaked my spine. "O-okay."

He smiled, but his face looked like it was about to crack. He slapped his thigh. "All right kid. Stay put. You need anything?"

My eyes were glued to the floor.

"Derek. Hey."

I shook my head and folded my arms over my chest.

"Derek, forget about it. Put that troublemaker out of your mind." His voice grew stronger. "One day, you'll meet a nice girl, marry her, and have a whole bunch of kids. This is gonna be like a nightmare that happened to somebody else. Okay? Trust me. It's over now."

Officer Di Paglio hesitated by the door, staring into my eyes, and then disappeared.

I waited again.

I watched a spider crawl across the floor.

Fiddled with my gown.

Counted the blue tiles.

Minutes passed.

The long kind.

Then the door swung open. "Baby!" screamed Aunt Frannie, rushing to me like I was on fire. "Honey. Red. Baby!" She was crying, snotting and shaking. "Why would you hurt yourself this way?"

Officer Di Paglio reached out and tried to peel her off me a little. "Ms. Saint-Jacques—"

"You could have killed yourself!"

Officer Di Paglio repeated, "Ms. Saint-Jacques—"

But Aunt Frannie couldn't hear anything over the sound of her own crying. Her tears were warm on my neck and cheek. "Oh, Red." A sob exploded out of her mouth, and spit shot out of her wet lips.

"Francine." Johan had appeared in the doorway. "Be still." It looked like the wind had been knocked out of him. His hair was disheveled. His blue eyes shone with tenderness. "Francine," he said again. His voice carried everything safe back to me, and my shoulders sank.

Johan quietly entered the room and set his robust hands on Aunt Frannie's shoulders. "Come with me."

His gaze met mine. "Let's get you into some clothes." He then faced Officer Di Paglio. "I'm taking them home."

Finally.

"Mr. Lund—"

"Enough." Johan's jaw set. "Give me your card, Officer. This is a family matter, is it not? This boy needs some rest." Johan tugged on my arm. "Come, Derek."

Aunt Frannie stopped whimpering. She spoke more coherently. "Red, let's go."

I glanced up to Officer Di Paglio, but his eyes quickly strayed, and he nodded. "Okay. Go home, but I'll be in touch in the next twelve hours." His attention shifted to Johan's face. "Before you go, I'd like to talk to you and Mrs. Saint-Jacques. *Privately.*"

Why?

My heart pummeled my chest, and I shot my aunt a nervous glance, fidgeting by the door. "Can we go—"

"Yes, baby. Just a minute okay? Why don't you find Nick?" Her cheeks darkened as she said Nick's name, and she and Johan exchanged a strange look.

Why?

Aunt Frannie gently pushed me out of the room. "He's sitting in the ER, right by the coffee machine. He's got your clothes."

At the mention of Nick's name, my heart picked up the pace.

My body twitched. "Okay."

I walked down the crowded hallway, with my gown coming undone in the back, and I shuffled my feet, avoiding eye contact with anyone wearing white.

I passed a washroom and stopped by the door.

I had to see what I looked like.

When my eyes caught sight of the boy in the reflection, they nearly popped out of my skull.

My nostrils were crusty. My lips were swollen and purple. It looked like I had a golf ball tucked under my left cheek. There was an imprint of my hand on the bottom of my neck.

I don't know why I had to go and paint all this misery on my face. Bad enough I'm a redhead.

I ran the water and cleaned my nose, then slicked my hair down.

I tied up my gown and took a deep breath.

Finding Nick didn't seem like such a fantastic idea after all, but he had my clothes and I needed those very badly, so I turned away from the mirror and walked slowly to the main waiting room.

There he was.

Sleeping.

Snoring really. He was half falling out of his chair. His long legs were stretched over another chair, and this didn't seem to please the old lady sitting by his feet. She kept staring at the hole in Nick's sock. His big toe stuck out of it.

I chewed on my lip, debating, then looked around for my clothes.

I found them quick enough.

They were folded neatly. *On Nick's lap.*

I tiptoed to him, trying to steady my heart, and carefully reached for my pants.

The old woman jerked in her chair. "Hey! What are you doing there, young man?"

I pressed a finger to my lips. "These clothes are mi-mine—"

Nick cracked an eye open and gave a startle. "What the fuck. Jesus. You fucking scared me." He ran a swift hand over his sleepy features, and sat up. "O'Reilly, you're so quiet. You're deadly, man."

I lifted the corners of my mouth, trying to smile. "So-sorry."

"It's cool. No worries." Nick's eyes moved over my bare legs. "Want your pants, I guess, huh."

"Yes Please."

"Here. 'Fore you blind us all."

I slipped them on right there. My shirt was dirty with blood, so I kept the gown on, but at least my bum wasn't exposed anymore.

Nick stretched his arms and neck. "Sit down, O'Reilly. You look like shit."

I obeyed.

He looked around, and sighed explosively. "I fucking hate hospitals." He stuffed a hand into his front pocket, digging for something, and pulled out a Twinkie. It looked more like cake batter in a plastic bag, but my stomach gnawed regardless.

"Want some?"

I nodded.

He laughed. "Jesus. You really don't say much, but tell you what. This here little shit show you just pulled sure got everybody's attention. I'll give you that." He unwrapped the package and slid the squashed mess out of it. "Here. Enjoy. See, you don't even have to chew it."

The first bite made my mouth water.

Nick lay back into the chair and let out a long breath.

I tried to keep my eyes on the TV beaming in the corner. The man on the screen was cutting wood with these special knifes and kept asking people to call in *now*. But my eyes kept straying. To the right, then down. Nick's thigh brushed mine.

All I wanted was to lay my head on it. To rest my face against the bulge in his jeans.

Nurses were coming and going. Some man came in on a stretcher, but he didn't look sick, on account of all his yelling and thrashing. Police officers helped roll him down the hall. His bloody screams echoed for minutes.

Nick whistled. "Nut case."

A giggle escaped my mouth.

Nick looked over at me. "Think that's funny, huh?"

I smiled.

His face became serious. That ice storm blew through his eyes again. "Yeah well. You keep Jean-Claude Van Damme-ing your ass, and they'll be rolling you down same as that guy. No?" He shook his head, running his tongue over his lips. "O'Reilly, keep pushin' shit down, it keeps floatin' back up. Only uglier. Trust me. I know."

My gaze found the TV again, and this time, my eyes didn't stray.

Officer Di Paglio told Nick I beat myself up. Yes, he did.

C'est la vie.

My hands had begun pulsing again, around the knuckles. My lips seem to have a heartbeat of their own, and my chest was very sore. I tried ignoring the sensations, but with every breath, they only grew stronger. I sank back into the chair, easing my body into a more comfortable position, but a moan had drifted out of my throat.

Nick looked over. "Don't feel too hot, huh?"

I shrugged.

Something like a shadow moved through Nick's eyes." Your hand hurts." He glanced around the room.

Then his hand touched mine.

I froze.

Nick's skin is warm and soft like my favorite fleece blanket.

His fingers folded over mine, and he bent his face to my ear. "O'Reilly." His whisper smelled like sugar. "There's nothing wrong with us."

I turned my face up to him. "I—"

"Sit tight." His fingers left my hand, and he rose, found his boots, and then slipped them on. He didn't bother with the shoelaces. "I'm gonna score you some relief."

Relief.

I need you. I need you. I need you.

Please. Talk to me. Hold my hand.

"Okay."

I watched him until he was out of sight.

Nick walks like he knows exactly where he's going, but doesn't know what he might do when he gets there.

"Hey, hon."

I had fallen asleep in my chair.

I opened my eyes to find Johan and Aunt Frannie both smiling down at me. "Let's go, baby. Let's go home."

Was this time the real deal? Or would I be spending the sixth grade in a hospital? "No-Now?"

"Yes, baby. Now. Can you walk?"

Johan reached his hand out, and before I knew it, I was leaning up against his chest, being escorted down the hall.

Out of the waiting room.

Out of the ugly.

Nick was outside. I don't think Johan saw the cigarette on his lip, but I sure did. Nick flicked it over his shoulder just as we were coming on him. He popped a gum stick into his mouth, and handed his dad the keys.

"No. You drive." Johan pushed the keys back into Nick's hand.

Nick stared into Johan's eyes. He then slipped the keys out of his dad's fingers and walked around to the driver's side. We all followed.

I sat in the back with Aunt Frannie and Johan sat up front.

Nick turned the engine on.

"Seat belt," said Johan.

Nick looked over to his dad.

"Seat belt," Johan repeated without returning Nick's cold stare.

Nick pulled the belt over his shoulder.

He then set his hand on the stick.

"Mirrors."

Nick sighed impatiently. He checked the side mirror and adjusted it. He then glanced up to the rearview mirror, but I didn't have the chance to look away before his blue eyes caught mine staring back. I quickly turned my face to the window, and tried to keep from puking.

Nick finally put the van in reverse and pulled out of the parking lot.

"Watch the Pontiac."

"Dad. I got it."

Aunt Frannie's cold fingers set themselves on my hand, and she squeezed it gently. I glanced over and tried to smile. She tried to smile back.

Her makeup had run, but she still looked pretty.

"Nick. Slow down."

"I'm going the speed limit. I'm going forty, Dad, this is a fifty—"

"Slow down."

I watched the street. It was afternoon now. School was out. Kids were walking home, lugging their heavy schoolbags, throwing dirty snow at each other. Laughing.

I looked up to the white sky instead.

"Give the guy some space. Back off a little."

"I'm five feet from his bumper—"

"Back off, Nicolai."

"Dad, you gonna lemme drive or what?"

Aunt Frannie leaned her head back against the seat and closed her eyes. I stared down at my hands. They were pretty beaten up.

"Keep right here, it's the next light."

"I'll change over when I get a chance—"

"Keep right—"

"Fuck this."

We came to a grinding halt. My seat belt tightened like a vise around my neck, pressing down on the bruise there.

Aunt Frannie gasped. "Goodness."

We were stopped.

"What are you doing!" cried Johan.

I slipped my fingers between the seat belt and my neck, and caught a breath. I watched Nick climb out of the van. Johan honked and rolled down the window. "Nicolai Lund, where the hell do you think you're going! We're in the middle of the road."

Nick spun on himself, threw his middle finger up, then stuffed his hands deep into his pockets and walked away.

My jaw hung down like it was broken. I looked over at Aunt Frannie. She was trying to keep from laughing. But when the corners of her mouth lifted, a huge, belting laugh flew out of me. It was the kind of laugh you can't stop. The kind that hurts. Aunt Frannie covered her mouth with her hand, but her shoulders shook up and down, and tears were rolling down her cheeks on account of how hard she was laughing behind her palm.

Johan turned around. His eyebrows met over his nose. His eyes were two slits of disapproval. "Having fun back there?"

Aunt Frannie's laughter shot out so violently that it caused her hand to fly off her mouth.

Johan's lips moved a little. His eyes widened, then his whole face came undone, like the anger had fallen right off it. He chuckled softly at first, but slowly, his chuckles turned into full, heaving rumbles of laughter.

Finally, we all got our wits back.

Aunt Frannie blew her nose as I took a few painful breaths.

Johan leaned back into his seat and sighed. "That kid's got his mother's temper. Nicolai was born looking for the edge, and I don't even know what he'll do once he meets it." Johan slid into the driver's seat and we drove away.

That was four days ago.

I haven't seen Nick since then.

No one wants to talk about it.

Everyone just keeps their head down.

David is gone too.

Vanished.

❖

Today is the day.

In two hours, I will be in Boone's house.

Like a child coming home from a long field trip, I am running in my heart, with my eyes on that door, that safe, familiar door.

And I don't care if Nathan sulks all evening. I can't let him ruin this gift.

"So, tell me about this Boone guy."

We were having breakfast. Wheat cereal for Nathan. Peanut butter and jelly sandwich for me.

"You haven't seen him in how long?"

I washed down the head rush with a glass of milk. "Told you, seventeen years."

Nathan licked his finger and flipped to the business section. "And he was your best friend? Why did you guys drift apart like that?"

I set my plate in the sink. Saturdays, Nathan is on dish duty. I was itching to jump in the shower and go for a ride. "I told you, they moved."

"Right. I get that. But, you never looked him up, or—"

"No."

Nathan's expression was somewhere in between befuddled and suspicious. "Strange."

Some of the world's most precious treasures have turned to dust at the slightest touch. Sometimes, the past is better left undisturbed.

"So he's a cop, huh?"

I nodded and headed for the washroom, but Nathan slipped his fingers around my wrist. "He straight?" His fierce gaze punctured my confidence.

"He's married, Nate, I told you—"

"Well, that means squat."

"Trust me," I returned, freeing myself from his clutch. "There isn't a queer thing about Boone Lund."

I ran the shower as hot as I could take it and stood under the water with my eyes closed.

"Do you mind if I join you?" Nathan's voice pulled me out of my reverie.

I should learn to lock the door.

"No," I lied.

He slid the glass shower door open and stepped into the marble stall.

In some countries, our shower is a hotel.

I turned around.

There it was. His big throbbing morning salute.

His mouth tasted like Scope and newspaper ink. He kissed me on the lips, and then moved down to my neck. He nibbled on my left earlobe for approximately twenty seconds, in which time I heard him panting over the pulsing sound of the water. "Derek, turn around."

My eyes darted down to his erection. My buttocks instantly cramped up.

No way. Not today. *Nah-huh.*

His tongue worked at my sealed lips. "Baby, it's been so long, I wanna feel you from the inside. I wanna fuck you, Derek. Turn around, come on—"

When Nate begins to talk dirty, I have a tendency to look around for the cameraman.

"No," I carefully returned, retracting to the corner.

"No? Why?" He moved in closer, and his fingers began to crawl down my stomach. I was about as hard as a steamed zucchini. "What's wrong?" he asked as he circled his fingers around the obvious problem. "Did you just jerk off?"

I had been in the shower for less than twenty seconds before he came in. I've been known to provide myself with phenomenally quick self-gratification, but twenty seconds, that, I've never accomplished. "Just tired."

"Tired?" His fingers grazed my flaccid cock. "Sure?" His voice was thick with need. "I bet I can change your mind before the hot water runs out."

Maybe.

"Come here." His hands were hard pressed on my skin. His eyes, veiled with desire. "Blow me, come on, Der."

I'm the catcher in this relationship. I understand the limitation of this position. I read the fine print when I signed up for it, but lately, I've been feeling more and more like a boy blow-up doll.

"Nate—"

"Come on, baby. Look at me, two minutes and I'll come like—"

"Nathan. No." I freed myself from his embrace. "I'm not feeling it. Okay?"

His eyes hardened as he yanked my hand down. "At least gimme a hand job—"

I snatched my hand away and shot him a murderous look.

He brusquely reached for the dial and turned the water off. "What the fuck is wrong with you Derek? You're acting like a wife, you know that? Like I'm supposed to beg for sex? You know how hard I work for you? The shit I put myself through to satisfy your every little selfish need—"

"Na-Nathan, do-do not go there—"

"Yes-yes I will-will," he mocked.

That line? No, don't mind it. Go ahead and cross it.

It's just a little thing called respect.

My mouth popped open, but nothing but a gasp came out. I bolted out of the stall, jerked a towel off the shelf, and slammed the bedroom door behind me. Those years of repressing anything remotely close to an emotional outburst had to serve some kind of purpose. I bit down hard on my lip and clasped my unsteady hands together.

"Der, I'm sorry." Nathan stood in the doorway, a towel wrapped around his waist.

The man is absolutely breathtaking. Sexy mouth. Penetrating eyes. Thick dark hair. Not to mention, well hung. But the very idea of sucking him off makes me gag sometimes.

And I'm marrying him?

"I don't know why you bring the worst out in me." Nathan drew in a deep breath, and I watched his chest heave up and down. He's a bit too hairy for my taste, but I don't mind as much as I thought I would. "Derek, look, I don't know how to say this without hurting you." He closed his eyes for a moment, and I braced myself for a confession. "Baby, I think you're frigid. You know, I've been reading up on HSDD and I think you may suffer from this disorder."

I fell back on the bed, staring up at the ceiling. "Dear Lord, what are you talking about?"

"Hypoactive Sexual Desire Disorder. It's fairly rare, but it does occur in some young men, and you have most of the symptoms."

"Please, I'm dying to know what they are." My tone was charged with potent sarcasm.

Of course, self-centered people are immune to it.

"For instance, intimacy difficulty, relationship problems, you know, things of that nature." He cleared his throat. "Lack of sexual appetite is another."

I chuckled instead of punching him in the nose.

"Don't laugh, Derek, this is serious stuff."

I groaned and rubbed my face. "I'm going for a drive." I sat up and shook my head. "I'm going to stop at the S.A.Q., need anything?" Out of the corner of my eye, I caught him folding his arms over his bare chest, shaking his head in utmost disapproval. I ignored him.

Of course he wasn't satisfied. "I think you should see someone."

I flinched but kept my cool.

I slowly unfastened the towel around my waist and let it drop to the floor. Naked, I took my sweet time walking to the closet, making sure I was giving him an eyeful of my finest assets. If he was going to try to psychobabble me into sex, then I had every right to torment him.

His stare was hot on my skin. I could feel it roaming over my body. "You're cold, Der. Real cold. I'd even say you're a bit of a cocktease." The hurt in his voice caused my brow to scowl, but I remained immobile, as supple as I could, staring at the contents of our closet.

"Okay," he said, walking away. "You win. I can't fight your silence. I can't get past the walls you've built around you."

I stiffened, holding in my breath and indignation.

I'm cold?

Nathan took a call last night. One that dragged him out of bed, to the terrace, where he stayed for over ten minutes.

I checked his phone this morning, just before he opened his lying eyes.

I dialed the last number. Some guy answered with sleep lingering in his young, crystalline voice.

You know who he sounded like?

Sounded like that bloody bellboy.

❖

We had created a circle of flesh and salt water. Until, like a light being flicked on, Helga's strong, authoritative voice cast the darkness out of our thoughts. "Drink!" she ordered, wiping her polar eyes. "While it's still cold."

The first to laugh was Lene, followed by Boone; then Nathan, who had never witnessed such emotion from me, chuckled a little, and I let my shoulders sink, leaning back into my chair.

Boone blew his nose into his napkin. "Jesus."

I smiled. "Sorry."

Johan plopped back down into his chair and let out an explosive sigh. "Don't apologize. We all needed a good cry." He raised his glass, and I witnessed a shadow move over his aging, but handsome face. "To family."

As we all brought the deathly strong alcohol to our lips, he added, more somberly, "To Nicolai."

The cold alcohol shot down my throat, burning through my chest, and Nick's voice echoed through my mind. *"I'll see you around,"* he had said, that night, by my bed.

That was the last time I heard Nick's smooth voice.

When Nathan and I left Boone and Kenya's home, the sky was pink at the horizon.

"We're doing this again soon," Boone said, leaning against the doorway with Kenya half-asleep in his arms.

"We'll be back tonight," I teased.

Kenya popped an eye open. "To clean, you mean."

Our laughter rippled through the empty street.

Nathan threw the rest of his espresso back. "Okay, babe, let's go before I lose my second wind." He shook Boone's hand. "Thanks for a wonderful evening."

Boone nodded, but his gaze quickly flicked to my face, as if he couldn't be bothered. "Come here, you," he said, tugging on my sleeve. I fell into his grip like a rag doll. I was completely spent, but so very alive.

He released me. "Call me, okay?"

I smiled.

He then grabbed my hand and shook it vigorously. "Okay, kiddo. Take care."

Boone had slipped a piece of paper inside my hand. I discreetly folded my fingers over it, and tucked my hand into my pocket. "I'll see you soon, good-bye Kenya." My voice was weak with fatigue and emotion. "Thank you."

That note scorched my skin through my jacket all the way home.

As the scarlet sun inundated my room, I turned to watch Nathan. He was fast asleep.

I carefully pried myself loose from the blankets and tiptoed to the entrance, where I pulled the note out of my coat pocket.

I unfolded it as if it held the instructions to Paradise Lost.

Boone's handwriting brought a smile to my face. He writes like he's holding his pen with a nostril.

> *Split is on DuPort Street, in the Old Port. Just off Saint-Paul. Monday afternoons are quiet for Nico. I haven't told him about you. Thought you'd like to surprise him.*

> *Maverick*

❖

Dear Bump,

Boone broke his arm.

He was taking a nap and fell off his bunk bed. He says he was dreaming about punching Johnathan Dupuis in the mouth. Johnathan is the jock taking Kenya to the Valentine's dance.

When it happened, I was in the living room, changing the shoelaces on my new running shoes. The ones that came with the shoes were white, so I was replacing them with the black ones from Dad's old army boots.

I'm tired of my clothes.

I look like the boy in the Sears catalog.

The one from 1985.

Wish we could go shopping somewhere else. Aunt Frannie bought me a new jogging suit. All white. But that's not the worse part. No. She had Corey Hart's face printed on the sweater. "Thought you liked him," she said, flapping the sweater around like a flag. "You're always running into the living room whenever they play his video."

I wasn't in a very good mood, lacing my new shoes.

I heard some commotion, coming from the Lunds' side of the building. As always. I didn't make too much out of it because it was around dinnertime, and that's when things get really crazy in their home. I kept sliding the lace into the holes, thinking about Dad coming home. About being a family again. Then I heard Boone screaming. Something something, *skade skade*. It sounded like someone was pushing thumbtacks under his nails. I pricked up my ears.

Watched the walls.

Aunt Frannie tumbled in. "Oh my, do you hear that?" She clutched her heart, wide-eyed.

I nodded.

Then, I heard their front door open. I sprang to my feet and shot to the window. Johan had Boone strapped over his shoulder, like some Norwegian sack of sweet potatoes, and a few steps behind, Mrs. Lund followed, wearing nothing but her pink dress and ballerina slippers. Johan pulled the back door open and struggled to slide Boone into the backseat. Mrs. Lund hovered over them both.

I threw my coat on and opened the front door. "Is Boo-boone okay?"

Mrs. Lund didn't acknowledge my question. She climbed into the front seat, and Johan bolted the van out of the driveway, whipping snow and ice with the tires. I watched them turn the corner, shivering in the doorway.

"Fuckin' Bunny boy."

Nick's voice.

To my left.

I shifted, but kept my eyes on the street.

"Could wallpaper the whole Parliament with that kid's hospital record." Nick's tone was flat. There was no smile in it.

I tried to catch sight of him out of the corner of my eye, but couldn't.

Aunt Frannie had come up on me. She wrapped her hands around my neck, and I jumped a little. "Hon," she said, "come inside. It's too cold." She poked her head over my shoulder, glancing left at the Lunds' front porch. "Oh, hello, Nicolas."

My heart leaped inside my chest. Could she feel it against her palms? I hoped not.

"What happened to your brother?" she asked.

Nick cleared his throat. "Well, Ms Saint-Jacques—" Against Aunt Frannie's crystalline timber, his was low, full of depth. "He fell out of his bed."

How could such a simple, basic explanation sound like someone recounting a religious experience on the church steps?

I wasn't the only one feeling it. There was a subtle change in Aunt Frannie's breathing, talking. "I see," she said, her voice thickening like molasses. "Didn't hit his head, I hope?"

"No ma'am. He wasn't making any sense, so looks like he's just fine."

Aunt Frannie's laughter shook my shoulders. "Where's your little sister?"

My stomach tightened.

Something in her tone was causing my face to harden.

"Inside. Painting ma'am."

Aunt Frannie's hands left my shoulders. "Oh. Did you guys have supper?"

"No ma'am. But—"

"Well, then, come on over. I insist. Your mom's gonna feel a lot better if she knows you guys are looked after while they're away."

Why would she do this to me?

I cringed, hoping Nick would decline her offer.

"Sounds nice," he said.

My mind raced. Nick Lund was going to be sitting at our kitchen table. *Eating.* And Lene was coming too.

There had to be a way to avoid this cataclysm.

Aunt Frannie pulled me inside. "Go get cleaned up." She hurried to the kitchen. "Why don't you put on the new jogging suit I bought you? You'd look so sweet."

I would rather stick my head inside a jet propeller.

"Do you think Nicolas likes meat pie?"

I shrugged. "Dunno."

She cocked her head. "What's wrong, hon?"

I chewed on my lip, feeling my eyes blaze.

"Derek?"

My face tingled. My cheeks were hot. "Why did you-ou have to invite them?"

Aunt Frannie's features softened, and her gaze roamed over my face for a moment, then she tousled my hair. "Thought we could try to get to know him better. He's so exciting, don't you think?"

We?

She spun around and went to the fridge. "Now, go and get washed up and bring back some ketchup from downstairs, please."

We?

I shuffled off, padding down the stairs, grumbling.

I pulled on the string that dangles from the bathroom's ceiling, and white light flooded the small room. I stood in front of the mirror, staring at myself.

The bruises on my face are faded yellow.

I look like I have jaundice, but only half of it.

I sighed and washed my face. I shot a breath into my hand. It smelled okay, but I brushed my teeth anyway, making sure I didn't have any toothpaste on my lips or chin. I pulled my sweater off.

The cold air immediately iced my skin. Made my nipples hurt.

I'm skinny. Really pale too. My belly button sticks out a little. My shoulders are twice as big as my waist. Makes me look like an upside-down triangle.

I went to my bedroom to find something to wear. Impossible. All my sweaters are ugly. All my pants are too short. All my button-up shirts are missing a button.

I stripped my pants off and plopped down on the edge of the bed, staring at my closet. The cold and humidity sank deep inside my bones, but for some reason, I didn't mind it so much. Actually, it felt kind of nice.

My skin had hardened, my nerves awakened.

My penis jumped inside my undies.

Like it needed to be somewhere and I wasn't invited.

I need you. I need you. I need you.

Those words danced around the fire in my head.

I glanced at the door.

Closed it.

My hand felt weighed down, like it had a mind of its own. I tried to focus my attention on the clothes hanging in my closet, really I did.

But my eyes kept straying, looking into space, staring at the blank wall. That wall had become a screen, and my eyes were the projector. The movie was of my own making, and the same scene played over and over. Though I hadn't actually seen Nick and Dave that night, in Nick's bedroom, trying to imagine what had gone on between them caused my heart to beat wildly, and my penis to swell.

What did Dave need from Nick? What had made his voice sound so different? His tone so desperate?

My fingers slipped inside my underwear.

I need you. But what do I need from you?

The top part of my penis was wet. It had leaked again. But it was still full.

Your attention. Your undivided attention. Your secrets. All of them.

I wrapped my hand around it and pulled a little.

I need you to see me.

I pulled harder, because something needed to come out, something pushing deep inside my belly.

My legs tensed. My calves were cramping up, but I couldn't stop pulling. I could hear myself breathing. Could hear the noises my penis made as my hand rubbed it up and down.

My toes curled.

Nothing had ever felt this good.

I wanted to cry out, but I tucked my chin in and held my breath instead.

And I knew. As that warm liquid softly pumped out of me, soiling my fingers, I knew.

I need Nick to do this to me.

And I want to do it to him.

"Hon?"

I sprung up and leaped to the door, leaning my weight on it. "I'm-I'm dressing."

"Okay, hurry up. Our guests are here."

I closed my eyes.

"Derek?"

"Ye-yes, I'm co-coming."

I paused on the second to last step. Listening.

Lene and Aunt Frannie were obviously enjoying each other's company. I supposed it can get pretty boring living with me.

Then I heard Nick. "Can I help with anything?"

"Oh no, it's fine. I've got everything going already."

I rolled my eyes. Her tone was *so* inappropriate.

"Why don't you go find Derek, he's downstairs, doing God knows what."

The image of me pulling on my penis instantly zapped behind my eyes. I shrank back and tiptoed down the stairs. I glanced around frantically and heard Nick opening the door.

I jumped on the couch and picked up a magazine.

Heard his footsteps.

Glued my eyes to the glossy paper.

It was upside down.

I hurriedly switched it around.

"O'Reilly, hey."

I wouldn't be able to do this. How could I? How could I be alone in my basement with Nick Lund after what I had just done to myself?

And what I had been thinking of as I had done it?

I clutched the edges of the magazine, my fingers imprinting them with sweat, and kept my heated face hidden behind it. "Hey."

A weight sank into the couch, a foot away from me, at my left. I guessed Nick must have sat down. I didn't care to check. Just wanted to keep from hurling.

"You like that stuff, huh?"

If someone prays to die really really hard, why can't God listen?

My eyes had been staring at the magazine, but they hadn't seen anything. Just colors. Out-of-focus faces. I realized now, I was holding Aunt Frannie's *Spin* magazine. I knew the cover. Had seen it lying around for the last two weeks. Michael Hutchence.

Jumping.

Wearing very tight leather pants.

"No-not really, just bo-bored."

The magazine was gently slipped out of my hands. "Do you mind?"

Nothing Nick does, I mind.

"You know INXS? They're pretty decent." Nick leafed through the magazine. His long fingers turned the pages, and his blue gaze moved over their content. "A little too pop for my taste, but there's a couple songs I like off their album." He glanced up. "You have it?"

I don't have anything. Why would I have something?

I shook my head.

He smiled. "Didn't think so."

I folded my arms around myself and curled my knees under me.

He stretched and yawned. "Got cable?"

I looked around.

We don't even have a TV downstairs.

Nick stood, and I watched him walk to the window. It's more like a ship porthole. No light comes through in winter, on account of the snow piling up against it. I noticed Nick had to tilt his head a little. Slouch down. He's taller than the basement ceiling.

How is that possible?

He was staring out, but there isn't anything there to look at. Just white.

"I like the smell in here," he said, half to himself.

What smell?

Nick walked off, heading straight to my bedroom. "This your bedroom?" He pushed on the door.

Nick Lund was in my bedroom.

I was frozen. Completely unable to move, or speak. I clutched the edge of my shirt, watching the open door.

Nick appeared in the doorway. He leaned on the frame, wearing a half-smile. "Nice Hot Wheels."

I don't even play with those anymore. Just rearrange them once in a while.

Heat shot up in my face, and I couldn't find anything to say.

Nick's smile straightened. "Nothin' to be embarrassed about." His eyes paused on my lips again. "You have a lot of books. Read a lot, huh?"

What else am I supposed to do with my time?

"That's cool. Probably why you're so smart." He turned away and went back into my bedroom.

I rose. The nervousness in my stomach was no match for the desire to be alone with him. In my bedroom of all places.

Nick sat by my bookshelf, with his back to my bed, fumbling through the books on the bottom shelf. That's where I keep all the ones I've read more than twice.

He plucked *Lord of the Flies* off the overpacked shelf and scanned the cover. "What's this one?"

I fidgeted by the bed, and sat down. "It's the-the-the sto-o-ory of—" I couldn't get any more words out. My stuttering was out of control. I knew exactly what I wanted to say, because I know that book by heart, but I couldn't relax my mouth and tongue.

Nick glanced up. His blond hair is coming in by the roots. "O'Reilly," he said softly. "Take a breath. Try one word at a time. Not the whole sentence."

Not the whole sentence.

I had never thought of that. I always think of the complete thing I want to say, never break it up into fragments. One word is easier than ten. Just like reading.

I tried again. "It's-the-story—of—these—school-boys—" I paused, stringing the words in order. "That-get-stranded-on-an-island-and-built-their-own-society."

Nick cracked a smile. "See. It's easier that way." He looked down at the book. "Sounds interesting."

"I eenjoy-oyed the-the—" I stopped, took a breath, and stared into his eyes, witnessing him staring right back. My throat loosened. "I-enjoyed-the-social-comment. Like-*Animal-Farm*."

Nick belted out a great big rumbling laugh and tossed the book back onto the shelf. "Social comment, huh? Fuck, man. You're something else."

Upstairs, Aunt Frannie was calling.

"Looks like dinner's up." Nick got to his feet.

I followed him out of the room and up the stairs.

Aunt Frannie pulled a chair out for Nick. "You can sit in John's seat."

Lene was already sitting. Her eyes flickered on my mouth for a second, and I cringed at sitting opposite her, but that was the only chair left, so I slid into it, trying to avoid her ardent stare. "Hello, Derek," she said. "I made the salad."

I looked down at my plate. The salad appeared normal enough.

She smiled. She's missing so many teeth. How does she manage to chew? Her smile broadened. "Did you know that Nicolai put blue ink under his skin, on his—"

"Lene, what did I say 'bout that?" Nick drove his fork into the meat pie. "Looks good Ms. Saint-Jacques." He was obviously trying to change the subject. "Real good, thank you."

Ink? I let my eyes roam over his arms and hands. Didn't see any ink there.

Aunt Frannie dabbed her painted lips with a napkin. "So, you're going off to Cegep next year, huh? What do you plan on studying, Nicolas?"

My eyes darted up to her face and Aunt Frannie caught my murderous glance. She shifted a little, smiling. "Or maybe you don't intend on going. At any rate, what are your plans for your future? What are you interested in?"

The meat pie was scalding hot. It fumed inside my mouth. I flicked my gaze to Nick's face. He was eating ferociously. Didn't seem to mind Aunt Frannie's interrogation.

"Traveling," he said with his mouth full.

Aunt Frannie livened up on her chair. "Oh, really? You'd like to be a travel agent? That's a solid choice, lots of potential for growth. Good money too."

I don't think Nick meant he wants to sell traveling to anyone.

Aunt Frannie wasn't finished. She took a long swill of her red wine and sharpened her gaze. "Ever think of modeling?"

Yes, Bump, modeling, she asked.

My eyes shot back to his face. I swallowed the salty contents of my mouth.

Nick raised a brow. His lips seem to glisten. "No ma'am."

Suddenly, I realized Aunt Frannie wore her blue blouse. The one with the missing button on top. She skimmed the rim of the glass with her red fingernail, and smiled. "Well," she breathed, "you should. You'd make a killing."

Something passed over Nick's features. His eyes moved over Aunt Frannie's mouth, then lowered their attention to the opening of her blouse. "You think?" he asked under a breath.

"Oh yes," said Aunt Frannie, her eyes devouring his face. "Would you like a small glass?" She pointed to the open bottle of Rioja wine on the table. "I know Johan let's you have beer once in a while—"

"That's right."

Oh, the nerve on her. She didn't hesitate for a second and poured a very generous dose of the red wine into his glass.

It wasn't small at all.

Nick immediately raised the glass to his nose. "Spanish. Oak aged. A bit of a vanilla taste. Dry enough. Good choice for a table wine, Ms Saint-Jacques."

My jaw hung loose.

Aunt Frannie gasped. "Oh my, you're quite the connoisseur. Where did you learn about wines?"

Nick took a mouthful of the wine. I watched his Adam's apple move up and down as he swallowed. "Drinking, ma'am."

I hadn't touched a bite. Nick was on his second serving.

Lene was busy feeding our baby. "Just another tidbit, Cassandra. And then you can have dessert."

Nick scooped the last of the mashed potatoes. "Lene, you're freakin' O'Reilly out. Eat your supper."

Lene pouted, but when Nick's eyes hardened, the fork jumped to her mouth, and she started eating with voracious appetite.

"Don't like the meat pie, hon?" Aunt Frannie's eyes were full of reproach.

I shrugged. "It's okay-kay."

"Nicolas seems to have enjoyed it," she said softly, watching Nick clean his plate.

"Yes ma'am. Just enough cloves and sariette to my liking."

Sariette? Cloves?

I wiped my mouth and pushed my plate up.

"Nicolas, please stop calling me ma'am."

My eyes nearly shot out of my head.

"All right," said Nick. "But only if you stop calling me Nicolas."

"What should I call you, then?" Aunt Frannie's voice was barely a whisper. Like her dress was on too tight.

Nick's eyes flickered with fun for a moment. Then he laughed.

Never answered her question, just laughed and winked.

Winked, Bump. *At Aunt Frannie.*

My fingers clasped the edges of the dish. I had an inclination to hurl it at her.

"Hon," she said, without making eye contact, "why don't you and Lene put on *The Grinch Who Stole Christmas* in the living room. Nicolas—*Nick* and I are going to clean up in here. Then I'll serve dessert."

"No." The word had gunned out of my mouth.

Aunt Frannie shrank back a little, setting her hand on her chest. "No need to yell, Derek." She turned to Nick and rolled her eyes. Not much. Not in a very noticeable way.

But I saw it. Yes I did.

Nick smiled. "Don't blame you, O'Reilly. That green freak gives me the willies too." Nick rose and pulled his chair up, then began gathering the plates. Aunt Frannie seemed to hesitate, but she soon followed his lead. Lene and I helped too.

While Aunt Frannie and Nick whispered at the table, Lene and I washed the dishes.

Lene pulled on my sleeve. "I have my Strawberry Shortcake panties on."

I stared into her face for a second, then went back to scrubbing the glasses.

She set her chubby fingers on my wrist. "I love you, Derek."

I glanced over at her.

She stood on the stool, rubbing the rag up and down the same spoon, like she hadn't even said it.

She's really pretty when she isn't talking. But I'm not going to marry her.

"Hello?" Aunt Frannie had picked up the phone. We all turned and watched her. "Oh good, then," she said. "Have they've got the cast on him already...Oh, I see." She gestured for me to get the cobbler out of the oven. "Right...Johan, listen, Nicolas and Lene are here. We've just finished dinner...No, please, it's my pleasure...Of course, yes... All right...We'll see you soon."

Nick cocked a brow. "So? Bunny boy okay?"

"Yes, he's fine. Your father says they expect to be home within the next two hours."

Two hours. 120 minutes. 7200 seconds.

"Watch it, hon, you're spilling the edges over."

pipes are cold, on account of it being winter and all, so I fiddled with the faucet until I got the right temperature. I took a sip. It was satisfactory.

When I came up to Mom and Dad's bedroom, I heard Aunt Frannie whispering to Nick. "Keep an eye on Red. His asthma pump is on the kitchen counter."

Great. Nick Lund was going to be babysitting me.

She waved to Nick. "Okay, be good." She kissed my forehead. "Don't stay up too late, hon."

"Don't worry, Ms. Saint-Jacques." Nick was smiling from ear to ear. "I'll make sure he brushes his teeth and everything."

Scott squinted suspiciously and pulled Aunt Frannie out the door. "Come on, or we'll miss the previews."

They shut the door behind them.

Brush my teeth?

I frowned and folded my arms over myself.

Nick glanced back at Lene. She was sleeping soundly, drowned in a sea of green flannel. "Okay," he whispered. "Go brush your teeth and get into bed."

The corners of my mouth sagged.

He walked off, heading for the kitchen. "O'Reilly," he said without looking back, "I'm fucking kiddin'. Get your ass in here."

My heart fluttered, but I followed.

"Think I can have the rest of this lemon pie?" Nick's head was inside the fridge.

I nodded.

His blue eyes appeared over the fridge door. "Did you say yeah?"

I nodded again, trying to steady my beating heart.

"Want some?" he asked, scooping the citrus mess into his hand.

That lemon pie had been on the shelf since Monday. It was yellow in the middle, but tawny at the edges.

Nick stuffed a whole piece inside his mouth, grimaced, and hurried to the cupboard. He fumbled for a glass and filled it with milk. "Wish I hadn't eaten that." He looked my way. "O'Reilly, you should have warned me." He wiped his mouth with the back of his hand, and a long shiver rattled him. "That was the nastiest lemon pie I ever had, and I've had my share of nasty food, trust me."

My shoulders shook a little as I held back a laugh.

Nick popped the pantry open. "Need to get this taste out of my mouth." He began rummaging through the cans and dry goods. "Let's see."

Unless Nick knew how to make something out of corn meal and old molasses, that lemon pie was going to be the last decent thing he would find in our house. Aunt Frannie doesn't believe in shopping for food. She likes to stop by the store after work and buy something for that night's dinner. No more, no less. Problem is, what am I supposed to eat in the remaining twenty-three hours?

"You got ten bucks?" Nick had emptied the contents of his wallet on the counter. I counted twenty-seven cents.

I shrugged.

"Forget it." He rubbed his chin, staring out into space. "Bad idea anyway. I'm just food trippin'. It'll pass."

Food tripping?

"You got a tape deck?" He was flicking lights on in the living room. "Some tapes or records?"

I pointed to my dad's sound system. I'm not allowed to play it.

Nick crouched down next to it. "Sweet." He looked up. "You got some tapes?"

There's a box of them in Dad's closet.

"In-in my pa-pa-par—"

"O'Reilly. Take a breath. Your parents' room?"

I nodded. "Clo-closet."

Nick got to his feet and disappeared into the hall. I chewed on my lip, watching the snow fall, trying not to see the redheaded boy in the window's reflection. I couldn't believe that boy was me. So insignificant looking.

So mediocre.

"All right, let's see what we can find." Nick had found the big red box and set it on his lap. He pulled a cassette out and flipped it around. His blond eyebrows met as he stared at the white label. He shrugged, tossing the tape back into the box. I watched him do this for twelve minutes. Finally, he had exhausted the box's contents. "Your dad a religious nut or something?"

I've never thought of that.

Perhaps.

"The only thing I wouldn't mind popping in the deck is this one. Not so bad, I guess. Used to listen to this when I was a kid." He slid the cassette in the deck and pushed the rewind button.

I watched the light get caught in his hair, thinking about the sun streaming through the church's tainted windows. When my eyes moved over his mouth, my penis twitched a little, so I made myself imagine grandma's avocado green toilet seat.

Then Elvis began singing.

Something-something wise men don't rush into things.

Nick jumped to his feet. "Fuck, this man can belt out a song!"

I guess so.

I noticed Nick's eyes were different. They were two gigantic swimming pools. Like the ones in the ads Aunt Frannie always sighs over. "Come to the Caribbean," so on, so forth. Yes, his eyes looked just like those turquoise pools. So fresh and inviting. There was something dancing in them too. Something wild.

I stood in the living room, trying not to look stupid.

Nick plopped down on the couch, staring up. "You know O'Reilly, I'm gonna split one day. Gonna live in Greece." He closed his eyes for a second. "And own a resort. Just off the shore. Call it Blue Dreams."

My saliva had run out. Or maybe all of it had drained into the creases of my palms. "Ni-i-ice."

Nick cracked an eye open. "Yeah." He sat up, pulling something from his back pocket. "So, what do you wanna do, O'Reilly, you know, after you've made it out of this shithole of a town?"

My cheeks scorched, but I don't know why. "I wa-wanna be an accountant."

Nick cocked his head. "Yeah? Good stuff. You like math?"

I nodded.

"Yeah, well—" Nick was dropping some green stuff into a small paper, "I take it English isn't your strongest subject."

Actually, I'm quite good in English. If I'm not asked to speak any of it.

Nick ran his tongue along the side of the skinny cigarette he had rolled up. He rose. "I'm gonna smoke this on the porch. Be right back."

"I'll co-come."

Why I say these things. I don't know.

Nick looked me up and down, and smiled. "Okay, but don't ask me what it is, or if you can try some, okay? I don't intend on floatin' up in the canal in three weeks."

I suppose he meant Officer Di Paglio and his new protective interest in me.

"Put a coat on." Nick stuffed his feet inside his big black boots, but didn't bother with lacing them up. "And button it up too. All the way."

I slipped on my coat and even wrapped a scarf around my neck.

We stepped out on the back porch.

As soon as I shut the door behind me, the cold wind whipped my face, and in an instant, every muscle in my body had tensed. I began shivering.

"Oh fuck me." Nick was trying to light his cigarette, shifting his weight from leg to leg. "It's deadly out here. You should go back inside."

"No, it's o-okay."

He finally lit the slim white tube, and I watched him suck on it. Nick held his breath in for a long time, like he wasn't sure where it was suppose to go, before slowly letting some of the smoke out. It streamed out of his nose and lips, making clouds of white vapor around his face. He sucked on it another time, then carefully extinguished the end of it between his wet fingers and tucked it back into a plastic bag, which he stuffed into his back pocket. "All right," he said against the howling wind. "Let's go back inside. My dick's gettin' freezer burn."

Inside, Nick let out a cry of relief. "Wow, that was brutal." His smile was a little crooked, and his pupils had overflowed into the blue ocean around them. "Oh man, I love this song." He made his way back to the living room. "Let's see how good your old man's sound system is. Lene sleeps like the dead anyway."

Within seconds, the walls were shaking. The floor under my feet trembled.

I rushed to the living room, firmly intended on turning the volume down before Mrs. Markov, our upstairs neighbor, called the police. But I stopped short.

Nick was dancing.

Singing too.

Something-something desk clerk in black.

He knew all the words, like he had written the song himself. Then the guitar broke out, some piano too. Nick climbed on top of our coffee table, and with a sway of his hips, began stroking an invisible guitar. His eyes were closed, and I was glad they were, because mine were wide-open, drinking in this unexpected vision. I had never seen anyone move like that. Not even Uncle Ted, and he's won a few dancing contests, or so Aunt Frannie says. Nick's hips rolled and swung from side to side as if his feet had eyes of their own. As I watched him skid up and down that table, my own feet seemed to come alive.

But I clenched my toes and stuffed my hands into my pockets.

Then another song came on, and this one sent Nick into some kind of dancing trance. Something about rocking in a prison. Nick howled just like a werewolf and jumped off the table, shaking his body like he had been electrocuted. I shrank back a little. "Come on, O'Reilly!" he screamed over the music. He was out of breath and wild-eyed. Before I knew it, my hand was in his and he had spun me around a few times.

For a second, the floor was where the ceiling should have been, and my brain felt loose inside my skull.

The music thundered inside me, like it was moving up my limbs and shaking all their contents. Nick hadn't let go of my hand. His long fingers were wrapped around mine and he was jerking me around like a noodle. "Let's see your moves, little man."

My moves?

Nick laughed and spun me around again. "Like this," he said over the blasting music. His fingers let go of mine, and as soon as they did, I missed them, but within seconds, his hands were pressed against my hips. "Go with it. Dancing is about pushing and pulling." I was stiffer than an iron stick, but Nick began swaying again, only this time, he locked me in, and I had no choice but to follow his movements. "Relax." He pressed his hot mouth against my ear, sending shivers down my shoulders. "Listen, O'Reilly."

The music had a fast tempo, but the baseline was smooth, slower, and that's the beat we were following. I began hearing it better, as if it had disconnected itself from the rest of the instruments, and suddenly, my hips could hear it too. "Oh yeah, you're gettin' it now." Nick laughed, and my heart leaped at the sight of his perfect smile. He released his grip on my waist only to enclose my hand in his again, and in brusque movements, he pulled me in, then set me loose, pulled me in, then out again. Spun me around, then pulled me in, pushed me out, then spun me around in the other direction. The colors had all blended in. The living room lamp was at one time to my left, at another, at my right. Once in a while, I caught our reflection in the window, but I couldn't believe it was ours. The more he pushed and pulled on me, the more limber I got. I couldn't feel anything else but his chest and hands. His laughter was mad, and it shook me deep, until it broke a smile out of me. Nick spun me around one last time before gently releasing me, but the dancing wasn't over. No. We both had lost our minds, it seemed. We ran around the living room, jumping over the furniture, climbing on the couches, bouncing off the walls like we had stolen away from Never Land.

The music wasn't important anymore.

We were tuned in to something else.

My lips tasted like sweat, and my breath was short, but nothing of that mattered. I was insane with freedom. Nick had found Aunt Frannie's broom and was singing into it, putting Elvis to shame.

This lasted until I couldn't remember what life was really about.

But soon, a quiet song came on, and we both glanced over at each other. I could see Nick's chest heave. Mine hurt a little. "Well, shit," he said, grinning. "Your body sure knows what to do."

Nick turned the volume down before going into the kitchen.

I stood still in the middle of the room, letting my body recover from this new experience.

Nick soon came back with two tall glasses of water. I drank mine in three deep gulps.

"I wanna show you somethin'," he said, still trying to catch his breath.

I swallowed.

Nick winked. "Check this out." In one quick motion, he pulled his sweater over his head.

My eyes immediately darted to the floor. My mouth filled with saliva, but I couldn't make myself look up.

"You like it? It's a rune. It symbolizes travel. A journey. Personal rhythm."

I nodded. "It's ni-i-ice."

"O'Reilly, you haven't even looked."

Well. I didn't need to.

The way Nick had whispered those words had shot a dose of

excitement inside my belly. I blinked, slowly raising my gaze. As my eyes passed his leather studded belt, they hesitated, but curiosity egged them on higher, over his flat stomach, which had a fine line of blond fuzz shooting down into his jeans, then higher, over his chest.

When my eyes reached his nipples, the heat inside my stomach made me a little nauseous.

Nick's chest looks like a man's chest, but without the hair.

"So, what do you think? Pretty cool, huh?"

Above his left nipple was a blue *R*. Just a letter. And the letter *R*, of all letters. Not very moving. "You-your mom-mom know about—it?"

Nick shrugged. "I don't give a flying fuck what my old lady says," he sneered. "I'm gonna be outta here soon anyway."

My teeth found my lip.

Nick slipped back into his sweater. "I remind her of her dad. Or something." His eyes glimmered. "Better off this way."

Why couldn't I find something to say to him? Something meaningful.

Nick ran his hand over his face and smiled, but there was a hint of sadness in that smile. "Where does your aunt keep her makeup?"

He was already making his way to the bathroom.

I followed.

I paused in the doorway, watching Nick rummage through the cabinets. "Here it is."

Makeup.

What now?

"Sit down." Nick pointed to the closed lid.

I hesitated, but soon obeyed. How could I refuse him anything?

"Look up."

I raised my chin. Nick towered over me. His stomach was at my eye level, but I lifted my gaze to his face.

"Don't move," he whispered. His breath seemed short. "I don't wanna put your eye out." He plucked the tip off Aunt Frannie's black eyeliner with his teeth. "Don't worry, I'm pretty good at this."

I held my breath.

Nick brought the sharp point of the black crayon to the corner of my eye. I drew back a little at the sharpness of it. "O'Reilly, trust me." I could smell the lemon on his breath. "Keep your eyes wide open and keep looking up." As he ran the tip of the eyeliner all along the edge of my eye, his hands were surprisingly steady. "Oh man—" He stepped back to assess his work. "Your eyes look fucking wicked." He pulled me up and turned me around.

When I caught sight of myself in the mirror, I immediately frowned.

Nick laughed. "What? You look super trash."

I came in closer, studying my eyes with wonder. The black contour made the green of my irises shine. Like my eyes were radioactive, almost phosphorescent.

Supernatural.

"Ah, I can tell." Nick watched me in the mirror. "You like it. Don't deny it."

I shrugged, but couldn't tear my eyes away from our reflection.

"You wanna try some lipstick?"

There was something in Nick's tone, something tense, and suddenly, I realized what we were doing might be wrong. Nick shut the door. "Just the light shades, no red or anything." He began twisting caps off the lipstick tubes, apparently looking for the right color. "Here we go," he whispered, settling on a blush tone. "Let's go with this one."

I instinctively sealed my lips shut.

Nick touched my arm. "It's cool, man, I do this to Dave all the time. He does a lot of plays and stuff."

My lips were still sealed.

"O'Reilly, don't fucking look at me like that." He laughed. "You've got a pretty intimidating stare, you know that? Anyways, it's not like I'm gonna tell anybody. It'll be our little secret."

My head was on an elevator ride without my body. The heat drained out of me.

My penis had stretched to the point of pain.

If he didn't touch me, I would die.

"Hey." Nick's voice had an urgency in it. "You okay?"

My hands shook. I know, because I couldn't wipe the makeup from my eyes.

"O'Reilly? Hey. Goddamn it, look at me." His hands hovered over my face, but he didn't touch my skin.

The bathroom didn't have a door anymore. It had lost its window. And there was no air.

No air.

"Calm down. O'Reilly, calm the fuck down. Oh shit, come on man, don't do this."

Heard him, yes, but couldn't answer. Couldn't stop shaking, thrashing.

Then Nick left.

He left me with the cold ceramic under my feet. I clasped my fingers around the towel rack, trying to stop the room from spinning, trying to take one breath. If I could take one lousy breath, then I would know I wasn't going to die.

"Open your mouth." Nick was pushing something on my lips. "Open your mouth, goddamn you. Open."

My fingers ripped at his and my feet kicked at his calves.

"Calm the fuck down!" Nick's voice was strained, thick with panic, but my hands tore at his clothes, and my mouth remained shut tight.

"O'Reilly! You're having an asthma attack, you need to suck on this, *now*. Please. Open your mouth, please, O'Reilly." His voice softened. "Please. Open your mouth, Derek, come on, one big fucking breath and it's over."

My eyes had been running wildly along the bathroom walls, but slowly, they began to regain some of their focus, and as I locked my gaze to Nick's, my lips drooped open a little.

"Look at me, O'Reilly. Breathe. Please. Look at me and breathe."

Softly, Nick pushed the edge of the inhaler into my mouth. "Please."

I kept my eyes on his and sucked in a small dose. Then another. Slowly, my airways relaxed.

"Good boy." Nick's fingers released their grip on my shirt, and he slumped back down against the wall, cradling his face inside the fold of his arms. "Fuck," he mumbled. "You're so intense."

I was going to say something, but without a warning, a giant sob shot out of my mouth. It had the force of a shove propelling me two steps ahead. I clutched my mouth, but it was no use. The tears were gunning out of my eyes like liquid bullets.

Nick glanced up. "Hey—"

The surprise on his face caused me to bolt out of the bathroom.

I pulled the basement door open and skidded down the stairs, running for my bedroom where I could be alone.

Safe.

I couldn't find any tissues in my bedroom, so I wiped my face, makeup and all, with a T-shirt. My throat was scratchy on account of that runaway sob. I hurriedly pulled my clothes off and jumped into my pajamas.

I glanced at the door.

Would Nick be knocking on it soon?

I pushed my dresser against the door, and leaned a chair against that.

Good. I would be undisturbed.

I lay on my bed, staring up at the ceiling, trying to slow my heart down to an acceptable pace.

"O'Reilly. Come on, you freak, open the door."

I shut my eyes.

"I fuckin' mean it. Open the door."

I popped an eye open.

"I swear to God, you've got five seconds to open this door."

I sat up.

Debated.

"NOW, O'REILLY."

I jumped out of bed and worked at sliding the dresser away. I turned the doorknob, but leaped back into bed before Nick entered.

"I'm gonna talk to you and you're gonna listen." Nick had come into my bedroom again, and he sat on the floor, facing me, with his back against the wall. "Okay?"

I turned on my side, watching him. The wind rattled the window above my head, and at the sound of it, a shiver rippled down the small of my back. "O-okay."

"Good." Nick crossed his arms over his knees and sighed. "You know why you have these episodes? 'Cause you don't deal with things. That's why. Now, I don't know what brought this one on, but I have a feelin' you're not gonna be tellin' me anytime soon." He leaned his head back and my heart grew quiet. His voice tired. "I'm sorry, okay? Really. I didn't mean to freak you out." He paused, and his blue eyes scanned the dark room. They shone like a skating rink under the moon. "The last thing I wanna do is push you back farther into yourself. You get that don't you? I mean, shit, that's what the dancin' and makeup was for, just lettin' out a little steam, that's all."

Silence filled my bedroom.

And I almost told him.

But how do you say these things? How?

I don't even know how to say anything.

"O'Reilly, I know things are pretty tough for you right now, but I have a good feelin' about you." Nick locked his eyes to mine and smiled. "You're one of those. You know? The ones that come out of things stronger." He got to his knees and made his way to the edge of my bed. His mouth touched my ear. "I see you, O'Reilly. The way you watch me." I could feel his breath in my hair. "We're of the same kind."

My soul exploded inside my chest.

Nick got to his feet. "Get some rest. I'll clean up and make sure everything is the way it was before your aunt gets home, okay?"

I need you. *Please.*

"All right, sleep tight, little man."

No. Stay. Oh God, please.

"Sweet dreams."

I love you.

Stay with me.

Always.

Don't leave me, Nick.

"I'll see you around, O'Reilly."

I woke up to the sound of Boone scratching on my small windowpane.

The orange sun filtered through the glass, creating patterns of light on my bedroom floor.

Where had winter gone? The chilling winds? The piles of snow?

Had the morning been so gentle?

I rubbed the sleep out of my eyes and stood on my bed, looking out to Boone.

He wasn't smiling.

My heart broke out into an uneven rhythm.

"Nick's gone again," he shouted against the glass. "Dave too."

This time, Nick isn't coming back.

CHAPTER SEVEN

I was at my desk this afternoon, and I'm sure, to others, my appearance was absolutely unworthy of attention.

My fingertips tapped the keyboard.

My eyes fixed the screen.

I sat in a regular, natural way, but something had not been detected by my colleagues—I had turned into a mere hologram.

My body was present, but every single cell of its composition had drifted with my soul. For hours, I had been sitting at my desk, pretending to be there, when really, I had long ago flown out the window and was soaring through the Montreal sky, letting the wind carry me to DuPort Street.

"What the fuck is up with you."

Shot down, I crashed back into my limbs. "Huh?"

Jake bounced an eyebrow. "You're typing into oblivion." His slim index pointed to my screen, and I realized I had been tossed out of the accounting program by an intrusive pop-up letting me know I had new mail. Oblivious to it, I had been plugging in information into "The Nothing" for the last ten minutes.

"Is that your lunch?"

I looked over at my open Tupperware. Moss would have been more appealing. I shrugged. "Yeah."

"You disgust me." Jake smiled. "Let's go Chez Loulou and eat Jello out of the stripper's navel."

I couldn't help chuckling. "Lots of work. Sorry."

"You're *so* gay." Jake winked and kicked my chair. "Drinks later?"

My mind had begun drifting again, but I held on to reality long enough to acquiesce.

"Good," he said, leaving me to my inner debate. "I'll catch you later."

Please do.

Yank me down to earth.

Hammer reason into me.

My eyes shifted to the screen again, but I knew very well I had lost this battle, and slowly, as if I might trip myself up, I gathered my bag and jacket and discreetly left the office.

❖

Dear Bump,

Dad has gained a million pounds.

His beard is thick and red like my hair. He smells like charcoal. "Look at you," he keeps saying. "You've grown an inch or two for sure." I think it's just wishful thinking on Dad's part. I haven't grown at all.

Matter of fact, I think I'm still shrinking.

"What happened to your good grades, boy?"

We were having dinner. Guess what was on my plate? Yes, Bump, sloppy joes.

"Oh Johnny, he's just been distracted with everything," answered Aunt Frannie in my place. "It'll come back to him, now that you're here and Dolores will soon be."

No. Never. Won't ever be good in school ever again. Hate it. Hate it more than I hate sloppy joes.

"What about that chess tournament, beat that little chink yet?"

Some sauce sat on the edge of Dad's mouth, hanging on his beard.

"He-he's mo-o-ving—"

"For Pete's sake, spit it out, Red. Fran, didn't you say you were gonna get that boy some help?"

I pushed a piece of bread around on my plate. Not like I was going to let it anywhere near my mouth, but if I push it long enough, Dad starts thinking that I'm eating.

"Well, John," Aunt Frannie's eyes shone a little, "those things cost a lot of money and—"

"Woman, I've been sending you half my darn pay—"

"I know, but the winter was really cold, that heating bill nearly ate all of—"

"All right. All right, spare me." Dad threw back the rest of his Irish coffee and rose. "Help your auntie with the dishes."

I've been helping Aunt Frannie with the dishes since day one. If he had been here, he would know that.

I waited until he had disappeared, then slid out of my chair with a sigh.

Aunt Frannie squeezed my shoulder. "He's just worried 'bout your mom, that's all."

I don't care. I don't mind. I only want to go lie down in my bed and stare at the wall.

Pretend Nick is still sitting up against it, whispering to me.

It's been two weeks. No one knows where Nick and David went.

Boone says a detective couldn't figure out where these two ran to.

Though I have a hunch.

But I'm not gonna tell anyone.

Not even you, Bump.

Nope.

No one.

❖

When I straddled my motorcycle, the afternoon was a crystal blue promise made up of silver cement and yellow skies.

I rode down Saint-Denis, squeezing through the midday traffic of delivery trucks and salespeople, with my mind drawing up a million different possible scenarios. Would Nick be there? What would he say? Would he touch me?

Could I stand it?

Before I knew it, I had reached Saint-Paul Street. I slipped the bike between a Mercedes and a BMW and climbed off.

The Old Port.

It had been a while since I had walked down its cobblestone

streets. As I passed art galleries, quaint boutique hotels, and bistros packed with power eaters, I smiled to myself. Of all the places to open a restaurant, Nick had to pick the trendiest, most sought-after street of Montreal. Nothing here is mediocre. Especially not the people. In the five minutes it took to reach DuPort Street, I had seen more beautiful, fashionable people than I would have if I had been leafing through a *Glamour* magazine.

At the corner, I stopped.

There it was.

Split.

From what I could see, it was a fairly small place, wedged between two much larger restaurants, one a Mediterranean place I had heard of, famous for its grilled squid, and the other a bar/restaurant that appeared to be closed for renovations. I took a shy step forward, and then paused again.

I watched Split's front window.

The glass was tinted, but not too darkly. I could see the interior of the restaurant quite well. There were approximately twenty-five tables, mainly designed for two and four, and at the back was a larger table for six. A corner bar filled a third of the dining room, and behind it, I caught sight of a man.

My heart popped up inside my mouth and I instinctively shrank back, hiding behind the corner wall of the Urban Galleria.

But it couldn't be Nick.

Didn't look like Nick at all.

I ordered myself to get a grip, and drew in a long, cleansing breath.

I wiped my clammy palms down my thighs and shook my shoulders loose. "Okay," I whispered. "Okay."

I peeked into the window again.

The man had disappeared. There were no customers.

I noticed the menu pinned to the door. I wanted to browse through the items and familiarize myself with every single one of Nick's dishes, but I had forgotten how to read. I could feel my shirt breathing against my chest, on account of my heart pounding so dangerously hard. I looked into the window again.

I let out an impatient sigh.

How long was I going to stand at Nick's door?

I pulled on the handle, but when the door opened, my body shook as if I had been zapped.

I hadn't expected to actually walk in.

But I had.

I was inside Split.

Outside, the sunlight had been quite blinding, and as my eyes adjusted to the dim lighting of the interior, I let my nose and ears take over. I heard pots clanking. Some voices carried to me from behind the kitchen's swinging metal door. I tensed. One of them was deeper than the rest.

Could it be Nick's?

I inhaled, and the scents of coconut and wild orchid appeased my nervousness.

Finally, my eyes had regained their purpose, and I let them roam over the room. The tables were covered with fern green cloth, and atop every one was a set of mahogany candle holders, in which stood thick, round almond-colored candles.

My gaze wandered across to the bar.

It was a half-circle hugging the corner of the room, with seven high stools tucked neatly under its rustic, wooden bar top. The back wall was filled with every possible thing one might need to throw the finest party in less than a minute. It was a laboratory of color and decadence. An alchemist's dream.

Under my feet, the dark hardwood floor shone. A string of thin white lights zigzagged across the ceiling above, creating a soothing, almost moonlike effect of light and shadow. The walls were painted a lighter shade of apple green, which could have been tacky, but against the lacquered dark wood that covered the bottom part of the walls, the green had become a pale leaf one wanted to wrap oneself into. The Caribbean had obviously influenced Nick in his choice of accessories and decor. But there was more to the place than that.

Split was exactly that.

Divided.

Modern and conservative. Welcoming, but a bit pretentious. Classic, yet criant.

A rain forest where all the tree trunks were metal rods.

"*Oui?*"

My eyes darted in the young voice's direction. A boy, no more than eighteen, stood a few steps in front of me. His black eyes scrutinized my face. *"J'peux vous aider?"*

"Um—" Whenever I attempt to speak the French language, I sound as if I've just had a root canal and am still under the analgesic. *"Je cherche—"* I realized I was gesturing as if the young man was deaf. *"Je cherche Nicolas Lund,"* I said coherently enough.

His eyes sharpened and his pretty young face soured. He looked me up and down with mild disgust, as if I smelled of guano. *"Un instant."* He spun on himself, going back to the kitchen.

My teeth dug into my bottom lip with enough ardor to startle me. I had nearly drawn blood. I tried to suck in a few breaths, and fastened my gaze to the kitchen door.

I held on, bracing myself for the tsunami of sensations that would soon wash over me.

The door swung open.

The tidal wave crashed into me. It tore into my very skin, pouring into my nose, eyes, and mouth. I could neither breathe nor speak. I had been knocked out by the sheer force of its revelation.

Nick was more beautiful than I could bear, but still, I hadn't truly seen him.

Just caught sight of the *nature* of him.

"Tu m'donnes de papiers, pis tu sacres ton camp okay?"

Something-something, gimme the fucking papers.

My mouth moved, but before I could retort, Nick had snapped my bag off my shoulder. Quite hard too.

"I agreed to the test, what the fuck does she want?" He was fumbling through the contents of my Swiss Army bag, but there's nothing in there but boredom.

"You know, I told Mona—" Nick pulled a beige folder out and slapped it on the bar. "Tell her we can do without the—"

"Nick." Some alien voice had streamed out of my throat.

His blond eyebrows met, and he ran his tongue over his sculpted lips, then squinted.

I watched a subtle transformation come about his face.

Oh, and what a face. Makes you believe in God.

Nick cocked his head a little and looked down at my bag.

"Nick, you-ou don't—don't—" I took a breath, and tried one word at a time. "You don't recognize me?"

His arctic gaze slowly moved over my body, as if I were an empty canvas he needed to fill. "O'Reilly?"

To hear Nick speak my name after all these years cut the last string that held me to the ground. "Yes," I whispered.

Nick slammed his palm down on the bar counter. "Fuck me! No fucking way." His features softened. "No way," he said again, more softly.

He came in closer. "No way," he whispered, his eyes burning my mouth.

Could he see how flustered I had become?

I could barely hold myself together.

He took another step to me. "O'Reilly."

Nick makes my name sound like a Celtic prayer.

I lifted my eyes to meet his piercing gaze. "Nick," I almost moaned.

He bent his face to mine, and I froze, besieged with an overwhelming physical want. His fingers skimmed the edge of my face. "Same wicked eyes," he murmured, his breath warming my hungry lips.

I could not take my eyes off his smile. "Nick." His name I had not said, but *pleaded*.

Nick's eyes dimmed, and he pulled away.

He found refuge behind the bar, pulling a bottle of whiskey off the shelf. "Drink?"

I nodded.

I watched him pour the amber whiskey into two shot glasses. "Straight?" A provocative smile turned up on his sensuous lips. "Well." He laughed.

His laughter shook me out of my mild trance, and I walked, more like wobbled, to the bar, and leaned in, using the counter to hold my weight. "Thank you."

Nick set the glass before me. "Welcome." We raised our glasses, and again, his eyes met mine. "Cheers," he said quietly.

"Cheers," I echoed before downing the delicious Connemara.

He leaned back against the small sink, studying me. "You're all grown up."

Was I imagining the sensuality in his voice?

He cracked a smile. "How'd you know how to find me?"

"Your brother tried to arrest me."

Nick chuckled. "Fuckin' Bunny boy." He picked up the bottle and poured two other shots. "So you guys are hanging out again. Good stuff."

"Yes—" I noticed the tension in my voice had let out. I felt calmer. More together. "Just recently. We were over for supper at his house. Lene and your parents—"

"We?"

Had I said we? I dug my fingernails into my palms.

Nick threw back his shot and glanced down at the silver band around my finger.

I inwardly cursed myself to the pyres of hell.

"You married?"

The question sounded more like an accusation.

"No-no."

"Didn't think so." He lolled his head, peering into my heated face. "Are you a fag?"

I have always hated that cursed word.

Why does Nick make it sound like a sexy triple chocolate fudge cake?

Oh yes, baby. I am a fag.

A smile was my only reply.

"So who's *we*?"

"Chef Nicolas, le gars d'la ville est là pour les tuyaux." The young man who had greeted me with disdain stood by the kitchen's open door.

Nick glanced over and gave him a quick nod. The boy hesitated by the door, his eyes lingering on every fantastic line of Nick's body, then he spun around, and disappeared.

I pushed the glass up. "You're busy. I should go."

"What? Him?" Nick rubbed his chin, laughing.

"Would you like to ha-have din-in-ner maybe?"

I had meant to stutter *drinks*, but my soul had betrayed me.

Nick moistened his lips again, then pressed them together, watching me. He bounced off the sink, and without a word, headed for the kitchen.

My mouth sagged, and my eyes followed him out.

What had just happened?

I stared down at the empty shot glasses, trying to put everything back together in my frazzled mind. I waited, glancing at the kitchen door every other second. Then, after five minutes of this torture, with a heavy hand, I gathered my bag off the counter.

I shuffled to the front door.

"O'Reilly."

My pulse quickened, but I didn't turn around. "Yes?"

Nick's voice rustled at the edge of my ear. He had walked up to me. "Gimme your number," he ordered.

I turned around. "I'll give you my card—"

"No cards, I fucking hate cards. Shoot." He punched my number into his phone. "All right," he said before turning back. "I'll see you around."

At the sound of those words, a chill surged through me.

❖

Dear Bump,

Officer Di Paglio asked Aunt Frannie to marry him, but she said no.

She's been crying for two days. Dad keeps shuffling his feet around, watching her out of the corner of his eye.

She's going to be moving out. Somewhere near the Jolicoeur metro, you know, the one we never get off at.

"It isn't very far from here hon, just on the other side of the canal, 'bout ten minutes."

She was folding some clothes, making neat little stacks of them.

"But why do you-ou have to-to?"

"It isn't right for an unmarried woman to live with her sister and her husband. Just not right."

"Why don't you ma-marry Scott, then?"

Her hands stopped folding, but her eyes remained glued to the sweater in her fingers. "Because that's not the life I want, baby. I don't have the nerves to be a cop's wife. And I enjoy my freedom. Though it comes at high price. Someday you'll understand."

What do nerves have to do with anything?

"Besides, your mom's coming home next week. You don't need me here anymore."

How could I not need Aunt Frannie? That's ridiculous.

"Can I-I co-come with you?"

Tears twinkled in her pale green eyes. "Hon," she whispered, "you don't know how much I want to take you with me. I dream of it, baby. You're my special boy, my friend too." She blinked and the tears ran down her powdered cheeks. "Oh, Red, why do people keep hurting you all the time?"

Dunno.

"I'm going to miss you more than you'll ever really understand." She took a deep breath and wiped her eyes. "Derek. Life is like a staring contest. One blink and it's over, baby. So don't blink, okay? I want you to stare life right in the face until she gives you what you want. What you need."

Whatever that means.

❖

As I ran down the hallway of the infamous cancer ward of the Hotel Dieu hospital, memories raced beside me.

One in particular gained momentum.

A boy with a fat lip wandering the halls in search of his clothes.

I turned the corner in haste, skidding down the white linoleum floor, and for a moment, I wondered, was I running to or from?

"Aunt Fran?" The door was ajar, but I had yet to enter.

A voice cackled. "You better have some booze."

I pushed on the door and walked in with dread tightening my jaw.

The woman whom the bed had swallowed whole wasn't my auntie.

No.

"Don't look at me like that," the feverish-eyed skeleton said. "It's not as bad as I look."

My kneecaps locked. And I hugged myself. "Why didn't you-ou tell-tell me? How could—"

"Hush, baby."

She tried to sit up, and I tried to stand.

"Hon, come here." Her voice was strained. "Come closer."

A cruel, sadistic sorrow bit the back of my throat, and once again, I was propelled into the past.

In our kitchen on First Avenue.

"You gotta let the sauce boil a little first, hon."

"Do you-ou think it'll co-come out good?"

"Oh, hon, everything you pour your little heart into comes out good."

By Aunt Fran's hospital bed, I realized, I haven't poured my heart into anything for the last decade.

I sat in the chair, at her bedside, and reached for her fingers. "Aunt Frannie—" But I was too choked up to speak.

"How was it, hon?" Her eyes had livened, and it gave me strength. "How was the dinner party? How is Boone? Lene? Everybody?"

I swallowed the grief and squeezed her bony fingers. "It was magical, Aunt Fran. Really."

She smiled. Her gums were white. "And did you see him? Did you see Nicolas?"

There was urgency to her tone.

I leaned in. "Yes, I have."

She tightened her grip around my fingers, as if she might fall off a cliff if she ever let me go. "And? Is he still dangerous?"

I thought of Nick's eyes as they had roamed over me.

The effect of them.

"Oh yes, he is, Aunt Fran. More than ever."

Aunt Fran is dying.

I'm not going to let her do this alone, no matter how much cynicism and false confidence she throws my way.

Because I know she's scared.

"You're gonna get yourself fired, Derek."

Nathan and I were getting ready for bed.

"I don't care, Nate."

"You said Goldman asked you to—"

"She's more important."

Nathan's eyes flared up. "You could visit her in the evenings, or go there on your lunch hour."

"You don't understand." I crawled into bed, aligning my body at the very edge of it, and pulled the blanket over my ear. "She's the only person who's ever really loved me."

"How can you say that? How can you lie there and say something like that?"

I sighed, and pulled the blanket higher still. "Because it's true."

"What about me? I slave day in and day out for you, to please you, to—"

"Nathan," I snapped. "I can't hear this again."

He ripped the blanket off my face. "No? You can't be bothered with how I feel? Okay, all right. I'm getting pretty fucking tired of living with a ghost, you know that? Where are you, Derek? Where the hell are you!"

I cringed a little.

Nathan sighed deeply. "Every day, I tell myself that you're gonna change, that you're gonna realize what I do for you, but, Derek, every night, I go to bed feeling more and more disconnected from us." He crouched down at my side, and when I caught sight of his dark brown eyes, my heart warmed a little. "Der, do you love me?"

For two years I have managed to avoid that question.

My imagination is limitless when it comes to finding new ways to slither out of actually saying those three words.

"I need to know." His eyes insisted. "I need to hear you say it."

Nick.

To touch his glorious skin.

To hear him come.

For me.

"Derek? Do you?"

I couldn't do it. I couldn't dirty the words that belong to another.

Nathan slumped back against the nightstand, looking down at his hands. "I've been offered a job, Derek." He turned his face to mine. "A transfer, really. An opportunity to get out of the pressure cooker. Out of sales for good."

I frowned. "What?"

"International relations. Setting up some contacts in Europe, getting a feel for the market over there."

"Over there," I echoed meekly.

"Yeah, Der. *Over there*."

Europe.

Paris. London. Lisbon. Berlin.

Dublin, even.

"They wanna set me up in Milan. *Milan*, Derek. All expenses paid. A twelve to eighteen month contract. Do you know what that means? You and me, in Milan—" He stopped, and then added, more softly. "We could skip the engagement party and get married before November—"

"November?"

He nodded.

"Is that when—"

"I gotta let them know before the third week of October."

The walls leaned in on me, and I shut my eyes. "What about-bout the condo, my job…my aunt?"

And Nick.

Nathan drew in a long, hard breath. "The condo we can sublease. Your job? You just said you wanna take off for a few months, so what's the big deal? We can work something out after the wedding, get you a visa—"

"Oh my Go-god," I gasped. "You've already-dy planned all of this."

"I want you to come with me. I *need* you to come with me." He got to is knees and bent his face to mine. "Baby. Please. Don't make me choose."

And I'm supposed to?

❖

Lene and Boone accompanied me to the Hotel Dieu this afternoon.

We met in the lobby of the cancer ward.

As I walked up to them, I had an urge to grab hold of their beautiful smooth hands and run down the hall, until our feet left the ground, to leave Death far behind.

Let that miserable wretch eat our dust.

Boone came to me and squeezed my shoulder. "Hey. How are you?"

Lene had already wrapped herself around me. Her hot tears wet my neck. The news of Aunt Fran's imminent death has rattled Lene. She remembers her vividly.

Boone gently nudged her out of my embrace. "Come on, let's go say hello."

We huddled together and walked slowly to 1019.

As we came to Aunt Fran's door, Boone flinched, stepping back into the hall. "Wait," he whispered. "Can't do this—"

"Boone." Lene wrapped her fingers around her brother's. "It's okay." She pulled him closer. "Come on, she needs to see that life makes sense. Things go on."

His eyes found mine. "She real beat up?"

I nodded.

Boone rubbed his chin for a moment. He hadn't shaved, and the blond stubble covering his cheeks gave his face an air of weakening virility. How handsome Boone has become.

Testosterone soaks his every move.

"All right," he said at length.

Aunt Fran was sitting up in bed, leafing through a men's fashion magazine. Obviously, the cancer has yet to rob her of her phenomenal libido. At the sound of my voice, she peered over the glossy paper.

On the cover, a blond boy held on to his flimsy shirt as some kind of tornado blew through it. I caught a veiled annoyance in her green eyes.

I had snatched her out of her daydreaming.

Boone and Lene were a step behind, still out of view.

"Aunt Fran." I bent to kiss her sunken cheek. "Boone and Lene Lund are here to see you."

She slapped my hand. "Derek! I haven't even showered."

The woman amazes me.

I chuckled. "Stop it."

"Help me ease up," she said, primping her thinning auburn hair. "And fetch me my Air du Temps."

I handed her the perfume bottle. She poured a small amount onto her fingertips and dabbed her wrist and neck with them.

"Okay?"

"Okay."

Lene and Boone seemed to be a balm on Aunt Fran's spiritual wounds. She held their hands as if they carried absolution. She spoke softly, her eyes drinking in their beauty, and for the whole hour the Lunds were in her room, Aunt Fran's usual caustic tongue did not make an appearance.

I stood in the corner, watching youth and health seep back into her tired face, knowing very well that it was a temporary hallucination.

An illusion brought on by wishful thinking.

"And how's Scott?" Though she tried to sound uninterested, I had caught the anticipation in Aunt Fran's voice.

Boone laughed. "Di Paglio? Still busting my balls."

Aunt Fran fiddled with the edge of the sheet.

I watched her, amused by her little charade.

"Married?" she asked in the same disinterested tone.

Boone leaned in. "He was for a while, but he's recently divorced." He set his gigantic hand on Aunt Fran's arm. "I don't think he ever got over you, Ms. Saint-Jacques—"

Her gaze shifted to my face and I winked. She rolled her eyes. "Well, that was a long time ago. Anyway, he probably made his wife crazy."

"Actually," said Boone, "it was the other way around."

"I see." She quickly turned to Lene. "And you, my dear, no husband?"

Lene's cheeks glowed pink. "Busy, you know."

Aunt Fran scoffed. "Please, child. Ain't no such thing." She pursed her thin lips. "And Nicolas?"

Boone glanced over at me.

I shifted.

The mere mention of Nick's name is like a warm hand sliding down the front of my pants.

Lene tucked a blond curl behind her ear. "Nico isn't the settling-down type of guy, you know what I mean? He's—" She smiled. "Wild."

Wild.

Instantly, images of Nick's cock skimming my lips shot through my mind.

What does he sound like when he comes?

"Hon, you okay?"

My body pulsed with sex. I could hardy blink.

Boone laughed. "Don't worry, Ms. Saint-Jacques, Derek always looks like that when the subject of my crazy older brother comes up. Been like that since we were kids."

Lene squinted. "What are you talking about?" Her eyes queried mine. "Does Boone mean…?" She slapped her thigh. "That's why you always looked so shell-shocked when you sat at our table! You have a crush on Nicolai?"

I have a crush the same way a great white has dentures.

"When Derek was a boy," said Aunt Fran, a musing smile on her lips, "he used to draw everything in purple."

"Purple?" echoed Boone and Lene.

"Yes. Purple."

I remembered.

Purple trees. Purple cars. Purple stick men.

Purple hearts.

"Why?" asked Lene, watching me.

"I asked him that same question one day," returned Aunt Fran. "Oh and Lene, you should have seen those big emerald eyes, the way they shone. He said, "'Because I like mixing the red and blue.'"

Lene set her fingers on her lips, but a small gasp escaped them. "Red and Blue," she whispered.

Yes.

Red and Blue.

❖

I think Nathan is going to be leaving without me. I think I want him to.

He waits for me to deliver the final blow.

And I keep delaying it.

Why have you come back into my life?

Feels like you're on a mission to tear it down.

❖

Human resources declined my request for a temporary leave.

I had been harassing them for the last three days. I received an e-mail this morning: I can take the remainder of my vacation time, which adds up to eight days, or hand in my resignation. In the current situation, they cannot acquiesce to my request.

Eight days. That's not enough time.

I need more time. She needs more time.

Why can't we get more bloody time?

Aunt Fran suffers. She denies it, but I read it on her face every time she coughs, moves, breathes. They've upped the morphine dosage, but she refuses to let them reduce her to a "bag of bones and drool."

Today, I sat at her side, watching *The Ellen DeGeneres Show.*

"She's pretty, no?"

"Ellen?"

"Yes."

"Have you ever?"

"Have I ever what?"

"You know, hon, been with a woman?"

"No."

"Why?"

"I never wanted to."

With every commercial break, our relationship deepened.

"Derek, do you remember how beautiful I was?"

"Yes, Aunt Frannie."

"I once invited three men into my bedroom."

There were no taboos anymore. Nothing sacred.

As women washed their hair on the boob tube, I was explaining the pleasures of male anal sex.

Aunt Fran was curious and eager, and I offered her all of my answers on a plate of candor and truthfulness that I have never owned.

"Do you love Nathan?"

I sighed, fiddling with the silver band around my finger. "Aunt Fran, I said yes, when I shou-should have been say-saying no."

A flash of anger illuminated her green eyes. "You have been trespassed on. You hear me, Derek O'Reilly? Trespassed on!" Her voice had risen abruptly, and it startled me quiet. "I've been watching you, Red, all these years, and you have allowed every one of your greedy lovers to rummage through your temple, and without any consideration for your limits, or boundaries, you have let them claim it as their empire."

My lips parted.

Reality's icy fingers clasped the side of my head.

Be quiet.

Don't talk about this.

Be good.

Say yes.

Wear this. Wear that.

Eat this. Eat that.

Blow me.

Let me fuck you.

Turn around.

We don't need rubbers.

Open your mouth.

Shut up.

My jaw tightened, and a quiet but deadly rebellion inched up my spine.

Aunt Fran fell back onto the pillow. "Honey, promise me something." She closed her eyes, obviously exhausted. "Don't go to Milan." She opened her eyes. "Go to Split and kiss Nicolas Lund on the mouth."

I laughed.

It felt tremendously good.

"I'm serious, Derek. Enough already. You go there, grab hold of that magnificent beast, and you stick your tongue down his throat."

Laughter quenched my soul.

She smiled. "I bet you he'll let you," she said before dozing off into a morphine slumber. "I bet you that cold ocean could use a little of your warmth."

"O'Reilly."

I had just fallen asleep when Nick called.

I pressed the phone to my ear, and glanced at the clock. "Hi."

"Sleeping?"

"No," I lied.

It was ten p.m. How pathetic of me. How lame to have been reduced to falling asleep at this hour.

"You alone?"

I was. Nathan hadn't come home yet. He was still at the gym.

"Yes," I returned, feeling my body harden under the sheets. "How are you?"

"Good. Sorry 'bout not calling."

"It's okay. Figured you were bu-busy."

"I've got shit coming at me from every direction." He exhaled. I pictured him standing at Split's back door, looking like some kind of Dionysus. "I need to get out of the kitchen. I need to blow my lid, you in?"

I sat up, my groin filling with heat. "Yeah," I whispered in a breath. "I am."

"Good. Come, then."

I almost did. Right there in my pajama bottoms.

"Where do you-ou live?"

"Right on top of things. Split's second floor."

What a complete control freak Nick is.

"I'll be there in about —"

"Whatever, O'Reilly. Just *come*."

As I climbed up Split's iron staircase, I could almost hear my mind humming.

I paused on the last step, watching the door.

I looked down at myself.

I wore my black jeans and an army green shirt. That shirt is snug in all the right places, and my black jeans have gotten me more action than any other pair of pants I own.

I blew a breath into my cupped fingers. Spearmint.

I ran a nervous hand through my hair. Not much I could do about that.

I took a shallow breath and knocked.

Immediately, the most gruesome, hellish sound filtered through the thick wooden door. I shrank back from it, as if the very sound could tear my throat open.

"Quiet!" Nick's tone had a chilling authority to it. *"Stille."*

The thing, which I imagined was the offspring of Cujo and the devil, instantly stopped its barking.

Nick popped the door open. "Hey."

My eyes darted down to the monstrous animal he was holding back from murdering me.

"What is tha-that?"

"This is Escoffier. Don't worry, man, he's real sweet."

I smiled. "Sweet?"

"Yeah." Nick began petting the thing, rubbing its gigantic head with vigor. The thing, which is in fact a red nose pit bull, is Nick's "baby."

"Come in, he won't bite you. Well, only if you show weakness."

Then I was screwed.

I eased myself into the entrance, my eyes never leaving the dog's jaw.

"Put your hand out, let him smell you."

I was quite sure the dog could smell me just fine from where I stood, but Nick's blue eyes insisted, so I extended my hand, prepared to be carrying it in a bag of ice to the ER in a few seconds. The dog's nose was wet and cold. "He's very ni-ice."

Nick laughed. "Go on, Esco. *Get.*" The thing padded down the hall. "Go destroy my boots or something."

In the living area (everything is an *area*, as there are no rooms, no doors, just one huge space with scarcely any furniture), Nick pointed to the only chair in the place. "Sit down."

I did.

He went to a box and pulled out a bottle of wine. "Take your shoes off, relax."

I took my shoes off.

He then went to his laptop, which was set atop another box, this one wooden, and began scrolling down some list. His eyes were fixed to the screen, and I indulged myself while I could.

He wore faded blue jeans and a tight white T-shirt.

Nick's lines are graceful. Everything on him is long and hard.

His ass tortures me.

As my eyes wandered over every inch of his body, I remembered the L-shaped couch.

I recalled the blue ink that had stained my sweaty fingers that night.

"Wing it, O'Reilly."

Slowly, I loosened my grip on the moment and inhaled deeply.

Nick's hair is shorter now, but the ash blond strands still hang loosely around his face, reaching just above the neckline. He kept pushing it out of his translucent eyes. "Yeah, this is good," he whispered, stepping away from his computer.

David Usher's childlike voice streamed out of the various speakers scattered around the room. The acoustics in the loft are amazing.

Nick uncorked the wine bottle and flipped a thick, sturdy cardboard box upside down. He set the glasses on it.

"Just moved in?" I asked.

Nick sat on the floor, curling his long legs under him. "No."

I glanced around. "Okay."

He lit a thin cigar. "Do you mind? I quit smoking last year, and this is my last guilty pleasure."

I didn't mind, but every time his lips sucked on the cigar, I held my breath, trying to hold myself back from knocking the box over and ripping his jeans open with my teeth.

"So, you never answered my question." His blue eyes danced on my mouth. "Who's *we*?"

I took a generous swill of the wine. It was fantastic. Deep, rich, and earthy.

"Come on, O'Reilly, tell me all about Mr. Roboto."

I frowned.

"Boone told me. This Nathan guy, you live with him?"

I took another mouthful of the wine.

"So you guys are like, *monogamous* and everything?"

That word. That awful, awful word.

I shrugged. "Dunno."

Nick choked on the smoke." What do you mean, you don't know? Are you guys fucking other people or not?"

Mr. Smart-ass.

I sank the rest of my wine and rose.

There were some drawings taped to the brick wall. I wanted to get a closer look. "You made these?" I asked, hoping to stray away from the subject of my degrading sex life, or lack of it.

"No." There was a subtle tension in his voice. "Quit poking around my stuff," he added. "Sit down, O'Reilly, and I promise not to ask any more dumb questions."

The drawings were nothing but circles and lines. One of them looked like a face, but I wasn't sure. "Who's Spencer?" I asked, reading the name at the far corner of the paper.

"Nobody."

Nick's breath had warmed my ear.

And I turned around to find him standing less than two inches from me.

I hurt to taste him.

"Wow." He inhaled, skimming his nose along my neck. "I remember that smell."

His T-shirt grazed my shirt.

His breath caressed my nose.

I tensed, trying to keep control.

Carefully, Nick moved in closer, and when I felt his own desire, pressed hard against my lower stomach, a small moan escaped me. I leaned into him, pushing my face into his chest, getting high off the scent of his clothes. "Nick," I pleaded again. "Oh God, please. *Please.*"

His body tensed, and his mouth scorched my ear. "Don't, O'Reilly. No need to beg."

I turned my face to his voice, dying to catch his mouth with my lips. He clasped my arm, and slowly, he raised it over my head. Then the other. Nick held me tightly, trapping my body between him and the wall. My knees bent. His lips skimmed my skin, moving up my neck, pausing on my chin, heating my flesh with a paralyzing lust.

But he teased.

His mouth touched mine, but never fully quenched it. His fingers held me prisoner, yet it was his feverish blue gaze that bound me to him. His hips pushed into mine, and at the feel of his erection grinding up against mine, I shivered and cried out, mad with need.

His fingers released my wrists, but before I could plunge mine into his hair or jeans, he had slipped my shirt over my head and was working at my belt. "Help me with this—" The belt was stuck, and our fingers tore at it. "Fucking thing," cursed Nick under his breath. "This thing a chastity belt or what?"

I gently pushed his fingers away and yanked at the belt, then the zipper. Nick's warm fingers didn't hesitate for a minute. They dove inside my briefs and freed my swollen cock from its confinement.

At the touch of his fingers, I nearly came.

Slowly, Nick got to his knees, sliding his warm hands down my bare chest, and I leaned back on the wall, but refrained from closing my eyes.

No. I wanted to see.

His mouth steamed my skin. His velvet tongue glided along my erection—his desire obscene and raw.

There is no excuse on his tongue. There is no apology in Nick's sexuality.

As his ardor heightened and his lips raced along my erection, I became aware of every nerve under my skin—every breath moving my chest.

Every bloody minute I have ever wasted.

Our eyes met.

A surge of pleasure burned my loins, and I tried to pull away, afraid to soil his perfect lips, but his fingers dug into my ass to bind me to his mouth, and I touched his face as I came, letting the nirvana chill thunder through me, until it had left me limp. Spent of everything.

I leaned back, trying to steady my legs, and I caught the thing, Escoffier, watching me. "Your dog."

Nick rose, running his tongue along his swollen lips. "Don't worry about him. He likes you. Come here."

I fell into his hands.

Nick smiled. "Let me see those wicked green eyes." I looked up and playfully batted my eyelashes. His gaze clouded over, and he bent to me, cupping his fingers around my face. Again, his lips only grazed mine, but I would not be teased any longer. I drove my hands into his hair, and pulled him in. "Kiss me, Nick. And don't stop."

I needed everything. His tongue, fingers, cock inside me.

We tumbled to the mattress that serves as his bed, and as pants and underwear flew about, I gasped for a breath, but never could tear my mouth from his.

"Wait." He pulled away from me, and I watched him fumble through a small box. "Rubber." His voice was thick with lust.

I traced my fingers along the small of his back, my eyes roaming over his naked body. There is no sense in trying to be good, hoping to find myself back in God's grace, when Nick's skin makes heaven seem like a flooded trailer park.

"Got it." He ripped at the package with his teeth and dropped it in my hand.

I carefully eased the condom out, and with trembling fingers, rolled it down the most perfect cock I have seen. It is smaller than I had imagined, and a bit crooked, but if I could stare at it all day, I would.

His mouth found mine again, and as our tongues tangled and tasted each other, his fingers crawled around my inner thigh. "Can I?" he asked softly, gliding his index down my ass cheek.

"Yes."

His finger hurried a little, as if I could change my mind. "Can I?"

"Yes, Nick," I moaned.

I had never heard myself saying yes this much.

Without a word, nor a whisper, Nick made love to me. He fucked me slow and deep until we had both exhausted our bodies, and for purely mechanical reasons, had to release the other's limbs.

We lay quietly for a long time, waiting for our hearts to slow and our bodies to recover.

Nick turned to me and smiled. "Sleep?"

I thought of Nathan. I had left a note on the kitchen counter, letting him know I might be spending the night with Aunt Fran, but that I would call.

I glanced over at my pants, debating on that phone call.

"No?" asked Nick, peering into my eyes.

I nodded. "Yes. Sleep."

"Come closer."

I cradled myself against his smooth chest, with my cheek against his rune, and listened to the sound of his heart.

"Good night," he whispered.

The dog jumped up on the mattress, making a nest of blankets at my feet.

"Good night."

I closed my eyes, listening to the two of them breathe in sync.

This morning, Nick was gone.
I haven't heard from him since then.
But really, Bump, did you think I would?

CHAPTER EIGHT

Nathan has asked me to give him an answer before the end of the month.

I could give it to him now, and I should, but I cannot make myself care enough. I have no desire for confrontation; as a matter of fact, I have no desire for anything but Nick's skin.

I stumble through my days, with barely enough concentration to find a matching pair of socks.

Nick hasn't called.

And Aunt Fran is leaving me.

I was in that dreaded hospital room this morning, watching Aunt Fran challenge time with every painful breath.

"Call Nicolas," she insisted from under the oxygen mask. "Don't let the cloak of insecurity fall over his eyes."

Her sickness has blown poetry into my life. Her every word opens a closing door.

"I don't want to pu-push him," I argued weakly.

"Call him. Call *Nicolas*."

Aunt Fran can't understand. It doesn't work that way.

Right?

"Don't go to Milan." Her eyes scorched my face. "I don't—" She paused, struggling to suck in one salvaging breath.

I cringed, clutching the bed's metal post. "Aunt Frannie, don't talk, please."

She rolled her head on the pillow, and her gaze shrouded with fever and urgency. "Listen," she shot under a shallow breath. *"Listen to me."*

When I was a boy, I believed in the notion of restorative karma. Do good, and you shall be rewarded. After all, what is love but a warm look, a comforting touch, a word of praise? All those things Aunt Frannie has bestowed upon me when no one would? Francine St-Jacques has walked a line few people have. She has had gusto. Courage. Her straightforwardness has laid a foundation inside me, something solid I have been able to fall back on through the lonely, confusing years.

Many times, we have disagreed, but never about the important things.

In a world full of wannabes, posers, and fast-talking happiness pushers, Aunt Fran has been the only real deal.

I can't let her go.

I don't want to.

I'm not ready. I need more time. There's so many things I still need to learn from her.

And so many more I would like to teach her sometimes cynical heart.

"I'm so proud of you, Derek."

Why? What have I done but sink in my own troubled waters?

"Do you remember the man..." Her voice was barely a whisper, but she pressed on. "The man at the Dragon Hair counter, that day?"

I remembered.

The taste of sugar and oil filled my mouth, and I could almost smell the roasted peanuts.

"You *are* the sorcerer, my love." Aunt Fran held her fingers out, and I cupped them, letting the moment drown my mind in sorrow.

"You've remained unscathed, untouched by the ugly." She closed her eyes. "You've blessed my life, Derek O'Reilly. I wish you could have been my son."

A sob curled at the edge of my lips, but I shook my head, fighting it back, afraid I would collapse and steal this powerful, lucid instant from her. "Aunt Frannie—" But I could not speak.

"I won't leave you, Derek." Her eyes blazed. "I'll watch over you. You and Nicolas."

I fell on her hollowed belly, letting her fingers comb my hair. "Don't, Aunt Frannie. Don't go-go."

Her hand caressed my neck, and I heard the disease, that treacherous bastard of a disease, howling inside her chest.

"I'm so-so alone, Aunt Frannie. So alone."

"No." Her hand paused.

I lifted my blurry gaze to meet hers.

She tried to smile through her own tears. "No, honey. You're not alone. No. *No.* You never were. You have Nicolas. You hear me?" She closed her eyes. "You have Nicolas."

They believe she might make it through the weekend.

I'll be with her when it comes.

That murderous thief.

Nick and I were together again.

Yesterday.

In his bed.

"Don't squirm so much."

In that parallel universe disguised as a loft on Du Port Street.

"It tickles."

"Be still."

Nick's mouth, softer than cashmere, moved across my stomach. His eyes, like two giant Ulysses butterflies, fluttered above my skin, spying on me. "Feels nice, no?"

I closed my eyes. "Yes."

Nick says sex breathes and lives at the edges of our erogenous zones, and he was demonstrating the power of his theory. When his lips skimmed my inner thigh, I let out a small groan.

"No," he whispered, "no sounds."

Silence is key.

One must hear every heartbeat, every breath.

"Sorry," I said.

Nick flashed a smile, tucking a loose strand of hair behind his ear. "You're not ready." He stretched out next to me, nestling his face into the fold of neck. "You're still too grounded in what your cock wants."

I laughed. "Oh yeah?"

He kissed my ear. "Yeah." His fingers folded themselves around mine. "I don't know, something feels tense in there." He gently pushed his finger into my stomach.

My body stiffened against my will. "Sorry," I said weakly.

"Would you stop apologizing? It's nasty for your health."

I smiled against his silky hair and held his fingers more strongly.

Nick pulled away a little, glancing over at me. "I'm serious, O'Reilly."

The smile faded from my lips. "Sor—" I stopped.

"Look at me." Nick's eyes burnt my face. His blue stare leafed through the most hidden pages of my heart. He squinted. "Why did you beat yourself up that day?"

I nibbled on my lip.

"Why?" he insisted, looking around the bed as if he could find the culprit, hiding somewhere near.

I shrugged. "Doesn't ma-matter."

"Don't say that." He sat up, stealing the warmth off my skin.

"Please, Nick. I wanna leave it alone. It feels so much better when I leave it alone."

Nick fell back on the pillow and turned his piercing eyes to me. "I've been thinking about you and all my fucking sauces have been splitting. O'Reilly, everything you don't say speaks to something gentle in me. Something I thought I'd choked."

I wrapped myself around his beautiful chest, remembering what it had felt like to wake up with my head on his lap, and the winter sky rolling pass my eyes. "Nathan wants me to go to Milan with him."

"Of course." Nick's fingers curled around a strand of my hair and he lifted it to the pale light filtering through the room. "O'Reilly," he murmured. "He'd be fuckin' crazy not to want you there. Every day. Every night." Against my arm, his heart thumped. "He'd be stupid not to want to wake up to your wicked green eyes. Those eyes that make him feel like he's paid his dues. Like he's finally finished with living off God's fucking redemption crumbs."

I held my breath.

Nick tensed. "Are you gonna go?"

I couldn't speak.

"Well? Are you?"

I chewed on my lip.

"O'Reilly. Hello? You're gonna marry Nathan and go to fuckin' Milan? You're gonna play boy toy, maybe let the jerk dress you up and take you out to see a show when he isn't too busy tappin' every loose ass in Italy?"

When Nick makes a point, it makes a hole in the paper.

My pulse flew into a rage. "No, Nick. I won't go. I won't marry him, because I love—"

"Don't, O'Reilly. Not now. Don't say it now." Nick's eyes darkened. "Not right now."

"But I—"

"Look, I need to take care of something. Something important. I'm gonna be out of town for a few days."

"What's wrong?"

"Just kiss me." His heart had begun pounding. "You gotta bear with me, O'Reilly. Can you bear with me?"

Bear with him?

If Nick would ask me to meet him on the other side of an erupting volcano, and I had just been decapitated, my body would still find a way to his.

"O'Reilly," he murmured into my hair. "Don't go to Milan. Please. I'll make it worth your while. But you gotta gimme some time. This is big."

❖

Like glass, Nathan's fragile idealism has shattered.

I spend my days sweeping up the broken pieces, yet I sense that I've neglected one, and its ragged edge will soon slice my skin.

"You were in there for thirty minutes."

Lately, I've been spending a lot of time in the washroom.

I sit on the toilet lid and watch the wall.

"What were you doing in there anyway?"

Nathan's moue of disdain snatched a chuckle out of me.

"What's so funny?"

My eyes strayed to the television.

"Derek?"

It was golf. Again.

"Babe, do you know where my Raffaello shirt is?"

I can't glimpse Nathan's love for me through the thickness of our faults.

"So, are we going to Oliver's on Christmas Eve or not?"

Oliver?

Is he a friend of ours, or a restaurant?

"Derek, I told my mother we would drive up to the cabin on the twenty-sixth. Should I cancel the holidays?"

The holidays can probably do without us.

"Der, if you don't talk to me in the next two minutes, I'm gonna put my fist through a wall."

If I could get a refund on my thoughts, I would gladly turn them in.

"I live with an apparition. You know that, don't you? I fuck a ghost."

"Hanging on the doorknob."

"What?"

"Your shirt."

Nathan's eyes swept my face. His features hardened. "The bedroom?"

"Yes."

He hesitated, watching me suspiciously, and slowly walked backward to our bedroom.

My attention strayed to the sky. Crimson clouds streaked the horizon.

Nick.

My beautiful wreck.

"Found it." Nathan's cold lips wet my cheek. "Can we look at the Hotel Saint-James pamphlet—"

"Nathan—"

"Der, I know you're feeling overwhelmed with your auntie."

"Nathan. I want you to look at me." I sat on the couch with my back to the world outside our window and my face turned upward to the man I have been kissing, holding, and sucking off for the last two years. "Please."

Nathan's eyebrows met. He smiled, but his arms had folded over his chest. "What do you mean?"

"Do you see me?"

"Derek."

"Nathan."

He sat by me and sighed. "Are you having a nervous breakdown?"

Where have all the shades of gray gone?

"I don't want to get married, Nate. I don't want to be—"

"Sadistic?"

"I'm sor-sorry—"

"No, Derek. You're a haunted house. That's what you are." His gaze drifted for a moment. "You know, sometimes when I've been chasing a deal down for too long, I get sick of the sale. The fresh ink on the contract reminds me of what I could have been doing with my goddamn days."

"Nathan, I need to be on my own."

His dark eyes set themselves on my mouth. "Oh God, I'm obsessed with you."

"I know."

He hid his hands in his face. "Fuck."

I reached out.

He flinched, then rose. "We're not breaking up yet. No one splits over a trip to Milan."

❖

Francine St-Jacques went slowly, as though creeping to a strange, open door.

"It's over." Johan's hand rested on my shoulder. "She's gone."

Mom's whimpering caused my jaw to harden.

"Leave me." I slapped Johan's hand off my shoulder. My fists clenched. "Go."

Their quiet footsteps unnerved me.

I waited, staring into the one face that has known me.

Me.

The authentic me.

The boy.

The man.

I watched her lips, praying for one final word out of them.

I stayed by her side, until I could smell the end on her.

When I stepped out of her room, I found everyone waiting.
Nathan took a shy step toward me. "Derek—"
I flinched. "Go home."
He shrank back and retreated to the corner of the lobby. I watched him hesitate by the door, as if he might actually listen to me, but he sat in one of the lobby chairs instead.
Why would he start considering any of my needs now?
"Derek—" Boone reached out for me. "I'm sorry."
"Why are you he-here? Huh?" My voice cracked. "Why are any of you here?"
"Stop it, Derek," cried Lene. "We all loved her too."
"Yeah?" I mocked, feeling the rage course through me. "Where the fuck were you all these years, huh? Huh, Lene? You and your perfect fuck-fucking family. You and-and your—"
"Derek, calm down." Johan's voice boomed through the empty lobby. "Let's get you home."
"Home? Ho-home?" I grabbed my head. "Don't you get it! She was my home! She was the-the only one who ca-cared—"
"Derek! Enough!" Mom had grabbed my arm and was trying to wrap her hypocrite arms around me, but I jerked myself away from her phony embrace and threw my finger up in her face. "You!"
Yellow breath.
Empty mornings of muted cartoons.
Silent threats of abandonment.
"You don't touch-touch me-me!"
Dad's palm whipped the air out of my throat. The strike caused me to tumble back, then, before Johan could restrain me, I had lunged at Dad, shoving him into the wall, shouting until my vision blurred. "Fuck you!" The anger burned my throat. "Go fuck you-yourself!" I beat his chest, slamming my fist down into him. "I ha-hate you, I fucking ha-hate you."
Dad's eyes stared blankly as I pummeled his chest.
Johan and Boone's hands tore at me, trying to pull me off him.
Then Nick's voice shot my fury dead. "O'Reilly."
He had come.
Nick had come for me.

My muscles loosened.

My fists opened.

Boone's arms circled my shoulders. "Easy now. Easy." He then turned to Nick with surprise in his eyes. "Take him, please. Get him outta here."

Nathan hurried to me and intercepted Nick, forcing himself between us. "I got it, thank you." He then turned to me. "Come on, baby, it's okay. Let's go downstairs and get you some water."

I shook all over. My teeth clattered. I could barely hold my own weight. "Nick," I managed to plead. "Nick."

Nathan's eyes flicked to Nick's face, then back to mine. "Derek—"

"Nick," I said more forcefully.

"You're Nick?" Nathan's question carried all of the answers.

Boone coughed.

Lene seemed to hold her breath.

Johan shifted, reaching out for Nick's arm. "Be still," he whispered to him. "Be still, Nicolai."

Nick stared Nathan down, and nodded quietly. "That's right." His gaze blazed with defiance.

Nathan stiffened, but held on to my limp hand. "Okay. Well, *whatever*. I'm Nathan, and I'm taking him home. So you mind?" He pulled me near.

I resisted. "Nick," I said again.

"Derek, let Nathan take you home. No more trouble from you, please. Nicolai, go find some coffee for John."

My legs felt stronger. "Nick, please."

Nick's eyes roamed over my face. He rubbed his chin, exhaling a long, hard breath.

"Nicolai." Johan's tone was authoritative. "No. Go find the coffee. Now."

Nick didn't move.

We stood, face-to-face, with Nathan fidgeting at our side. "Der, what's going on here?"

"I'm not going home with you, Nathan." My voice was quiet. I held Nick's cold blue stare.

"Derek, now is not the time to cause a scene, son."

But I didn't heed Johan's careful words.

I took another step in Nick's direction.

Finally, Nick set his fingers on my hand. "Come," he murmured. "Come with me, O'Reilly."

Nathan slapped his hand off mine. "Who the fuck do you think you are? Get your hands off him—"

"Nathan," warned Boone. "You don't wanna do that."

Nick flinched. His jaw tightened, and I witnessed the violence rising inside him.

I remembered the rumors that had been whispered about him, a long time ago, and reached out for his hand again. "Don't, Nick. Let's go, plea-ease."

"You're gonna walk away like this?" Nathan's face was twisted with indignation.

Not hurt, or loss.

Indignation.

As if I were a prize he had won, only to find out I was broken.

"You're gonna end us like this?"

Gently, Nick's hand drew me close to his chest, binding me to him.

At last, I was in his arms.

Johan sighed. "All right. Go, you two." He slowly shook his head at Nick. "I miss you. My Nicolai." His kind eyes twinkled with tears.

"*We* miss you. We need to see you, Nicolai. So much more."

Helga extended her long fingers, but never touched her stubborn son. "Come by sometime. Our door is open."

"Maybe I will," was Nick's only reply.

I let him escort me down the hall, and didn't turn back once.

Nathan never even chased me.

I suppose a closer knows when the deal has soured.

As Nick and I passed through the cancer ward's final door, Aunt Frannie's last words forced my drowsy inner eye to open.

"Keep staring, hon. And don't you dare blink, baby. Don't you dare."

I squeezed Nick's hand.

CHAPTER NINE

November is here, and with it comes the end of many things. Beginnings come too. No matter how slowly they seem to crawl, when I would like them to sprint, they are still promises of something new.

Let me knock you out of your dancing shoes.

I live with Lene Lund. In her one-bedroom apartment in the Mile-End district. And no, she hasn't ravished me yet. Of course, this living arrangement, as pleasant as it is, is only temporary. I'm looking for an apartment.

And... *a job.*

Three days after Aunt Fran's funeral, I handed my resignation to Mr. Goldman, who, only a few weeks before, had praised me for my "quiet leadership." He called me Eric through the whole private meeting; it was very anticlimactic.

Jake spotted me emptying my desk. "Where you going, man?"

"Quit."

His face turned a vibrant shade of red, and he rubbed his dark hair back, then jumped up and down as if his team had won the cup. Jake's arms stretched above his head in sign of victory. "Oh yes, my man! You fucking rock! Oh yes! Give it to the man! Up his ass!"

I chuckled.

It took a little convincing on my part to keep Jake from feeding his tie to the shredder and following me on my reckless whim. I'll miss him, I think.

Not sure.

What I do know is that whatever Jake does, he'll manage to screw it up fantastically, but will always be forgiven for it.

I remember walking home that afternoon, carrying a box of useless things, feeling strangely calm. I had no money saved up. No other job waiting for me on the next Monday. The Ducati's insurance was going to be up in less than two months, and I couldn't afford half of it. I would have to store my sexy red toy in Boone's dirt basement.

When Nathan left (first class, Milan), I had exactly three days to "get my shit out" of *his* condo. Those last brittle days were terrible. I slept on the couch, with my eyes open for a few nights, scanning the darkness for a shiny blade. Thankfully, Nathan was too busy with transferring accounts, shipping furniture out, and tying up loose ends to stab me seventeen times in the throat.

I wanted to drive him to the airport.

"I have someone to drive me to the fucking airport, Derek," he said.

More like *snarled.*

"I'm sorry," I lied, thinking about the bellboy, whose name is Joaquim.

They met in Toronto. Joaquim breeds dogs.

I hope he enjoys sushi and dry fucks.

"For what, Derek? You think you broke my heart?"

I would like to think that I did, at least a tiny fragment of it.

Nathan picked up his Delsey suitcase. "No, Derek," he reminded me before stepping into another life, one I have been written out of. "You didn't break my heart." His dark eyes gleamed, and this time, I caught a wolf in them.

Yes. *A wolf.*

These last two years, I have been Red, prancing about, like some adolescent idiot, waiting for Nathan to swallow me whole in the name of mainstream love.

"Derek, you didn't. Okay? All you did was waste my goddamn time." He shut the front door behind him.

I stared at that door for a long time, and then spent the next five minutes hurling shoes at it.

Lene showed up at my doorstep the very next day. "Our baby misses you."

❖

I moved in on a Tuesday.

It took less than ten minutes. I had exactly two boxes, and that's counting the one from the office.

I thought I owned more. Every thing in my life was borrowed.

Lene and I get along fabulously. I supposed we always did, in our own demented, asocial way. She works evenings; I lounge days.

I walk around.

Sit around.

Pine around.

Wait for Nick to call.

Which he hasn't.

❖

Lene and I were eating nectarine and almond couscous in her eclectic kitchen this afternoon.

That's all she eats, really. That and chocolate chip cookies.

"You could go into income taxes, you know, open your little office and do people's taxes."

"Dr. Lund, you've just depressed me." I dragged my fork across the orange mess.

"No? Not taxes? Okay—" She bit down on her lip and nodded, seeming to have a conversation with herself. She does that. The first night after I moved in, I stayed awake, staring up at the ceiling, listening to Lene debate the importance of democratic psychiatry.

With herself.

"How 'bout you set up a website, and—"

"Offer my queer Irish ass up?"

She smiled. "Do you accept credit cards?" She reached for my hand. "Oh, Der, you'll find something."

I sighed. "Lene, I'm twenty-eight years old. I'm too old for the jobs that starve the wallet and challenge the mind, but still too young for the jobs that numb the brain and pack the pockets. I'm overqualified, overeducated, and underexperienced. Not too mention *unmotivated.*"

"You said that whole long boring thing without stuttering."

I glanced up. "Guess I did."

Since the wolf has left my land, I have been treading new ground. I feel fearless at times.

"I gotta go to work," she said, getting to her feet. "What are you gonna do?"

"Panhandle."

She slapped my hand, and kissed my hair. "Call Nico."

"Lene, it's Thursday. It would be easier to get a sample of the pope's shit."

"Right."

And that goes for every day of the week. The last time I tasted Nick's mouth was nine days ago.

"O'Reilly," he always says, jumping into his big black boots. "I'll see you around."

Boone and Kenya were over for dinner last night.

I cooked.

Then I called for Thai.

As Boone and Lene rummaged through Lene's boxes of past Christmas decorations, hard set on decorating the balcony before the first snow, Kenya and I sat at the kitchen table, whispering softly over black coffees.

Aunt Fran used to say, "To some people, a breath is nothing but a breath, until the last one comes."

For the best of us, that last breath comes way too soon.

David Pinet died in 1999.

David was twenty-seven years old.

A dancer and painter.

Nick's longtime lover and dear friend.

AIDS-related, yes.

When Kenya murmured those four deadly letters, my whole body tightened with dread. Her inky eyes shimmered. That homicidal virus has wiped out many of her spiritual kin as well. One thing gay men and African women share is this bloody waiting game.

How long? How many more?

My heart leaped.

Nick.

The breath caught in my throat.

"No, Derek. Nick is HIV free."

I closed my eyes. "How do you know?"

She smiled, glancing over at Lene and Boone. They were cursing under their breaths, trying to untangle a string of Christmas lights.

"In strict confidence," she said quietly, "I've been drawing Nicolai's blood every six months for the last five years. At his home. You know how Nick hates hospitals and clinics." She chuckled. "In exchange for my trouble, Nicolai whips me up a meal fit for Mami Wata, the Goddess of Beauty."

My shoulders sank with relief.

He had been spared.

"It was difficult for Nicolai. To see him go like that. To watch David wither away."

I remembered David's beautiful dark eyes, and for a moment. I was ashamed. Ashamed of my good health.

My complete lack of gratefulness for it.

"Nicolai stayed at his side until the very end. In David's home. In Victoria."

The last thing David had seen before leaving this plane, too young, too fast, was Nick Lund's savage eyes gazing back into his. That thought brought a small measure of comfort to me.

What were the last whispered words between them?

When David closed his eyes to the world, did Nick hold his hand through it?

And later, when everything had been put away, cleaned, and stored—all of Dave's costumes, pictures, music, books, those things that make us who we are—had Nick turned his back to that dreadful empty bed? Had he stared out the window, at the blue Pacific Ocean, and died a little?

"When Nicolai came back to us, he was possessed."

Had he wondered how to make every thing fit again?

Had he hurt for the ones who want so much, but never get?

The boys who give, but seldom take?

Had he looked east, and wondered about home?

"The spirits lived within him. I could see them breathing inside Nick's eyes."

Had he wondered about a redheaded boy?

"But he battled them Derek. One by one."

Had he heard that boy calling him home?

❖

Last night, I woke up to the sound of my own breathing.
I watched the sky through the window.
And sweetly, the purple night called to me.

When the cab pulled up by Split's back door, I slipped my hat off and turned my face up to Nick's window.
Through the thin curtains, I caught sight of Nick's dark silhouette moving along the loft's bare walls.
I slipped the driver a twenty and stepped out.
I pressed my hat against my chest, tapping my heel to the beat of my heart.
Finally, I climbed up the wrought-iron stairs.
I knocked twice.
The sound of Escoffier's threatening bark ripped the silence to shreds, and I tensed yet a little more, waiting for my lover to let me in.
Light flooded my eyes.
Nick's face appeared in the doorway. "O'Reilly." He leaned his head against the door frame and smiled. "Come."
I peeled my feet off the ground and took a step inside.
Escoffier welcomed me with a thorough examination, and after he had stuffed his snout in every possible crease of my jeans, he padded back to his cushion to keep watch.
The air was dense with humidity, and the scent of Ivory soap filled the loft.
Nick's hair was wet and slicked back. The white towel around his waist was his only garment. "I just got home." His hand swept the air, inviting me to enter. "Sit down."
My eyes would not leave his naked chest. "Thank you."
Nick laughed. "You're welcome."
I went to the living area. I stripped my jacket off and sat in the only real chair. "Hope you-ou don't mind that I—"
"No. I don't." Nick slowly unfastened the towel around his waist and let it drop to his feet.
My cock stretched to the point of burn.

Nick walked to the other end of the loft, and my eyes followed his bare skin until my breath scorched my chest.

I sat and stared at his mattress.

My body spoke hard sentences to my pounding heart, and I rose, nervously, with my hands clinging to my shirt. I let my fingers have their way, and watched them unfasten my shirt's buttons, one by one.

My eyes were fixed to the washroom's door as my hands stripped every useless layer of clothing that held my limbs prisoner. When my pants carried my underwear to the floor, I glanced down at my naked body and caught sight of my heart thumping under my bare skin.

I need you. I need you. I need you.

The air moved along my skin, and I turned my head to the window, studying the naked man in its reflection.

"Make your eyes see. You are the sorcerer. When are you gonna start working some of that magic of yours?"

Hesitantly, my fingers grazed my smooth chest.

I stood, revealed and engorged with need, watching the redheaded man in the window.

Sexuality wet my lips and cock.

I let my fingers roam. They were warm soldiers, tearing through my inhibitions.

"O'Reilly."

Nick stood a few feet away from me.

His eyes were two beams of blue light slicing through the night. "Show me," he murmured, moving closer to me. "Show me everything."

His fingers joined mine in search of the end of me.

I lifted my gaze to meet his and leaned my spinning head against his broad chest. "This is all there is, Nick. You can have it all."

His mouth hesitated over my shoulder. "I wanna kiss you—"

"Kiss me."

"But if I kiss you, then I'm not tasting this." His fingers glided down my ass and reached into me. "And if I'm tasting this, then I'm not fucking you. I want everything you have to give me, but I don't know how to take it."

Nick's body tensed, and his fingers left my skin.

"Nick—"

"I'm damaged, O'Reilly."

Damaged.

Tampered by karma.

"Lie with me, Nick. Turn the light off and lie with me."

His eyes glazed with tears.

Tears.

In Nicolai Lund's eyes.

How can sorrow and beauty coexist in such a way?

My throat closed up.

"You're one of those, O'Reilly, the ones that come out of things stronger."

And what kind is Nick?

"Come," I whispered. "Come Nick."

Nick wrapped himself around me, hiding his face between my neck and shoulder. "I'm scared, O'Reilly."

"Everybody's scared, Nick. Everybody."

I pulled him to the mattress, and we fell onto it.

I turned my head to the light, and flicked it off.

Darkness shrouded us.

Our breaths echoed each other.

Nick warmed my skin with his.

I closed my eyes to the world and spoke quietly. "Your father used to wonder what you would do when you came to the edge." My fingers combed his silky hair. "Did you find it Nick? Did you find the edge?"

I felt his wounds under my palms. These invisible scars, hardened by time.

"No, O'Reilly. It was the edge that found me."

And when the last breath had streamed out of David's lips, had Nick stepped off it?

"Nick—"

"Ease my pain."

"Nick—"

"I cheated and lied."

"David's death isn't your fau-fault—"

Nick's body stiffened against mine. "I killed him." He pushed his face into my shoulder, and I held him.

"Oh God," he moaned, clutching my hand. "Oh God."

David was a melody.

I know that now.

Nick never could learn that tune.

"Listen to me, Nick." Nick's pain burned my flesh. "Every day is a new promise. We die with the sun, and receive a clean slate when—"

"I don't want a fucking clean slate." Nick's tears choked his voice. "I wanna feel it." He slapped his chest. "In here." His body quivered next to mine. "I wanna feel it, O'Reilly. Every goddamn minute I stole from him. Every fucking empty night I gave him. Every letter I didn't bother opening. Davie spent his good years sitting in airports, waiting for me to give him a smile, but I was so caught up—"

"Shh. Enough, Nick. Enough—"

"His mistakes were mine, but I got lucky O'Reilly. Oh fuck." Nick shook violently, and I held him tighter. "I watched David die and I packed my life into a duffel bag…" His voice died, and at last, tears snuffed the poisonous words out of him.

I rocked Nick all through the night, and my lover came undone for me.

I woke up to the sound of the radio and squinted at the clock.

It was ten past noon.

Against the vivid blue sky, the sun was a faded primrose.

I sat up and glanced around.

Escoffier cocked his head, watching me scan the empty apartment.

I raised a brow. "Where's our man?"

The dog barked, then sighed.

I stripped the sheets off my legs and picked up my jeans off the floor.

Escoffier sprung for the door before I heard the key turning in the lock.

Nick pushed the door open with his thigh and set down what appeared to be three years' worth of groceries. "Good. You're up."

I smiled. "Why didn't you wake—"

"'Cause you reminded me of a Botticelli painting." He bent to my head and kissed it. "Hungry?"

Every one of my senses was. "A little."

Nick lugged the bags to the kitchen area and rolled up his sleeves. "Okay then."

For the next half hour, I sat in my undies, watching him do what he does best. To Nick, cooking is part dance, part battle, and part sleight of hand.

Finally, he set a plate of debauchery under my watering mouth. My fork hesitated over the fluffy orange zest waffles, but I picked up a spoon and dove into the ginger ice cream instead. As the homemade ice cream melted in my mouth, I glanced up. "You're not eating?" I asked, wiping my cold lips with the back of my hand.

Nick drank the last of his black coffee. "I don't do sweets."

"But why did you—"

"'Cause I remembered how much you like sugar." He winked. "Especially my mom's tapioca pudding."

Heat filled my cheeks, and I stuffed a piece of waffle into my mouth.

"Oh," teased Nick, "there's the O'Reilly I remember." He leaned in, and with a sensuality that bent my knees, ran the tip of his tongue along my lips, gathering the last of the ice cream off them. "You taste like innocence," he whispered, his eyes darkening again.

I remembered the night's confessions and folded my fingers over his. "Are you okay—"

"I feel a little raw."

"Can I say so-something—"

"Not yet."

My face hardened.

"O'Reilly, things are changing for me in a way I can't explain to you right now." Nick sighed, then softly kissed my fingertips. He glanced around. "I need to get some furniture soon." For a moment, his eyes seemed vacant, but slowly, his blue gaze met my stare. "And—" But he stopped.

"Tell me, Nick. You can talk to me."

"I know I can." He closed his eyes and leaned his forehead on mine. "That's why I need you in my life."

My mouth popped open.

He laughed, but his smile was tense. "I've never said that to anyone." He shook his head. "Holy fuck." He rubbed his face. "Shit."

I chewed on my lip.

"Do you remember when you had that asthma attack in your bathroom?" Nick asked.

"Yes."

"'Cause I'd tried to put makeup on your face."

"Yes, Nick. I remember."

Everything.

"Well." He frowned, staring into space again. "Don't freak out, but that night, I wanted to kiss you, or something." He inhaled deeply. "But you were just a kid, and I—"

"I would have let you."

"Yeah?"

A boyish giggle exploded out of my mouth, and I hid my face in my hands for a moment.

"What is it, O'Reilly?"

"If you knew half of the things I wanted you to do to me, you wouldn't be-be tasting innocence on my lips."

The sound of Nick's deep, resonant laugh spun my head with lust. I pushed my plate up and tugged on his T-shirt. "Do you have to be downstairs?"

"Not for another hour." He cracked a smile and jerked his head in the bed's direction. "Come?"

I laughed. "Oh yes."

CHAPTER TEN

There was a *Golden Girls* marathon this afternoon.
On my way to the couch, I passed the entrance mirror.
I paused and debated on a shower, but went back to the kitchen to pour myself another glass of Mountain Dew instead. I dropped some vanilla essence in it and rummaged through the fridge in search of something disgustingly unhealthy to sink my teeth into. I decided on cheese dip. I grabbed a spoon, a heavy-duty bag of chips, and my drink, then headed back to the couch.

It was Monday afternoon, and as I dug my way through the dip, trying to keep the crumbing to a minimum, I knew I had officially stepped through the gates of Loserville.

I went through that bag of chips like a teenage boy goes through a box of tissues.

I glanced down at myself.

I was something you'd find at a thrift shop.

I leaned back and stared up at the ceiling.

My phone jingled.

I answered Nick with a breath.

"O'Reilly, hey."

My heart banged up against my chest. "Nick."

"Listen. I need you to come over." I heard him exhale into the phone. "Come through Split's back door."

He hung up without bothering with good-bye.

I ran to the kitchen to get a garbage bag, and proceeded to dump the chips, dip, and my "clinically depressed" uniform into it.

I ran back to the main closet and pulled the vacuum out, running it up and down the couch, like some kind of coked-up Martha Stewart. I ran back to the closet and tossed the loaded vacuum into it.

I jumped into the shower, washed, rinsed, and scrubbed all at once, then threw a gray T-shirt on and slipped into my good black jeans.

I bolted out into the street, with my winter coat hanging off my sleeve, and tossed myself at the first available cab.

"Wow. That was quick." Nick shut the back door behind us.

Immediately, I was entranced by the wonderful, rich scent of fresh salmon and dill. "Smells great, what—"

"Come." His fingers wrapped themselves around mine, and he tugged on me. "In here."

I followed him through the small kitchen.

It was immaculate. Cleaner than I could have imagined, and atop one of the industrial gas ovens, a huge pot filled to the rim with brown liquid, simmered gently. "What's that?"

"Brown stock." Nick pulled me away from the stove. "Come on, O'Reilly, I'll let you strain the fucking thing if you like it so much, but come now. Come on. *Come.*"

There was something almost mystic in Nick's smile.

We passed through the swinging doors into the dining room.

The larger back table was set. Candles flickered here and there, and in the middle, on a beautiful silver platter, a large pink salmon seemed to be sleeping in a bed of sea salt and fresh dill.

But that's not what had my attention.

"Say hello, Spencer." Nick had scooped up a child out of a colorful playpen and was holding his pudgy little hand, waving it up and down for me.

My jaw hung loose. I dropped my bag. "Nick?"

A shadow moved through Nick's eyes, but his smile did not fade. "O'Reilly. This is Spencer." Then Nick's voice weakened, as if it could not carry the weight of what he had to say. "My son."

The child squirmed inside his arms, and Nick combed the white-blond hair out of his eyes. "Where's your nukie?" Nick looked around, toting this little blond elf on his hip, fumbling through the toys and blocks in the playpen. "Where'd you put it, Spence?"

I stood, stiff as a mannequin, with my eyes pulsing inside my head.

Nick pulled a pacifier out of a toy truck and dangled it. "You want this?"

The boy smiled, jerking the pacifier out of Nick's fingers. He stuffed into his pink mouth.

"Okay, buddy." Nick set the child down into the play pen. "Give Daddy a minute, I gotta make sure O'Reilly's still breathing."

Daddy.

Daddy?

Nick carefully made his way to where I swayed. "I didn't know how to say it. I tried, but I just couldn't find the right time...I'm sorry. I just didn't know how to tell you. So I figured—"

"You figured you'd just invi-i-te me here and-and —"

"O'Reilly, listen, I—"

"You're a fa-father?" My eyes darted down to the child. Nick's child.

His son.

I shook my head, backing up to the door. "How could you-ou not tell me?"

"You think this is easy? You think—"

"But-ut—"

"O'Reilly. No one knows." He let out a long sigh. "I didn't know myself. Not until six months ago." He peered into my face, searching for something. "She never told me. One May morning, she shows up at Split, and makes me look at this kid's eyes, telling me he's my son. My boy."

I closed my eyes, sick with emotion.

"The paternity test came out positive. I'm Spencer's dad." Nick sighed deeply. "She was a fling. You know? I met her during a catering gig, and we told our sob stories and fucked around for a few days. I never even knew her last name." He looked over at the baby. At Spencer. "I get to see him every few weeks. Until we figure something out, her and me." He took a step closer, and I felt his body trembling. "O'Reilly, I don't know what I'm doing half of the goddamn time."

Nick's eyes were full of truth.

At our feet, the baby babbled.

Nick leaned into me. "He's a good kid, O'Reilly. Not like his old man."

I shot the baby a glance. "He looks like your mother."

That's all I could say.

Nick watched his son try to push a square block into a round one, and shook his head. "I've got some *major* karma issues." He paused, letting the silence give us repose, then added, "O'Reilly, I'm gonna tell 'em all. Don't worry. Just need to figure something out with my schedule, and—"

"Your life."

"Right." He rubbed his strong chin and nodded. "Right."

Nicolai Lund is a father.

A father.

Spencer, whose mother is a ballet dancer living in Trois-Rivières, is sixteen months old.

He was born in July of last year.

July is a good month to have a birthday.

Nick says, "Lately, I've been asking myself some important questions, and, O'Reilly, I'm getting high off their answers."

I think I know what he means.

It's done. Aunt Fran's apartment is empty.

There was a lot more in there than I had anticipated, and if it hadn't been for Boone and Lene's help, it would have taken much longer. Aunt Fran had so many clothes, shoes, and magazines that by midday, I had filled half of Nick's Econoline with items I know she would have agreed to donate.

Mom only wanted the pictures.

When we were finished, Boone shut the van doors and sighed. "Are you all right?"

I nodded.

I miss her so much.

Her voice.

Her ways.

"You wanna come by the house? Kenya would like that."

Lene kissed my ear. "Go, Der, I've got a date anyways."

I smiled. "Yeah?"

"Yeah." She giggled, climbing into her Echo. "And no, he isn't a patient."

The radiant smile on her face killed Boone's and my inclination to mock.

"So," said Boone, watching his baby sister drive away. "Coming?"

I watched the sky.

The November wind flew into my jacket and blew my mind. "I think I'm going to go see your brother."

"Nico? Good luck, man, it's Saturday."

"I know."

Boone smiled. "All right then."

I shook Boone's hand. I held his great big paw inside my fingers for as long as he would let me, remembering how his blue eyes had rolled back into his head that afternoon, in our schoolyard.

"Here goes nothing."

"I love you, Boone." The words had leaked out of my mouth, and embarrassed, I glanced up to Boone's face. My cheeks scorched. "I meant—"

"Derek. Shut up." Boone grinned. "I love you too, man. You're like a brother to me." And quickly, he bent his scrubby face to mine and kissed my mouth.

It was only a dry peck. Nonetheless, the feel of his lips sent a pleasant chill rippling down my back.

Boone slapped my shoulder and laughed. "Always wondered what that would feel like."

I smiled. "And?"

"I prefer my Kenya." He pulled the passenger door open. "Come on, get in, I'll give you a ride. Besides, Nico owes me one fucking decent meal."

Split was jam packed.

I had never seen it at its peak. Every table was full, and at the bar, people, young and handsome, piled up against the counter.

I recognize the boy behind it. Andy, his name is. Nick says he's the only honest bartender he's come across, and that pretty Andy has won Flair competitions.

I watched the little tramp throw bottles around. Mr. Cocktail himself.

Boone pulled his cap off and ran his fingers through his disheveled hair. "Maybe I should have changed."

I looked him up and down. Probably.

"Yes?" The sultry hostess had a thick Eastern European accent. "I can help you, yes?"

Boone's eyes moved over her, but his stare was more boyish than disrespectful. "I'm the cook's brother, and he's his—" He winked. "Never mind. Can you get him, please?"

She squinted. "Cook?"

"Chef Lund. Tell him it's his lucky day. The police and tax man are here."

She didn't smile. Just made a little moue and turned on her spiked heels.

Boone whistled. "Nico sure runs a tight fucking ship." He nodded to the bar. "Let's get a drink."

I let Boone nudge his elbow through the sardined stools, and with his build, we had a nice, comfortable space in no time.

In the background, a remix of Bob Marley's "One Love" played.

Suddenly, I had an urge to ask for a lime daiquiri.

"Oui," snipped Andy.

Was Mr. Cocktail wearing a tank top, or red body paint?

Andy's mouth should be insured. It looks like a porthole to queer paradise.

Boone frowned. "Are you the barman here?" He seemed to be sizing the boy up. "How old are you, kid?"

I cocked my head, staring into Andy's face. "Yeah, how old *are* you?"

Andy pursed his pulpy lips. "What's it to you?"

Boone reached down into his pocket and pulled out his badge. "Seeing that we're law enforcement, I think you better answer my simple question."

I nearly came from sheer satisfaction.

I'm twenty-eight years old, but in gay years, that adds up to sixty-two.

Yes, I'm jealous. Bitterness is only one of the well-documented side effects.

Andy's eyes sharpened. He then glanced down at Boone's badge and shrugged. "I'm twenty-one. So what's your order? I've got a line of people here."

We'd each had three rum and Cokes.

My stomach gnawed, and I kept yawning, staring at the kitchen door. Every other minute, it swung open, and my heart leaped, but it was always some waiter carrying a tray of steaming plates. I tried to catch a glimpse of the kitchen, but never could.

"What the hell is taking him so long?" Boone was reading the menu again.

I had already memorized it.

Hot starters: Mussels with Aquavit and tarragon. Mushroom sandwich with rye bread, and maple syrup. Swedish meatballs.
Soups: Porcini consommé. Svalbard beet soup. Scandinavian pea soup.
Salads: Fresh asparagus and cucumber salad. Beet and orange salad. Danish potato salad.
Main dishes: Vodka-marinated sirloin served with potato gratin with parsnip and rutabaga. Gravlaks and mustard sauce. Creamy rice with parsnip puree and root vegetables. Orange chicken served with pasta, green vegetables and herbs.
Desserts : Veiled farm girls. Apple ice cream with rosemary and honey. Cream cake with berries.

Every time I glanced over at a table and caught sight of one of Nick's fabulous dishes (his presentation is flawless), my mouth salivated. "Should I just—"

"Yes. For fuck's sakes." Boone slapped the menu down. "Go and get his ass out here before I lose my cool and shoot somebody in the leg."

I laughed. "Be right back."

I slipped out of my seat and wiped my hands down my thighs. As I came to the kitchen's door, a waiter intercepted me. "Can't go in there."

"I'm a friend."

"Sorry, man, can't go in there."

I nodded. "Bathroom?"

He pointed to the back, and then hurriedly headed for the table of six.

I took a few steps back, springing through the kitchen door as he was jotting down orders.

As I did, another waiter, who looked like Al Pacino in his younger days, barked, "I need two and five for mains, and three is on desserts, no nuts on the veiled." He pushed the door open with his ass and screamed over the gigantic tray loaded with soups and salads. "Chef, I need four tossed back on the grill, the lady says too bloody—"

"What?" Nick's voice rose over the stove tops. "What the fuck! Goddamn it, Jimmy, can you check your fucking doneness—" Nick flipped a piece of salmon onto a plate, swung around to squeeze some oil into a scorching pan, then, with a steady hand, ladled some sauce over a sirloin steak. "Seven is up !" He tore a pink sheet off the pass and yelled, "Seven is up! Let's go! Where's Gab? Fuckin' better not be tokin' up in the back!"

The young man, whom I suspected was the said Gab, popped his head over the counter at my left. "No, Chef, I'm here, just—"

"Why aren't you at the pass?" Nick threw some green vegetables into the oiled pan and flipped a line of chicken breast on the grill. I could feel the scalding heat from where I stood.

What did it feel like over there?

All their faces gleamed with sweat, and everywhere I looked, gigantic bottles of Voss water stood empty—testaments to their parched mouths.

"Get your ass at the pass." Nick wiped his forehead with the back of his crisp white sleeve, squinting at the line of pink papers, and rubbed his chin. "We're doing three and two. I want it up in five."

A waiter flung the door open at my right, and I shrank back, hugging the wall.

I was in a war zone.

I glanced over at the blackboard above my head. On it were the names of the dishes, and next to every one of the day's dishes was a symbol.

I smiled.

That's how Nick gets through it.

One word at a time.

"Chef, where's my four!"

"Keep your cock in your pants." Nick was garnishing a dish with some pink foam. "Fuckin' comin'." He tore another pink slip off the pass. "Eleven is up. Go before my fuckin' foam collapses!"

"Who the hell is this?" The waiter's sweaty brow shone with sweat. He frowned at me. "Hello?"

"I'm—"

"O'Reilly. Goddamn it. No." Nick's voice, though contained, simmered with firm disapproval. "Not now. *Later.*"

"Boone is here."

Nick pushed a plate up on the pass. "Later!"

I chewed on my lip, looking around.

One of the line cooks gave me a cocky smile.

The waiter pushed the door open. "You heard the man. *Out.*"

I hesitated for a moment, and decided I was through with hesitation. Through with it for this life, and some of the next. "Nick," I said, quite steadily, to my surprise. "Your brother and I are in the dining room. We expect to be fed."

Nick's cold blue eyes darted up.

"And we'd like the chef to make an appearance within the next hour," I added boldly.

I winced a little, waiting for him to hurl a plate at me.

A disarming smile turned up on his lips. "Tony." Nick's gaze lingered on my mouth. "Take care of my brother and him."

Tony looked me up and down. "All right. Come on."

I found Boone at the bar, chatting it up with Andy.

Andy seemed to be hanging on his every word.

That's Boone for you. He must be very good at what he does.

"I got us a table."

Boone grinned. "Of course you did." He got to his feet and

wrapped his bulky arm around my shoulder, nearly squeezing the breath out of me. "My man Red. Good job. Where's Nico?"

"Trust me, Boone, your brother has his hands full."

"What's it like in there?"

"Ever seen *Apocalypse Now*?"

He chuckled. "Fuckin' Nico. Always has to live it up a notch."

"It's his nature." I thought of Nick's passion. His drive. "The man is incapable of mediocrity."

Boone bounced his eyebrows. "Is that why he's been doin' you?"

I gave him my best disapproving stare.

"What? You don't think I know you guys are jumping in each other's pants every other night?"

"You mean, every other week," I said, quite sourly.

"That's 'cause you let him get away with it."

I frowned.

"Derek, man," Boone leaned back into his chair. "how do you expect him to know how you feel if you never tell him? I mean, shit, how long have you been pining away for my brother? Ever think about lettin' him in on your little secret?"

"What secret?"

Boone's smile vanished. "That you're totally, madly, fucking crazy in love with him. Always have been. Always will be."

My heart jumped a little.

I would, if only Nick let me.

Nick never came out that night.

Boone and I did enjoy one of the best meals of our lives, and many more rum and Cokes, but we left just at the edge of midnight, exhausted and light-headed, without having been graced by Chef Lund's commanding presence.

This morning, I sank deeper into Lene's sofa-bed and rolled myself into the blanket.

Gently, the scent of cologne tickled my senses, and I cracked an eye open, watching the sun-drenched living room through a half-shut lid.

"Good morning." A man, shirtless and stunning, fumbled through the clutter on the coffee table. "Didn't mean to wake you."

I cleared my throat.

The stranger pulled a sweater over his olive-toned skin. "You're Derek."

I nodded.

The man's full lip stretched into a smile. "I'm Giovanni." He extended his hand.

I sat up, being careful not to let my morning wood tear through the blanket. "Nice to-to meet you."

He shook my hand, and I caught another gust of his subtle fragrance.

"So you're Cassandra's father." He laughed.

Lene still has that famous doll. Our plastic offspring sits on her commode, and with every passing day, I grow more and more fond of it. She even looks a little like me.

Living with a shrink has done nothing for my lucidity.

Giovanni ran his fingers through his curly brown hair. "Coffee?" He headed for the kitchen.

I wrapped the blanket around my shoulders and locked myself in the washroom.

When I stepped out, I found Lene and Giovanni nestled comfortably on the couch.

I had found one of Lene's T-shirts hanging on the towel rack and had hastily slipped it on.

It was two sizes too small.

"You've met Gio." Lene handed me a steaming cup. "Sorry we woke you." She smiled. "You look cute."

I glanced down at myself.

She laughed. "Sit down, let's talk."

Her man nodded. "I've heard so much about you."

I sat.

"I didn't think you would come home last night." Lene took a sip of her coffee, and winked. "How's Nico?"

Lene is an aunt.

An aunt.

And she doesn't even know it.

"He's busy," I returned, staring at my bare feet.

Giovanni set his cup on the table. "It's a tough business he's in."

"Gio knows," said Lene. "He used to be a dry cleaner."

I frowned.

Gio laughed. "I cleaned uniforms."

Gio's sexy smile could possibly sell Crest toothpaste to Colgate's chief financial officer.

"You can tell a lot about a job by the state the uniform's in at the end of a week. Chefs' uniforms are the worst of the lot. I've cleaned oil and blood out of them. And man, the burn marks, those never come out."

I smiled, but my heart had begun pounding.

Unfinished thoughts swarmed my head.

"Derek?" Lene's indigo blue eyes watched me. "Is everything all right?"

"Yes." I rose. "I'm going to get dressed."

"You don't want breakfast?"

I kissed her head. "Thank you."

She reached out and squeezed my hand. "Okay."

I hurried to the small room that serves as Lene's office and opened my closet, which in fact is my unpacked suitcase, and got dressed in more appropriate attire.

I stepped back into the living room. "Lene, I'm going to take that apartment on Sainte-Émilie."

Her smile turned upside down. "You don't have to move out."

Gio coughed. "I'm gonna go make some eggs." He eased himself out of the couch and Lene's embrace. "I'll put on another pot of coffee."

We both watched him disappear into the kitchen, and then Lene leaned in. "You can stay as long as you like."

"No, Lene. I need to grow up." I slipped my coat on. "And really fast too."

Her eyebrows met. "What do you mean?"

If Nick is a father, then what am I?

What's my place?

My contribution?

Do I have one?

I zipped up my coat. "I'm going to ask something of your brother."

Lene nodded. "All right, but can I give you some advice?"

I wrapped my scarf around my neck and smiled. "Please do, Dr. Lund."

"For once in your life, Derek, be fearless."

My skin warmed.

She held my inquisitive stare. "There's only one thing no one has ever asked of Nicolai."

My chest tightened. "And what is that?"

Lene threw her head back and laughed.

Then, her expression became somber. *"Everything,"* she said in a breath.

❖

"We're closed." Andy's tight little body guarded Split's entrance. I pushed on the door. "Good morning."

He rolled his eyes.

I stepped into the warm dining room and blew into my frozen hands.

Andy shut the door behind us. "Don't get snow on the floor." He turned the lock. "I just washed it."

I wiped my boots on the carpet. "Is he here?"

Andy had fled to the bar, and stood behind it, wiping glasses.

He poured orange juice into one of them. "Thirsty?"

I glanced down at my boots.

They dripped with melted brown snow.

Andy sighed impatiently. "Forget the floor."

I stared at the kitchen door. Nothing stirred behind it.

"He's in his office. Do you want this orange juice or not?"

I frowned.

"Eric, right?" Andy leaned on the bar top, studying me.

"Derek."

"Right." His lips formed a subtle smile. "Sit down." He pointed to a bar stool.

I hesitated and then walked to the bar.

This disguised duel was necessary.

Nathan always said, *"You can't beat the competition if you don't get close enough to touch it."*

Andy's eyes roamed over my face.

I reached for the glass and paused. "Will there be any suffering?"

His face opened with surprise, and he cocked his head. "What?"

My fingertip tapped the rim of the glass. "When the poison sets in."

His eyes widened, and a genuine smile lit up his features. "You're all right."

I took a generous gulp of the orange juice.

Andy watched me. "Come on, I'll show you to the office."

I set the glass down and smiled. "Thanks."

Andy sighed. "But I warn you, he's in one of his moods."

He paused by the closed office door. "This is as far as I go." He smiled. "Honestly."

I watched the door, listening.

Something something fuck shit goddamn it.

Andy cocked an eyebrow and walked away.

I knocked on the door. "Nick?"

I heard the lock slide, but the door remained closed. I pushed on it. "Hi."

Nick's azure eyes looked over a mountain of paper. "Do you see this?" He swept his hand across the desk, blowing sheets of paper through the cluttered office. "Look at this fucking mess." He jumped out of his chair. "Gimme that box."

"What box?" I glanced around.

"There." Nick let out an explosive sigh. "Give."

My mouth dried up, and I wondered, was I panicked or madly turned on? "Here," I whispered, handing him the box, my eyes fixed to his heated face.

Nick's long fingers slipped it out of my hand. "Thank you."

My breath left me, and I leaned up against the closed door, watching Nick toss half of his office into the large cardboard box. Every paper his fingers landed on was severely punished.

"Nick?"

"I'm supposed to be making at least three percent net profit a month." His voice was tense with restrained fury. "I'm making one percent." He threw his pen holder against the wall. "ONE!" He picked up the cracked pen holder and stomped his heel into it. "I'm fucking done with this restaurant," he screamed, slamming his palms against the file cabinet. "Fuck this shit!" His electric blue eyes scanned the room for a moment, and I braced myself. Then he pulled a pack of matches out of his front pocket. "I'm torching this place." He let out an unnerving chuckle and locked his eyes to mine. "Turn the gas on and pop all the oven doors open."

I smiled.

Nick slowly shook his head, and tossed the pack of matches on the desk. "I think I'm cracking." I witnessed the mighty fear clouding his gaze. "I have a son." For a while, he only rubbed his chin, staring blankly. "A *son,* O'Reilly."

"It's a lot to take in." I carefully moved closer to him. "But—"

"She wants me to be part of his life."

"Of course."

Nick plopped down on his desk. "O'Reilly, I've been running from the worst of myself all my life, and now it looks like the best of me just caught up."

"You mean Spencer."

He nodded. "And you."

My body tensed.

Nick reached out for my hand. "You're angry with me."

I frowned.

Yes. I was, and I hadn't felt it until Nick's words stirred the hidden feelings inside me.

Nick pulled on my hand, but I resisted. "No, Nick."

"Hey." His voice was soft. "You think I'm playing games with you?"

My jaw clenched.

"Is that what you think, O'Reilly?" Nick's eyes searched my face. "Well, you're wrong."

My gaze drifted from his, to the wall.

Nick's fingers skimmed my hand. "Man, you sure don't say much." He smiled, trying to make eye contact with me, but I dodged his blue stare.

Nick rose and neared my wired body. "You need more from me."

I need you. I love you.

I turned my face up to his, fighting the words I am still not allowed to say.

He burned my mouth with his feverish kiss. "Okay, O'Reilly. I hear you loud and clear."

❖

Last Monday, Mona, Spencer's mother, asked Nick to make up for lost time.

Tortured by curiosity, I had every intention of accompanying Nick to Trois-Rivières, but at the last minute changed my mind. Mona knows of my existence and seems to be quite accommodating, yet the idea of facing the person who could give Nick the one thing I cannot was beyond my abilities for the present time.

Upon his return, Nick took five consecutive days off to spend with his son and me. He hadn't taken time away from the kitchen in over seven years.

I spent those five days in the company of a whimsical child. A tiny blue-eyed creature who has figured out how to stir me up and pour me back into the world, more potent and tasty than I have ever been.

In Spencer's eyes I am no longer the mere son, I am so much more.

To myself as well.

The first night we spent together, all three of us hidden safely inside Nick's newly furnished loft, was the most challenging sequence of minutes I have ever lived through.

My eyes have opened to a world where trivial moments do not exist.

I have never been around toddlers. I have never paid attention to them. I know nothing of their species.

After ten hours in Spencer's company, I had run out of clean clothes and used my inhaler twice.

My nerves were so raw, I could almost hear the muted television across the street.

Thankfully, Nick's years of watching over Lene have taught him the basics of child care.

During Spencer's short stay, Nick and I ran the house like a two-soldier battalion.

"Where are the wipes?"

"In his bag."

"I looked, they're not there. Forget it. Get me a wet towel. Oh shit. Never mind."

"What?"

"Run a bath."

"Again?"

"Oh my God, what is that?"

"I don't know."

"It looks like—"

"It's the spaghetti he had. Run the bath, not too warm.

"I know. I know."

"And get the dry clothes out."

"I did already. Watch it, he's slipping."

"You've got something crusty on your shirt."

"Don't let him put that in his mouth. Give him to me."

"Here, wrap him up in this."

"Hand me his Mr. Bubble."

"Pour me a double, will you?"

"Double what?"

"It doesn't matter."

We got through it, one order at a time.

Later that night, after Spencer had finally fallen asleep in his new crib, I crept across the loft and found Nick standing by the window, staring at the charcoal sky.

I stood by him, watching the street lamp's yellow light lace the snow banks with diamond dust. "How do you feel?"

Nick looked over at me and cracked a tired smile. "I can't wait to go back to work so I can rest."

I smiled. "You did good today, Nick."

"You mean *we* did good."

I kissed his shoulder. "Let's go to bed."

"I think I'll just sleep here." He leaned his head on the glass. "Like this."

I tugged on his sleeve. "Come."

That word sparked passion in Nick's eyes, and he followed me to the bed, but dragged his feet all the way. He fell back on the covers, listless.

I laughed. "Look at you."

Nick cracked an eye open. "What?"

I plopped down next to him and cradled myself into his arms. "I think you're done throwing punches in the air."

Nick's fingers combed my hair. "Yeah."

I closed my eyes, remembering Nick as he was seventeen years ago.

Stormy.

The endless traveler.

Dangerous.

I nestled my face against his neck and inhaled the scent that has haunted me all these years. "Nick, I—"

"No, O'Reilly."

"But—"

"Not yet." Nick's warm hand glided down my stomach, and when his fingers skimmed the edge of my briefs, I let those three words sink to the bottom of my soul once more.

Sunday morning, we fastened Spence in his car seat, and climbed into Nick's old, beat-up van.

"You clipped the middle strap too?"

"Yes, Nick."

"You checked it? 'Cause it's a little loose."

"I checked it. Twice."

Nick stretched his neck and glanced up into the rearview mirror, watching his son. "Okay, buddy. Hope you're ready to be sucked into the vortex—"

"Nick. Stop it." I smiled. "That's not the right attitude."

"Yeah, well, easy for you to say." He put the van in gear. "You're not a fuckin' Lund."

"Language."

Nick glanced over at me. "Right."

I reached out for his hand. "It's gonna be okay."

"Don't say it's gonna be okay. I hate the fuck-*freakin'* clichés. You're better than that, O'Reilly."

I drew in a deep breath, watching the sunlight play hide and seek in Nick's eyes. "You're right. Maybe it's not going to be okay. Maybe it's going to be raw. Hardcore." I felt him tense under my hand and I smiled. "But there's also going to be some hugging, some tears of joy, and lots of support, which you need right now. Nick, no, you're right…I'm not a Lund."

Nick looked over at me.

"But *he* is," I added softly, watching Spencer dozing off in his car seat.

"How'd you get to be so freakin' eloquent anyway?"

I laughed. "One word at a time."

When we pulled up in front of Johan and Helga's bungalow, Nick turned the ignition off and leaned back into his seat.

Myself, I had lost my quiet composure.

I had an inclination to twist open the Aquavit bottle we had brought as a gift and chug whatever I could manage to get down without puking.

I nibbled on my lower lip instead, listening to Spencer's quiet breathing.

"I like it when you do that." Nick stared straight ahead.

"What? Sit here, and try not have a panic attack?"

"No. That. The lip thing. It's sexy."

When Nick says sexy, the world has an orgasm.

"Come here, O'Reilly."

I glanced around. "Me?"

"Yes. You. Come here."

I leaned in. "What?"

"I want you to hold my hand in there," he whispered deep into my ear.

"Yes, Nick."

"Let's go."

We passed the threshold and were welcomed by Lene.

She had met Spencer yesterday and had been preparing Helga and Johan, as well as Boone and Kenya, for this event.

"Nico—" She embraced him. She stood on her tiptoes and kissed him. "Dad's had a few drinks."

"And Mom?"

"Hasn't."

Nick exhaled a short breath. "All right."

"Derek." Lene squeezed my hand. "You wanna put Spencer in Mom and Dad's room?"

Spencer was still fast asleep in my arms, drooling on my shoulder.

Nick disagreed. "No, let's wake him up and do this."

I set Spencer down on the couch and began undressing him. When I pulled his sweater over his head, he popped an eye open. "Dwek."

I smiled. "Did you have a nice nap?"

Nick paced up and down. His nervous energy could have fueled a space shuttle. "Let's go. Let's go."

Spencer yawned and sat up. "Doggy."

"No. No doggy. Esco's at home." Nick scooped his son up. "You'll see him later—"

"Doggy."

Lene tousled Spencer's hair. "Later baby, later."

"DOGGY."

Nick shot me a glance that was between an SOS and a threat. "He's gonna flip his lid."

I had heard those words before, but they had always been whispered about Nick.

"Doggy! Doggy! Doggy!" Spencer's cries had become furious, and his cheeks were scarlet. "Doggy!"

Nick, who has been running a kitchen for the last ten years, thinks communication means barking out orders. "Quiet, Spencer! You'll see him later. Enough."

Spencer seems to find all of his father's triggers readily available for his entertainment. "DOGGY DOGGY!" He yelped and thrashed in Nick's arms.

As the fit came to its peak, Nick had clearly lost his cool.

That's when Johan and Helga walked in, with worry painted on their faces, and Helga rushing to the baby as if Nick had bit him.

"Oh my! Why is he so red? Why he is screaming like that?" Helga gently combed Spencer's bangs out of his eyes and pulled him out of Nick's arms. "Come here, honey." Her polar eyes warmed. "Oh, look at him. Oh, Johan, look at him—"

"Mom, he's fine."

She frowned. "Nicolai. He's more than fine." She smiled, staring at her grandson. "He's perfect."

Nick's eyes met mine, and I nodded.

Boone tapped Nick's shoulder. "See that?" he whispered, watching their mother carry Spencer from room to room, showing her grandson around the house. "I haven't seen her smile like that in a long time. Well, not since you left."

Nick looked over at Boone, and I stood, at a respectful distance, witnessing Johan, Boone, and Nick share a quiet moment.

"O'Reilly, come here." Nick's hand was extended to me.

I hesitated, but then took a step forward.

The Lund men pulled me into their embrace.

Deep into their wonderful puzzle of chests, arms and necks.

It was Johan's birthday on Tuesday.

Nick hadn't seen his gentle-mannered father blow out his candles in eleven years.

Slowly, with extreme caution, father and son have been tending to their once-powerful relationship, one careful word at a time.

Of course, Spencer has brought everyone together, yet I sense that Nick's son is a beautiful excuse, but not the cause of their reconciliation. When Nick and Johan are in a room together, I want to live forever.

And Helga?

She no longer merely extends her fingers to Nick. She touches her son's face, and every tender kiss she offers Spencer is a quiet apology to Nick.

Nicks says, "O'Reilly, happiness does eventually come, it just needs a lot of foreplay, that's all."

And what better lover could happiness find?

After we had all gorged ourselves on Nick's decadent Bløtkake, Nick slipped out the back door, to suck on his "second favorite thing."

Lene and Helga sat in the living room, sighing over Nick's travel pictures, and at the table, Boone and Johan were having another one of their heated political debates, with Kenya enjoying and fueling most it.

Suddenly, I felt a little out of place. The stranger again.

Looking on.

"Sit down, son."

"Red, are you actually washing the dishes?"

I was merely stacking. Not washing.

"Come help me here," said Johan. "Explain to my son that it isn't possible for the Québec government to—"

"Dad, if you think that the liberals have done anything remotely important for the Franco—"

"I am saying, that whatever your separatists, fascist—"

"Fascist? Okay. What government actually moved people out—"

They never get to hear the end of a sentence.

"Are you enjoying this as much as I am?" asked Kenya, leaning in.

I laughed. "Do they even know what they're arguing about?"

"This is not arguing, dear. This is *talking*. When they argue, they never interrupt. That's when you know things are going to get ugly." She bent to my ear. "So, you and Nicolai, is it as serious as it looks?"

I glanced over at the bay window, to the back porch, catching sight of my lover.

My wild, divine lover.

Nick puffed on his cigar, and his blue eyes seemed to be searching the evening sky.

Excitement raced through my veins. "I think so," I whispered, my eyes still roaming over Nick's regal profile.

Kenya's fingers skimmed my hand. "It's been a long road for him, Derek."

"Yes, it has."

"But Nicolai is home now."

"Yes."

"And so are you, child."

CHAPTER ELEVEN

I was at Nick's this afternoon.

I sat at the kitchen island (a piece of counter drilled into the middle of the kitchen area) watching Nick work his magic. His back was to me, and my eyes moved over his broad shoulders, his narrow hips, his tight, maddening ass. He swayed his hips as he tossed, chopped, and stirred. In the background, Elvis's reverberating voice swung me back and forth between that night, so very long ago, when Nick had spun me around the living room, and today, where Nick is still dancing me around.

Though he doesn't know it.

"Taste this." He pushed a spoon full of the most marvelous-looking sauce to my parted lips. "Tell me what you think."

He had been cooking all day, trying out his various spring recipes, with me playing the role of the very willing taster.

I gathered the sauce with my tongue, let it sit in my mouth for a moment, then swallowed the decadent thing. "Wow," was all I found to say.

Another success. He smiled, leaning back on the sink's edge. "Not missing anything? Sure?"

It's all there.

All of it.

"Escoffier, come here, boy." The dog lolled his head and shuffled to Nick. "Here." Nick dropped a piece of bone marrow into the dog's jaw. "Enjoy."

I smiled. "Is that how you get rid of your competitors?"

Nick laughed, throwing his head back, and my soul soared.

"So," he said, more seriously, "you like the new job? Must be exciting to plug in digits all day."

I plucked another Guinness out of the fridge. "Jealous?"

His eyes flickered on my lips, and my body quivered with desire.

"No, O'Reilly. Just been thinking, that's all."

My fingers froze on the can.

I waited.

"I mean, I don't know." He picked up some dirty plates off the mountain of soiled dishes and sunk them into the soapy water. "Maybe, we could figure out a more productive situation."

Yes my love.

Productive.

Whatever.

Ask me.

Say it.

"How much is a guy like you worth on today's market?" He grinned. "I mean, an accountant. O'Reilly. What's your going rate? Like for instance, if you were, let's say, keeping track of inventory, schedules, payroll, menu costing, suppliers, bar transfers… Could you do all that for forty-two grand a year?"

Could I?

"Look, I'm in over my head down there. You've seen my office. I need a numbers guy, someone with a good head on his shoulders." He stared into my eyes. "But most of all, I need someone I can trust. And there's Spence. When he's here, I might need you to—"

"Do you-you mean—"

"You wanna a job with Split? Look, it ain't the RBC, but I'd—"

"Yes."

"Yeah?" His breath caressed my lips. "Sure? 'Cause, I don't know, but I heard the chef is a real ball breaker. A bit of a control freak too."

I laughed. "Yes."

"Listen, O'Reilly, if we're gonna be doing this, we gotta lay down some kind of rules. Don't wanna be messing up a good thing, right? I mean, what we have is good, right?"

The insecurity in his voice caught me off guard.

"Listen, I know I'm not easy, but if you want, we could make a go at it. You and me. The whole deal. I'm ready for it, if you are."

I set the can down on the counter before it had a chance to slip out of my limp fingers.

He pulled me into his arms. "You're smooth, O'Reilly. Real smooth. You slow everything down around me. Always have."

Once, I had a small window overlooking a yard.

A yard with a sprinkler.

And sometimes, big blue eyes would appear at that window, calling my name.

Calling me back to the world.

In those days, I understood nothing but the color blue. One shade in particular. An icy shade of a northern sky. And each time my own eyes would meet that shade of blue, something false chipped away from me.

Yes, I was a boy in love with another.

But I was also a sorcerer, casting my own quiet spells.

I fell into Nick, feeling his heart thump against mine, and leaned my head against his chest. "I used to watch the night, hoping you'd come back."

"When?"

"When you left, Nick. After that night, after that night we dan-danced. You left. Never said good-bye—"

"O'Reilly."

"I hurt so much-much. So much, Nick. I was so lonely—"

"O'Reilly."

"I had-had no one. You were my world, my drea-dream—"

"O'Reilly."

"I've waited all my life for—"

"Hey." Nick's whisper warmed my neck. *"Stille."*

I pushed my face into his shoulder.

"O'Reilly. Look at me."

"No."

"I'm sorry, baby." His fingers crawled over my face as he lifted my chin. "I didn't know. I was young. I was angry. I had so many fucking demons working me…I'm sorry. I never meant to hurt you."

"Nick, I lo—"

"No." Nick's blue eyes shone like a skating rink under a cold winter moon again. "Don't you get it yet? Baby, you have to let me say it first."

And the past, like a mere cloud of gray dust, blew away at the corner of my eye.

"Derek." He smiled at the sound of my name out of his lips. "I love you."

❖

As we made our way through the Notre Dame des Neiges cemetery, the lemon sun dripped down on our heads.

"Here it is."

At a distance, a blue jay fitted across the summer sky.

"Do you need a minute?" Nick unfastened Spencer from his stroller.

I nodded. "Thank you."

I watched them walk away.

These two blond deities that have challenged the silence around me.

I let my eyes roam over Aunt Fran's picture. "Hello," I whispered. "It's me, Red."

The sound of Spencer's giggle rippled back to me.

"I just came by to—" I let out a determined breath. I had promised myself I was going to be strong. "I came by to say thank you. For everything. Every word. Every laugh."

I ran my fingers along her modest plot. "I miss you, Aunt Frannie."

I set the bouquet of fresh flowers on the trimmed grass. "But I'll see you around."

I found Nick and Spencer waiting by the van.

Nick's gaze scanned my teary eyes. "Okay?"

"Yes. Okay."

Spencer tugged on my shirt. "Dwek! Birthday!"

"Yes, Spence. We're going to Grandpa and Grandma's right now. They have a big cake waiting for you."

"The biggest," Nick stressed.

Spencer clapped his hands, then, like an arrow of youth, shot for Aunt Frannie's grave.

Nick and I followed.

"What is it, Spence?"

Spencer knelt by the flowers, pressing his tiny fingers into them. "Purple."

"Yes. That's right. *Purple.*"

"Let's go, guys." Nick was already on the move.

On to the next best thing.

"That cake isn't gonna decorate itself, you know."

Yes, my love.

My Nicolai.

My Nordic King.

My blue-eyed bum.

Let's go, you and I.

Let's go until we cannot go anymore.

Dear Bump,

Johan and Helga have asked Officer Di Paglio for help.

They've printed pictures of Nick and plastered them everywhere around the neighborhood.

Nick's face stares back at me every time I walk to school.

Mrs. Lund stopped doing hair.

Mom says she sits by the window a lot, watching the street. The last time I saw Mrs. Lund, she wasn't wearing any lipstick.

Boone says, "My brother's gonna come back when summer gets here. Nico likes to swim, and I bet there isn't a pool where he's at."

Spring is coming.

Mom's been opening the windows in the afternoons, trying to air the apartment out.

Her hair has grown back in. "My beautiful Red," she sometimes says, running her slim fingers through my hair, "I'm glad you're here."

Where else would I be?

Officer Di Paglio thinks Nick has gone south. Maybe New York.

"That's where all the teenagers go. They all want a piece of the action, you know, a chunk of the apple."

He and Aunt Frannie still see each other, but Aunt Frannie hasn't changed her mind yet. "He can piss and moan all he wants, but I'm not gonna be counting minutes by windows for the rest of my life."

I get to see Aunt Frannie often.

Mom lets me ride the bus there, on account of the maturity I've shown in the last month.

I was there yesterday.

Aunt Frannie made her famous meat pie. Again.

We sat in her tiny kitchen and had cranberry juice.

"So," she said, piling another piece on top of the one I hadn't even touched yet, "too bad you and Boone didn't go to the Valentine's dance. I'm sure it was a lot of fun." She took a bite, then washed it down with some juice. "You're telling me there isn't a single girl in that whole school worth dancing with?"

I picked at the pie, chewing on my lip.

"I bet Lene's going to be a knockout in a few years, and she likes you a whole lot. Maybe you'll be taking her to the prom."

I glanced up.

"No?" Aunt Frannie smiled and wiped her lips with a napkin. "Not your type, huh?" She set the napkin down gently and leaned back into her chair. Her eyes moved all over my face. "You miss him, don't you?"

I shut my eyes.

"And it's okay. Nothing wrong with missing him."

My heart accelerated, and I dared a glance her way.

"Tell me about it," she whispered. "Tell me how you feel about Nicolai Lund."

"No."

"No?"

She laughed a little and poured herself another glass of juice. "Well, then, it's worse than I thought."

I frowned. "I think I nuh-nuh-know where he-he is—"

"Yeah?"

I nodded.

She winked. "And now, my little sorcerer, where could that be?"

I thought of that night Nick and I had danced in the living room.
"You know, O'Reilly, one day I'm gonna split."
And I smiled.
"A place cuh-cuh-called Blue Dreams."

About the Author

Mel Bossa is the daughter of an Italian immigrant father and French Canadian mother. She studied language and literature in hopes of reconciling the francophone and anglophone worlds she struggled to fit into. Shortly after the Quebec Referendum, Mel left Quebec for New Orleans and then later, San Diego. She eventually returned to her hometown of Montreal and graduated from culinary school. After a short but intense relationship with the food industry, Mel decided to hang up the white jacket and go back to her first love: telling stories. *Split* is her first novel.

Books Available From Bold Strokes Books

True Confessions by PJ Trebelhorn. Lynn Patrick finally has a chance with the only woman she's ever loved, her lifelong friend Jessica Greenfield, but Jessie is still tormented by an abusive past. (978-1-60282-216-0)

Jane Doe by Lisa Girolami. On a getaway trip to Las Vegas, Emily Carver gambles on a chance for true love and discovers that sometimes in order to find yourself, you have to start from scratch. (978-1-60282-217-7)

Ghosts of Winter by Rebecca S. Buck. Can Ros Wynne, who has lost everything she thought defined her, find her true life—and her true love—surrounded by the lingering history of the once-grand Winter Manor? (978-1-60282-219-1)

Who I Am by M.L. Rice. Devin Kelly's senior year is a disaster. She's in a new school in a new town, and the school bully is making her life miserable—but then she meets his sister Melanie and realizes her feelings for her are more than platonic. (978-1-60282-231-3)

Call Me Softly by D. Jackson Leigh. Polo pony trainer Swain Butler finds that neither her heart nor her secret are safe when beautiful British heiress Lillie Wetherington arrives to bury her grandmother, Swain's employer. (978-1-60282-215-3)

Split by Mel Bossa. Weeks before Derek O'Reilly's engagement party, a chance meeting with Nick Lund, his teenage first love, catapults him into the past, where he relives that powerful relationship revealing what he and Nick were, still are, and might yet be to each other. (978-1-60282-220-7)

Blood Hunt by L.L. Raand. In the second Midnight Hunters Novel, Detective Jody Gates, heir to a powerful Vampire clan, forges an uneasy alliance with Sylvan, the Wolf Were Alpha, to battle a shadow army of humans and rogue Weres, while fighting her growing hunger for human reporter Becca Land. (978-1-60282-209-2)